# A NEW TWIST ON SOME OLD TALES—

Everyone knows that fairy tales, no matter how dark, will always come through with "happily ever after" resolutions, but are those endings happy for everyone involved? What about the witch, the wolf, the giant, and the other so-called villains who make their homes in the Enchanted Forest? And what happens when the excitement's over and the heroes and heroines have to live with the choices they've made? Here's your chance to find out in original twists on such treasured tales as:

"Puck in Boots, the True Story"—So you really believe in talking cats. Well, in fairy tales some of the players don't just dress up for Halloween. . . .

"True Love or The Many Brides of Prince Charming"— All Charming wanted was to find true love—he should have known that enchanted princesses aren't always what they seem to be. . . .

"Fifi's Tale"—As a wolf he'd made a few mistakes, but letting himself fall under that Snow White's spell had been the biggest error of his career. . . .

# TWICE UPON A TIME

# TWICE UPON A TIME

Edited by

Denise Little

WITHDRAWN

## DAW BOOKS INC.

DONALD A. WOLLHEIM, FOUNDER

375 Hudson Street, New York, NY 10014

ELIZABETH R. WOLLHEIM
SHEILA E. GILBERT
PUBLISHERS

ACKNOWLEDGMENTS

*Introduction* © 1999 by Denise Little.

*Spinning a Yarn* © 1999 by Jody Lynn Nye.

*How I Came to Marry a Herpetologist* © 1999 by Nina Kiriki Hoffman.

*Puck in Boots, the True Story* © 1999 by Connie Hirsch.

*Case #285B* © 1999 by Esther M. Friesner.

*The Beanstalk Incident* © 1999 by Jane Lindskold.

*Gilly the Goose Girl* © 1999 by Nancy Springer.

*Fifi's Tale* © 1999 by Alan Rodgers.

*Thy Golden Stair* © 1999 by Richard Parks.

*True Love or The Many Brides of Prince Charming* © 1999 by Todd Fahnestock and Giles Custer.

*Savior* © 1999 by John Helfers.

*Wolf at the Door* © 1999 by Lupita Shepard.

*The Castle and Jack* © 1999 by Tim Waggoner.

*Baron Boscov's Bastard* © 1999 by Jacey Bedford.

*The Emperor's New (and Improved) Clothes* © 1999 by Leslie What.

*One Fairy Tale, Hard-Boiled* © 1999 by P. Andrew Miller.

*Feeding Frenzy or The Further Adventures of the Frog Prince* © 1999 by Josepha Sherman.

*A Leg Up or The Constant Tin Soldier (Gonzo Version)* © 1999 by Gary Braunbeck.

*Mrs. Myrtle Montegrande vs. The Vegetable Stalker/Slayer* © 1999 by Elizabeth Ann Scarborough.

# CONTENTS

**CONTENTS**

# INTRODUCTION
## *by Denise Little*

*"Once upon a time, in a land far away . . ."*

How many times did you hear those words as a kid? How many bedtimes and rainy days did you spend in the company of the denizens of fairy tales? How many of your childhood dreams were shaped by those long ago tales of lost kingdoms, lonely princesses, and talking animals?

It almost seems absurd to write an introduction for a book about fairy tales. The stories are such a part of everyday life that we can't escape them, even when we want to. If parents don't read them to their children and schools don't teach them, the cartoon versions, even if they're interpreted as part of a kid's meal somewhere, will still get to nearly every child. I know this from personal experience. When I was two years old, Snow White's wicked stepmother scared me right down to my white leather high-top lace-ups. I worried for years that somebody was going to demand to see my heart in a box.

All my repeated attempts to duck out of future retellings were fruitless. The story was everywhere.

Recitations of *Cinderella, Snow White, Jack and the Beanstalk, Rumplestiltskin, Goldilocks and the Three Bears, Puss in Boots*, and many other common tales form a bond among us, provide universal prototypes that we all share. Just as the millions of big boxes of crayons sold every year imprint every English-speaking toddler with the same mental image of puce, evergreen, and tan, the fairy tales we're told as kids give us universal concepts that remain a part of our lives and our vocabularies forever.

Think about all the common phrases you hear today that are culled from those nursery tales and fables you heard as a kid. Prince Charming . . . sour grapes . . . MY, what BIG teeth you have . . . fairy godmother . . . and he huffed and he puffed and he blew the house in . . . kissed a lot of frogs before I found my prince . . . somebody's been sleeping in my bed . . . Fee Fie Fo Fum, I smell the blood of an Englishman . . . the sky is falling, the sky is falling . . . cry wolf . . . someday my prince will come . . . happily every after. . . .

It's hard to have an extended conversation without dragging in Hans Christian Anderson, Aesop, the Brothers Grimm, or Charles Perrault at least once.

But just because we all heard those stories as kids doesn't mean that we were satisfied with the way they turned out, then or now. Even as a kid, I always felt that the Three Bears got a bad rap, and that Jack the Giant Killer was a rather ungrateful (in fact, felonious) house guest. From a modern adult perspective, fairy tales leave quite a few questions unanswered. For one thing, it seems that the IRS would take more than a little interest in the sudden fortune displayed by a large number of fairy-tale heroes. And what in the world does Prince Charming plan to tell all those women he married? That he's taken up polygamy? There are characters in these stories who have a lot of explaining to do.

It turns out that I wasn't alone in my need to set the fairy-tale world on its ear. When the time came to revisit the Enchanted Forest and retell some of the old fairy tales with a bit of original spin and enough artistic license to tell them right, every writer I approached jumped at the chance.

And so, nestled in the pages of this book, brimming with humor, charm, a fine sense of justice, and more than a touch of tongue in cheek, are some of the tales you loved to hear so long ago, retold—sometimes beautifully, sometimes hilariously—by some of the best writers going. And this time, it all makes sense and the bad guys get it in the end!

So sit back and relax, and let us tell you a story. It begins this way:

*"Twice upon a time, in a land far away . . ."*

Enjoy!

# SPINNING A YARN
## by Jody Lynn Nye

Jody Lynn Nye lists her main career activity as "spoiling
cats." She lives near Chicago with two of the above and her
husband, SF author and editor Bill Fawcett. Among Jody's
novels are the *Mythology 101* series, *Taylor's Ark*, *Medicine
Show*, and four collaborations with Anne McCaffrey: *Crisis
on Doona*, *The Death of Sleep*, *The Ship Who Won*, and
*Treaty at Doona*. Recent works include *Waking in Dreamland*, *The Ship Errant*, and an anthology, *Don't Forget Your
Spacesuit, Dear!*

"**A**rlo Swidgemerlskong?"

"Aye," said the stocky, amiable man at the door.
He raised his eyebrows into his thinning hair. "Who
wants to know?"

The narrow-faced man in half-glasses and somber robes
put down the scroll case he was carrying and reached
into the scrip at his belt. From it, he presented a small
scroll to the man in the door of the grand house. "My cre-
dentials. Kingdom auditor."

"You're what?" asked Arlo in disbelief, unrolling the piece of paper in his large hands. The contents didn't make him any wiser. For all his newfound wealth, he still couldn't read.

"His Majesty's Revenue Service," intoned the thin man. "May I come in?" Though the phrase constituted a question, the auditor did not seem to have been issued an interrogative lift of tone for his voice. It sounded like an order. Arlo immediately jumped to one side. The auditor trudged inside. Arlo trailed after him.

"Look, what's this about?" Arlo asked. He could see the man studying the fancy hangings on the walls, the genuine tiles on the floor, even the brass bowl in the corner his wife had made him buy as soon as they had a tile floor. She called it a "spittoon," and expected him to use it. It looked exactly like the new "pissoir" in their chambers, only smaller, and he felt the two were largely interchangeable. The auditor turned and eyed him up and down, pausing on the rich, red cloth of Arlo's new houppelande. Arlo buried his hands in the folds of fabric over his ample belly and wished heartily he was wearing his old shirt.

"May I sit down?"

"Surely, surely, and welcome," Arlo said, projecting a geniality he didn't feel. The Revenue Service happened to other people. Rich people. With a twinge of fear, he suddenly remembered he now fit into that category. What should he do? He wished with all his heart his wife wasn't off visiting her people in the next village. She was the one with sense. "May I get you something to drink?"

"No." The auditor circled the sitting room and settled onto the hardest chair. He opened his scroll case. "Arlo *Swidgemerlskong*. That is your name?"

"Yes, yes," Arlo said, nervously rocking on his heels. "Paid for it fair and square, I did."

The man ran his eyes over one of his documents. "Three kopeck syllable tax paid, yes. Fifteen letters, and a nonstandard name requiring a variance." He peered at Arlo over his half-glasses. "Is that not extreme?"

"Well, we could afford it! I mean, yes, we could have gone with Neargoosepond, like me wife wanted, since we live near the pond; or Miller, 'cos I'm a miller, but that's too ordinary; or Formerlypeasant but that's like five syllables; but we really wanted something no one else had. I mean to say," Arlo said, warming to his topic and waving his arms, "everyone's called *Peasant,* and you get ripping sick of it. Swidgemerlskong, that don't sound nothing like Peasant, I thought it up meself," he finished proudly.

"I . . . see." The auditor went back to perusing his scrolls.

"You're not here about the name, are you?" Arlo asked nervously. He pulled the footstool away from the fireplace and sat down on it in front of the auditor's chair.

"No, I am here on a much more serious matter. The matter of unreported income."

"What unreported income? I sell flour, same as ever, year in, year out. Kingdom gets part of every sale, each and every time. I could hold up a grain of wheat and say, 'that bit's for the king, and that bit's for me. My wife sells the odd loaf of bread or cake, and an egg or so, but that's all in the returns."

"And your daughter?"

"What about her?"

"Spinning straw into gold?" Arlo started. It wasn't quite true, Vonaree couldn't really spin straw into gold, but it was what he'd told the king, a year or more ago. He'd happened to meet the king on the road one day, and knew the man was looking for a bride. He'd also known that King Boindal liked nothing in the world so much as gold. The girl hadn't done the spinning herself. I mean, she couldn't, could she? Magic didn't run in the family. She'd claimed it was done by that little man who came in the night. Took her necklace and ring in exchange.

"Er," Arlo said, as the auditor seemed to be waiting for an answer. "Yes?"

"And where did this gold go?"

"Well, she gave it to the king, didn't she?" Arlo said proudly. "Kept at it morning and night, she did, just like the king asked, right here in our cellar. Gave a little bit of it to her old pa—but that was *our* straw, mind, not kingdom straw. Good girl. She's queen, now, you know."

"Yes," the auditor said dryly. "We know. So you admit to receiving unreported gifts of value exceeding more than ten kopecks per person per annum."

"She's me daughter! She can give me gold if she wants to!" Arlo shouted.

". . . Not to mention flagrant violation of the labor laws," the narrow-faced man continued, as if Arlo had never spoken, "including those of legal working hours, allowable breaks, and fair compensation. You can also be charged with child endangerment, unlawful restraint, mental cruelty, and imprisonment. The reeve is considering a whole catalog of serious sweatshop violations against you."

"No, it wasn't like that," Arlo protested, becoming frightened. "We was poor, you see! Dirt poor. You don't know what that's like. I just wanted my little girl to have the best. Make her stand out before the king, you understand, but in a nice way. He needed to get married, and I thought Vonaree would be a rare prize as his bride! I, uh, got a little carried away describing her talents," he added, lowering his head so he was mumbling into his gold-embroidered collar. "Worked out all right, didn't it?"

"You have precipitated a crisis in the kingdom, do you know that? A serious violation." The auditor held up another scroll. Arlo peered at the parts of it that were marked off on the left with large black dots. He couldn't understand it, but he was worried by the words written in red.

"What crisis?"

The thin man brandished the parchment. "The heinous crime of falsely inflating the value of a commodity. The price of straw has rocketed since everyone heard it could be turned into gold. Eight hundred percent inflation, in a single year! Not to mention flooding the kingdom with new gold, diluting the currency! A fine mess, valuable straw and worthless gold! You could get thirty lashes for that as well as a week on the rack. Is . . . er, the creation of gold a *hereditary* skill?" He leaned forward with an avid gleam.

"Well, she couldn't do it before that gnome came to visit," Arlo said, carefully sidestepping the question. Nor after neither, truth be told, but that he didn't dare say. Vonaree would never forgive him if the king set her aside for not having the talent that Arlo'd said she had, even though she hadn't had it in the first place. It'd be criminal, what with the new baby and all.

"The gnome," the auditor said. He peered at Arlo over his spectacles and his eyes shone coldly like glass. "We *want* that gnome. He, too, has many charges pending

against him: counterfeiting; contributing to the delin-
quency of a minor; extortion; mental distress; and now,
attempted kidnapping."

"Kidnapping? Who?"

"The royal child, Prince Mafti."

"No!" Arlo was genuinely horrified. His grandbaby in
danger?

"The queen claims he approached her this morning
and demanded the child as payment for *services rendered*," the auditor said, looking steadily at Arlo. "We
need his name. We have two more days before he attempts to make good on his threat. Help us, and your own
case will be dismissed."

"His *name?*"

"That's right. His name."

"But surely my daughter has told you what it is," Arlo
said, puzzled. "She's the only one who's seen him."

The auditor pursed his lips, turning the skin around his
mouth into a converging mass of lines. "She claims she
doesn't know it. It is something . . . nonstandard, like
Swidgemerlskong. That is all we know. We can't prosecute him without a name on the indictment. Such is the
nature of Kingdom Law. And if we can't prosecute him,
we must find damages against his co-conspirator. You."

"Me! I didn't do nothing." And then he remembered,
well, yes, he had. Among his sins was lying to the king.
Keeping the girl in the cellar for weeks, no, he admitted it
to himself, months. At the time, the wealth had blinded
him. Now he was pretty ashamed of himself. And he'd
cheated a little on kingdom taxes. His wife had insisted.
But blood was thicker than near anything else. If he had
to go find that magical creature, then off he must go.

"Two days, miller," the auditor said, turning to point a bony finger as he crossed the threshold.

Where did you find a magic gnome who could spin straw into gold? If he was anything like Arlo, he'd be living in a fancy castle twice the size of the king's. But the little man was a demon about his privacy, and people living in castles tended to get talked about. Moreover, if he was of a fixed and obvious address, they wouldn't need Arlo to find him. But where to begin?

He went down to his local pub for a restorative mug of beer. Since his windfall wealth, Arlo had become a very popular man, especially in the company of the alehouse. At the long table in the middle of the murky room, he had the innkeeper set out a round of drinks for the house.

"To my new grandson," he said, aiming a keen gaze to each face in turn to see if any of them reacted negatively to the sentiment. Not a bit of it; everyone cheered the new prince.

"Good girl, your Vonaree," said Gaffer Thobsen, the baker, lifting his glass in salute.

"Little lad will be ten days old pretty soon," Arlo said. "We're invited to the naming ceremony. My wife's to have a new dress as a gift from the king." A few envious sneers from the women in the room, but the men nodded. "Someone's got to invite the good fairies so that the lad will have health and wealth and a long life. I suppose it's me who's got to ask them, as the only surviving grandsire . . . don't suppose anyone knows where you go looking for the fairy creatures?"

"Up in the sky's all I know," shrilled Goodwife Saria. "They don't have no feet, see, so they live on clouds."

Clouds? That'd do Arlo no good. "Um, the fairy godmothers have got feet, Saria. Er, I've seen 'em. I'm sure they have houses, same as you or me."

"Well, you know," said the innkeeper, laying a finger alongside his bulbous, red nose. "There's only one place hereabouts the magical folk live, and that's the Enchanted Forest." He nodded several times. "Odd things there."

"Aye," everyone said, draining their mugs of beer and looking at Arlo for a refill. "That's the very place."

The gnarled branches of the trees rose dark and threatening over his head, and the leafy canopy blocked out much of the sun. Like most of the folks in his village, Arlo didn't often go to the Enchanted Forest. It was just too magical for him. He avoided anything so associated with danger as this place. Still, it wasn't far from home, and a lot of people used the forest paths as a shortcut between his village and others in the kingdom. He brought along a stout walking staff, although he doubted it would do much good against werewolves and banshees.

Arlo trod the shadowy path with caution. The Forest was a big place. He wasn't going to find the little man without help. Fortunately, the roads were well sign-posted. "To Gingerbread Cottage," said one finger. "To Grandmother's House," said another. The latter sounded less threatening, so Arlo went that way. He could ask the grandmother if she knew of a man who could spin gold.

He passed plenty of other people walking in the woods. A girl in a hood skipped by him carrying a picnic basket. He nodded politely to a family of bears just leaving their neat little cottage. They gave him a suspicious look and reached back to shake the knob of the cottage door to make certain it was locked. A pair of sisters almost as

pretty as his daughter sat on a log by a stream, one girl
with snow-white skin, the other with rose-red cheeks.
They were spitting frogs and precious stones. He thought
of offering them the name of a local herb woman, but decided that she wasn't up to a case like theirs. And on the
river itself, seven dancing swans were performing an
elaborate water ballet. He'd seen them before, but they'd
gotten up some new choreography. He regretted that he
couldn't stop to watch. He must find the gnome as soon
as possible.

The grandmother wasn't much help. She was having
tea with a wolf and a woodsman, and none of them had
ever heard of the gnome. Arlo went past a handsome
stick-built house with a sign in front of it that had a picture of three pigs.

At last, he stopped an old crone with a basket on her
arm heading in the opposite direction. "Do you know a
gnome that can spin straw into gold?"

"No, I don't know him," the ancient woman replied.
She pointed in the direction from which she had just
come. "You can try back there." Her gnarled, wispy hand
reached into her basket and emerged with a shining red
globe. She thrust it at him. "Apple?"

"No, thank you, goodwife," Arlo said. She limped
away. Arlo followed the path farther, until he came to a
sprawling, shabby, thatched-top cottage with a polished
brass sign over the mailbox that had several names all
alike on it. Underneath was a much smaller box, almost
feminine looking.

He knocked on the door, which swung open at once.

"Excuse me, can you tell me . . . ?" Arlo started to ask
the dwarf who answered the door. "I, er . . . oh, I'm terribly sorry."

The inside of the house was a complete surprise after the shabby exterior. The paneled walls were made of walnut, stained very dark brown and polished to a glossy finish. Along the cornices and trim around the panels, sparkling gems as big as his fist had been inset into the wood. In the center of the chamber were six other little men, all wearing dusty work clothes. They stood with their heads bowed around a table upon which lay a pretty, pale-skinned girl with her hands folded over her heart. Arlo snatched his hat from his head.

"I beg your pardon. I didn't realize this was a house of mourning. I didn't mean to intrude."

The little, bearded dwarf who answered the door didn't speak, but looked a question.

"Sorry," Arlo said. "Seeing as you're also in the precious materials trade, might you know the location of a gnome who can spin straw into gold?"

The dwarf looked curiously at him and held out his hand. At once Arlo reached out to take it, but the little man dropped his hand without touching him. He figured out Arlo was not in the trade. He didn't know the secret handshake. Arlo hastened to reassure him.

"It's a personal matter. To his interest. All I want to do is talk to him."

The dwarf nodded. He went into a cubbyhole and came back with a map. He unrolled it. Arlo peered at it with relief. At least he didn't have to depend upon words. This was a first-class pictorial chart. The dwarf pointed to a cottage, then pointed at the floor. That represented this house. Then his finger traced a complicated pattern through the winding paths over hills and rivers on the map, until it stopped in the middle of a section of deep forest adorned with pictures of bats, wolves, and a skeleton or two.

"There? He lives there?" Arlo asked skeptically. Didn't look like a place where a man who could get rich off a twist of dried grass would live. Then he remembered the dead girl and lowered his voice. "Thank you, friend," he said. "I'm sorry for your loss."

The little man didn't reply. He nodded, tears gathering in his eyes and spilling down his cheeks. Arlo removed himself hastily.

The sun was more than halfway down the sky by the time Arlo reached the clearing the dwarf had shown him. No one was there, but this had to be the place. The wee hut beside the fire pit in the clearing only came up to Arlo's knee. Inside it was a pillow-sized mattress and blanket, and a drop-spindle with a hank of hay half spun into gold. Arlo looked around. He was tempted to unwind the gold strands and take them away with him, but he could almost feel the eyes of the auditor boring into his back.

Under the mattress were two thick books printed in tiny letters, but he suspected from the moss growing on the covers that the gnome used them for padding and not education. Arlo couldn't find a single thing with writing on it that would tell him the little man's name, even if Arlo could read it. He only needed the name, but he needed it badly.

Arlo sat down on a flat stone near the fire pit to wait. He looked longingly at the big iron cook pot sitting on the dead ashes and thought of dinner, which he wouldn't get now for hours. He lingered, getting up once in a while to pace and restore the circulation to his legs. It must be too late in the day to find the gnome at home. He was off elsewhere making mischief for some other well-meaning peasant. He'd be back soon. Arlo stretched his arms and shoulders, pretending he felt comfortable waiting around in a clearing for a strange magical being. And what would he say to him when he got back?

The sun peeking at him through the tree branches sank lower and lower until it was gone, and the Enchanted Forest grew uncomfortably dark. A whisper sounded out of the darkness.

"Go . . ." Arlo jumped.

"No, I'm staying," he said, sitting down on his stone, clutching the folds of his tunic with both hands. "Determined to stay. Yes. I'm here for the night. Got to see the gnome, I do."

As if in answer, wild, maniacal laughter bubbled up out of the woods around him, followed by bloodcurdling howls, owl shrieks, and sinister whispers. Arlo swallowed hard. He couldn't see what was making the noises, and he truly didn't want to.

"All right," he said, rising. "If he's too busy to see me tonight, I'll come back in the morning. I should have made an *appointment*." The shrill merriment rose even higher.

Dogged by his invisible tormentors, he strode out of the clearing, and hurried away. It was just too dangerous to stay in the Enchanted Forest overnight. He might be laughed to death, and that'd be no good for his grandson.

Arlo got little rest that night. He wiggled and fidgeted in the wide bed. His head ached as much as his legs. He wished with all his heart that his wife was home. She was the clever one. He'd send a message to her, but it wouldn't reach her in her parents' village for a couple of days. By then, the gnome would have claimed their grandson, and it would be all Arlo's fault.

A day wasted already. He couldn't think what he ought to do. He'd find the gnome, and ask for his name, and the little creature would tell him to stow his request where the light never shone. And then what? Try to beat it out of him? Attacking magical beings was dangerous. They'd find Arlo's body in the forest, trussed up with ropes made of solid gold.

There should be some official way to investigate the name of a magical creature. Official.

Miserable and exhausted, he fell asleep about an hour before cockcrow.

At the first cry of the rooster next door, Arlo sat bolt upright in his bed. Official, that was it! He could make an official request! It could work.

He threw aside his covers and ran to the table where his wife kept all their documents. He might not be able to read, but he remembered things. Somewhere in the piles of parchments they'd acquired with their new wealth was a page with an empty signature blank. He turned over the box of documents and pawed through the avalanche of papers until he found what he was looking for. This was a most important-looking decree, with fancy capital letters and pictures in the margin. There was a red stamp mark on the top. He recognized that it had four letters in it, traced them with his finger, COPY, and wished his wife was home to tell him if his idea was a good one or not. He shook the paper, feeling elation and hope.

He had his trap. All he needed now was to have the little man fill it in. But how to convince him? Bribery? All he had in the world was his mill, his wife, and his daughter. Now, the one was mad at him, the other was out of town, and the most important was threatened with seizure. Mill! Yes, that was a good notion. He must go to the mill.

He ran down the sloping street toward the river and the sound of the wheel turning the heavy grinding stones. Inside the white-painted building, his apprentice, a burly young man, was hard at work filling huge cloth bags from the hopper. Since Arlo had gotten rich, he hadn't spent as much time in the mill as he used to, but Edrit never seemed to mind. He was conscientious and he liked tedious work. You couldn't bore him even if you recited the same word over and over every day for a year.

Arlo waved a hand before his face to clear the flour out of the air. "Edrit!"

"Hey-o, master!" Edrit said, waving one of his big, flat hands. "How be ye?"

"Well, boy. Well enough. I need some flour!" Arlo picked up the first full bag on the top of the heap and hefted it.

"Hey," Edrit said, over his shoulder, "that's for Goodwife Marmite. "She asked for extra fine barley flour."

Arlo threw it aside and touched the next.

"That's the goldsmith's oatmeal!"

"Do we have any bags that aren't bespoken?" Arlo asked in despair. His grandson was in danger, and Edrit was worrying about goldsmiths and barley. Edrit stopped to think, a ponderous task for him. He scratched his head, dislodging some of the flour from his mop of dark hair.

"Yes!" he said, holding out the bag he was filling. "This one!"

The moment it was full, Arlo seized it from Edrit and

tied up its mouth with a practiced twist. With the document in one hand and the heavy sack of flour on his shoulder, he set out for the forest.

The sounds of laughter were ringing in the trees when Arlo came near the clearing. The voice sounded tinnier, though. Cautiously, Arlo lowered the big bag to the ground and peered between the black trunks of the trees.

Be danged if there *wasn't* a little bugger no larger than a cat flying around the iron pot on a cooking spoon! Vonaree's gnome was a tiny man with huge eyes and a mop of silver hair, and so thin in the body that the wind could carry him away with a strong gust. Vonaree had had larger dolls as a child. The gnome was waving a spindle in one hand, twisting a shining coil around it as he flew. So Vonaree had been telling the truth all along. This was the greedy little pest who wanted to steal his grandchild. But caution, Arlo, he told himself, caution. You can't stop magical creatures by wringing their necks, much as you'd like to. The little man was singing a high-pitched ditty. It sounded like nonsense to him. All Arlo could tell for sure was that it rhymed.

He shouldered the bag of flour and walked into the clearing. As soon as he spotted Arlo, the gnome hid the spindle in his shirt.

"Hail, fellow," Arlo said, pretending he'd seen nothing. "I come from the king." That was half-true, anyhow. He was thankful that he had never met the gnome before. Plausible deniability, that was what he had. Still looking suspicious, the little man brought his spoon down for a three-point landing: left foot, right foot, and bowl. "A present for you from your sovereign. As a magical subject, you are on the rolls for the surplus produce distribution scheme."

"What?"

"I've brought you a bag of flour, mate. Free. From the king," Arlo said. He brandished the document and a stick of charcoal his wife used for doing calculations. "Sign here."

Grumbling about government bureaucracy, the little man scratched a series of letters on the page.

"Is that handwritin'?" Arlo asked anxiously. "Make sure it's neat." The gnome threw the pencil at him and started jumping up and down on the bag. It emitted little puffs of starch out of the sewn corners. The gnome got more height with every bounce. At the top of the highest jump, he turned a somersault in the air before landing on his feet.

"Very nice," the little man said. "Yes. A useful present." He looked up at Arlo, and brandished the cooking spoon between his doll's hands like a bludgeon. "Are you still here?"

"No, laddie, I'm gone," Arlo said. Clutching the precious document, he turned and ran out of the clearing.

Arlo ran all the way from the clearing to the castle without stopping. The wind lifted particles of charcoal off the page, and he worried that the characters would vanish.

"I've got it!" he cried, as he went by the sentries, who stood tall and saluted the grandfather of the heir to the crown.

"I've got it!" he cried, as he ran up the stairs past a clutch of scholars in long black robes and black hats that tied under their chins.

"I've got it!" he cried, racing into the throne room.

Vonaree, sitting on her throne at the left hand of the king, rose and ran to him. She looked quite lovely in her rich, blue silk robes. On her thick chestnut hair, her little gold crown had knots and spindles for points, as a kind of reminder how the king had met her in the first place.

"Papa! Oh, Pa, are you sure?" she asked, looking at the paper with desperate eyes. "That little man was here again this morning. I have tried every name anyone has ever heard of. We have only one day left, and then he'll take Mafti!"

After a quick bow to the king, Arlo took his daughter in his arms and kissed her on the forehead, just like he used to when she was a little girl.

"I got it, my sweetling. It's right there, on that paper."

"Let me see that," King Boindal said, rising from his gold throne. Arlo admired his royal son-in-law. He was a handsome man. His black beard and mustache were clipped closely around a strong chin. His eyes were a noble blue, and his nose was a curled hawk's beak. Thankfully, their child favored Vonaree. "Rumplestiltskin? Are you sure this is the right name?"

"He wrote it himself," Arlo assured him.

"It's not a . . . standard name," Boindal said.

"Maybe he made it up," Arlo said. "Us creative folks don't like standard names, you know."

"Well, thank heavens," Vonaree said, reading over her husband's shoulder and sounding out the name on the page. "How strange. Rim pole fits skin. No. Rumpole of the bailey. No. Rumpled bed sheets?"

"Just a moment, Your Highness," said a dry voice. The auditor stepped forward from the side of the throne room, where Arlo had not even seen him standing. "May I see that?"

The king handed him the paper. The auditor straightened his glasses on his nose. After he read it he looked up at Arlo. "This is a tax receipt for a three-syllable name. The name on this page has four syllables. There's still one kopeck syllable tax lacking, plus penalties for failure to file properly."

"But it's the name," Arlo insisted. "You asked me to get it, and I got it." He explained his great idea, puffing out his chest when he told them how he'd fooled the gnome into writing on a piece of paper.

"Oh, Papa, that's clever," Vonaree said. Even the king gave him a grudging nod of approval.

"This is highly irregular," the auditor said, and Arlo's face fell. "You impersonated a kingdom official. You have filled out a document improperly. This is a copy. Where is the original?"

"There is no original," Arlo said. "This is the only paper I've got. It's the gnome's name!"

The auditor regarded him without pity. "For improper use of kingdom documents, you are sentenced to one day in the stocks."

"Your Highness!" Arlo protested to the king.

Boindal shrugged. "It's the law, miller. Nothing I can do. It's only one night."

He reached for the paper, but the auditor pulled it away. "You may not be able to use it, Your Highness. It is filed incorrectly. We may have to destroy it and start again with the correct form, PT-903, Registration for a Magical Kingdom Resident."

"Don't be silly," the king said. "My son's safety is at stake." He snatched the paper from the auditor's fingers, and nodded to Arlo. "Come and visit with Mafti. My men can take you down to the stocks after dinner."

                              *    *    *

Arlo spent a moderately uncomfortable night with his head resting on the top board of the stocks. As the king's father-in-law, only nobles were allowed to throw old fruit and dead cats at him, and their aim was uniformly awful. Before sentence was passed, he got to dandle his grandson. Mafti was a beautiful child, with a fancier wardrobe than any fairy queen. Arlo didn't hold with designer fashions for infants, they grew out of them so fast, But Vonaree was just like her mother. She did impractical things.

When morning came, the men-at-arms unlocked the frame and helped him up. They gave him only a few moments to massage life back into his limbs. Then he was hauled back to the throne room, without so much as a by-your-leave, nor breakfast neither. Vonaree was already there, pacing nervously. Boindal sat on his throne with one leg propped over an armrest. The men-at-arms marched him over to the king's throne. He bowed to Boindal.

"I don't need to tell you, miller, that you'll be thrown into the dungeon forever if this wretched little wart steals my son."

"No, Your Highness," Arlo said. The guards removed him to a corner to wait. Vonaree walked up and down, occasionally flitting back to the cradle to make sure her son was still in it. The next time she passed him, Arlo whispered to her.

"Sweetling, why didn't you come to me in the first place and tell me what was happening? I would have gotten you out of this situation."

"You put me into the situation in the first place with your wild stories," she hissed, all the while keeping a smile on her face for the king, who sat out of earshot.

"Vona, love, you're not still angry with me for bragging about you? I mean, if there's a girl in the kingdom who should have been able to spin gold, it surely would be you."

"I should almost be grateful to the gnome, whatever his name is, for making your silly tale come true." Vonaree still showed her teeth prettily. Arlo smiled and bowed to his sovereign.

"You're benefiting handsomely," he muttered back.

"Not if they take my baby."

"Well, I've seen to that, my dear."

"I hope so!" she whispered furiously.

"What was that, my dear?" the king asked, as her voice rose until it was almost audible in the rest of the chamber.

"Oh, nothing, my beloved lord," Vonaree said. She dropped him a graceful curtsy. Arlo was impressed. She'd learned a lot of court ways in a year. He wondered if his wife could get her knees around a tricky move like that. He was glad all he had to do was bow, which he did. "I was telling my father that I'm nervous about remembering the name properly to say it."

"Never fear," the king said, snapping his fingers. "I had the scribes write it out for you." A young monk in brown robes stepped forward and handed the queen a small parchment. "Why don't you practice it for a while?"

Vonaree resumed her pacing, mouthing the word over and over again to herself. She had only one chance to say it to save her baby. A page in a white tabard marched into the room and blew on a long brass trumpet.

"A visitor to see the Queen," he announced.

"Who is it?" King Boindal asked.

"He won't give a name," the boy said. "Says you'll know, or you won't."

"Well, Your Highness?" the little man said, marching in on the heels of the page. He put his hands on his hips and threw back his head. "Guess my name!"

His daughter was wily, as befit a daughter of Arlo Formerlypeasant Swidgemerlskong. Vonaree was in a temper, but she played the little man like a puppet.

"Well, I tried the most complicated names I knew yesterday," she said, with a pretty smile. The gnome looked skeptical. "So it must be a simple one. Are you Phil?"

"No!" the gnome crackled. He hopped over to peer down on the baby in his cradle.

"Bill?"

"No!" He played a little with the ruffles on the cradle's bonnet.

"Will?"

"No, no, and no!" The gnome said, and started to reach for the infant.

"Well, then," Vonaree said, throwing her arms in the air. "You must be Rumplestiltskin!" The gnome turned, his eyes popping so wide they looked as if they'd fall right out of his head.

"The devil told you that! No," he said, recognizing Arlo all of a sudden. "*You* did, flour man. You tricked me! You tricked me!" He lunged for Arlo, twenty pounds of rage, but the guards at Arlo's side leaped forward to grab him.

The court proceedings again the gnome Rumplestiltskin were spectacular. Peasants and nobles alike fought for places in the tiers of seats in the grand, tapestry-lined courtroom for three days to hear the heralds read it all out

from a scroll over sixty feet long to three judges in long
white wigs, and twenty red-robed jurors of the highest
rank in the land. He was indicted on 1,200 counts of fraud,
counterfeiting, practicing alchemy, extortion, attempted
kidnapping, inflating the cost of a commodity, and flying a spoon without a license. If Arlo could think of it,
they charged the gnome with it. A complete audit was
performed on any holdings that were under the name
Rumplestiltskin or even any name remotely like it, and
the assets confiscated by the court in the name of the
crown.

The prisoner was extremely uncooperative. It took
two wizards to keep the little man in the chamber during
the proceedings. They ended up sealing him into the
dock inside an invisible box that did nothing to deaden
his shrill shouts and ravings. They little man lashed out at
the king, the auditors, the guardsmen, everyone, including and especially Arlo and his daughter, the queen. Arlo
took all the abuse without wincing, hoping that the jury
would concentrate upon the gnome, and leave him alone.

The king gave his bride a couple of hard looks when
Rumplestiltskin testified under a geas that he was indeed
the one who had spun the straw into gold. Arlo could see
that Boindal was mentally toting up the value of the gold
Vonaree had given him, against how much he thought he
could get her to make in the future. *Settle for what you've
got,* Arlo prayed. *You've got a fine son, and she'll be a
loving wife the rest of your days.* More than anything else,
Arlo wanted to avoid having Vonaree coming back to be
another millstone round his neck. One set, of genuine
rock, was plenty.

It took another two days for the heralds to read out all

the counts of "guilty," and the crowd was hanging on avidly to hear the sentencing. Then Rumplestiltskin's attorney, a man in an elaborately rolled hat and a houppelande twice as elegant as Arlo's best, who had been appointed for the gnome by the court in a semblance of fairness, rose to reply to the verdict.

"Your Highness, my lords, noble members of the jury. You have heard these proceedings, and found against my client on every count. Under normal circumstances, he could be made to suffer terrible fates, including whipping, boiling in oil, hanging, drawing, quartering, beheading, exposure, imprisonment, flaying, and defenestration. I must point out to you, however, that my client is protected under the Kingdom Residents With Disabilities Act. Since he clearly is a crazed magical being as well as being severely vertically challenged, he cannot be held to the same standards as anyone else." As majestically as he had arisen, he sat down. To his left, Rumplestiltskin continued to carry on screaming and trying to fight his way free of his magical bonds. The judges looked at him, looked at the defense attorney, looked at the king, and scribbled on their slates. King Boindal leaned over and spoke in a low voice to one of his pages, who ran to the judges and whispered urgently. The most ponderous of them rose and read from a scroll.

". . . In the name of the crown, we find the gnome Rumplestiltskin guilty. He will not have to serve time, providing he will never again get within three hundred ells of a spinning wheel or any other device for turning plant matter into precious metals. All existing gold will be confiscated and added to the royal treasury." There was cheering in the gallery, and the king wore a smug smile. The judges had to pound their gavels on the table to be heard. "Take him away," said the chief judge. But as soon as they released the magical bonds, the gnome vanished in a cloud of smoke and obscenities. "Arlo Swidgemerlskong."

Surprised, Arlo rose. The judge peered at him short-sightedly.

"For your part in these proceedings, because you have cooperated with the crown, your only punishment will be a fine, in the amount of, er, however much magical gold you still maintain in your possession. After that, you will be free to go."

Arlo sat down. Well, it wasn't so bad. The fine was almost certainly Boindal's way of getting even with him for making him look like a fool, as well as getting his hands on the rest of the gnome's gold. Boindal was a greedy beggar, but he was smart. So long as he made the punishment sound legal, he could get away with anything he wanted.

Arlo stood in the sitting room of his fine house after the bailiff's men had left. He still had his mill, his wife, his daughter, his grandson, and his new name. That, the king had left him, since the tax had been paid on it, and all. You couldn't say fairer than that.

"Arlo!" He heard bustling sounds in the foyer, and went to greet his wife. For all her extra twenty years, Elyn was still as beautiful as Vonaree. "What in heaven's name has been going on here?"

While she unpacked, he told her all the events of the last three days. Elyn slapped her empty bag down on the floor.

"And you say that that was *all* the king confiscated?

Gold? Arlo, you are a fool. Without gold how can we keep up the appearance we are expected to maintain as the grandparents of a prince? We should have spent more! I told you at the time investment's better than saving. And now it's all gone!"

She surely had the better business head between the two of them, Arlo thought, bending his own head in shame.

"It could be far worse, my love," he offered, to no avail. She rounded on him.

"*How?* How could you be so stupid! You should have accepted a whipping, or even a month in the dungeon," she added, poking his round belly. "Wouldn't do your waistline a bit of harm, and we could have kept the cash."

"Yes, my love," Arlo said, wandering disconsolately out of the room. "I'm glad you're back, love. I wish you'd been here to tell me what to do."

"So do I!" she called. "Heavens above, what will we do? There's the naming ball next month, and before you know it, Mafti's first birthday. . . ."

To escape the sound of her voice, Arlo went down the cellar steps. He'd been poor before, and it didn't much bother him, but he saw his wife's point. Maybe the spinning wheel had given them too much too soon, and he'd wasted his opportunities just letting the wealth sit.

There, in the little room where he'd kept his daughter locked up for months, sat the spinning wheel. A spider had woven a web between the spindle and spool. He brushed it away with an idle hand. With a look over his shoulder to make sure no one was watching him, Arlo straddled the seat and twirled the wheel. There was plenty of straw down here. If he could figure out how to make the wheel work again, he would get out of all his troubles. Only, this time, he'd pay taxes on all that he made, so that auditor wouldn't have a thing they could hold over him again. Then, his wife would be proud of him for once.

"Rumplestiltskin," he whispered.

# HOW I CAME TO MARRY A HERPETOLOGIST
## by *Nina Kiriki Hoffman*

Nina Kiriki Hoffman has been pursuing a writing career for fifteen years and has sold more than 150 stories; two short story collections; two novels, *The Thread that Binds the Bones*, winner of the Bram Stoker Award for best first novel, and *The Silent Strength of Stones;* one novella, *Unmasking;* and one collaborative young adult novel with Tad Williams, *Child of an Ancient City*. Currently she almost makes a living writing scary books for kids.

When I first spoke in toads and snakes, I hated them and tried to kill them. They rendered me unfit for human company; I blamed them for everything.

But centuries passed, and I learned many things.

Above all, I learned to keep my own counsel.

Most of the people who knew me thought I could not speak. I worked in a library. When people asked me questions, I pointed.

I only let myself speak during my lunch break and at home. I took my sack lunch down to the riverfront park every day, so any amphibians I produced had somewhere safe to go.

On a day not so long ago, I sat on my favorite bench overlooking the river. The sky was pale blue with spring, and birds called in the quickening air. Light green flowers dangled from the branches of the maple trees. Paperwhites bloomed in shaded hollows.

I ate my yogurt and banana, then got out my list of unspoken words. I tried six. "Legume." A small brown toad with golden eyes. "Dobro." A spotted lizard with brown and white stripes across the back of its neck. "Protuberance." A tan serpent with a black head. "Spavin." A diamond-backed rattlesnake. "Upanishad." A fire-red salamander with black spots. "Concupiscence." A green-backed bullfrog.

The toad sat in my hand. The others raced, ran, or hopped away.

Sometimes I looked them up in books, but I usually couldn't identify them with certainty. A color would be different, size wrong, feature changed. Perhaps a function of magic.

I set my hand on the ground, and the toad, with one last long look into my eyes, hopped off.

And then a thing I dreaded happened for the first time in a long while.

With a rustle, a young man emerged from the bushes. (Later, I learned that he often observed wildlife from hiding.) He overflowed with questions and became irate when I wouldn't answer.

He had seen me speak. He wanted me to do it again.

I packed my trash, glanced around to see that all my animals had disappeared, and walked away from him, not answering.

He saw my name tag, FANCHON BUFO, though, and from there derived my telephone number, and then he gave me no peace.

"How is it that each one is different?" the young man asked me.

Evening shut down the sky outside, and streetlights drove back darkness. We sat at a table in a deserted coffee shop. My choice of meeting ground. Our reflections gradually displaced pieces of view where it was darkest outside. Steam rose from our coffee cups, possible prayers, doubled in the window's world.

After that one encounter, he had kept calling me and begging me to talk to him, and every "no" I gave him left me with another marine toad, the largest of all toads, and not so easy to care for, since it needs salt water. I had finally said "all right" (two small garter snakes), and picked a place to meet that wasn't home.

"It's a marvelous thing," he said, peering through his glasses at me. His brown hair was shaved short on the sides and left long enough on top to flop forward and obscure his vision. Through the lenses of his glasses his eyes looked pale and strange.

I shook my head. I sipped coffee. He wouldn't call it marvelous if he had lived with it for four centuries.

"But each word, a different species," he said. "That it happens at all is amazing. That it happens with such variety is—is stupendous!" He reached across the table and touched my hand.

No one in all my life had looked at me with such longing and appreciation.

I am not by nature fair in any way. My countenance is, at best, pinched; my eyes are narrow, as are my lips; my form is thin and bony; my hair long, but not thick or wavy, a dull dark-brown color with no interesting words to describe it.

My best feature may be my hands, with their long narrow fingers, or perhaps my long narrow feet and dexterous toes, though no one other than myself had seen my feet in an age.

Across the years I have done many things to change my appearance, sometimes wishing to render myself more attractive, sometimes less. I have cut my hair; grown it; dyed it; braided it; shaved half off and stiffened the other half with hairspray. Why not? I seem condemned to live forever; I may as well experiment.

I have had adventures as a result of some of these looks and my silence. The best I store, and the rest I forget.

I thought of my diamond-and-pearl-speaking sister, who married a prince. What a beauty she was. How could any man resist a woman who was beautiful and spat wealth with every word?

Did she ever know she was loved for her own self?

Did she even care?

Ah, well. That was *her* story.

Mine was different.

"Talk to me. *Please,*" the young man begged, stroking the back of my hand.

I shook my head. I stared at him across the Formica-topped table. I glanced down to where his soft, pale fingers touched the back of my hand, and wondered what I felt. Not attracted, not repulsed; but a little less weary, perhaps.

"Say something," he whispered, "anything. Please."

A car drifted by in the street outside, headlights glaring then gone.

"Something," I said. A small green tree frog plopped to the tabletop.

The young man caught his breath, held it behind his teeth.

"Riggit," said the frog, looking here and there.

My water glass was filled with ice. No safe haven there. I put out a hand to the tiny creature and it hopped up onto my palm. We were too far from a stream; I wouldn't have picked this place to meet if I had suspected I would speak. Maybe I should only use snake words. I couldn't always remember which words produced what.

The young man leaped up and went to the counter. He got a glass half full of tap water with no ice in it from the waitress, and floated a piece of toast on top. The tree frog was happy in the glass.

I smiled at this young man.

He smiled back. His face turned sweet. I saw something there I liked.

So our courtship began.

His name was Newton. He lived on an estate with his parents. Soon I went there to visit and found ponds and marshes and woodlands all looking as nature had left them, and inside the mansion a wing of rooms where Newton studied cold-blooded animals without killing them. Those from other climates had comfortable terrariums full of the plants and soils and temperature of their homelands.

All his life he had been fascinated by reptiles and amphibians, he told me.

He waited for my every word.

At home, with my orange teakettle, my slippers, my books, and my nineteen-inch television, I sat with my feet propped on the ottoman and considered options.

My sister had married a man who treasured the jewels she spoke. If I accepted Newton's proposal, would I not be doing the same cowardly thing?

When had I ever had such an opportunity before? Would there ever come another? Why not be loved, even if not for myself?

"My prince," I said to my room. Two brilliantly colored poison arrow frogs. "I love you." "I" was a snapping turtle; "you," a gila monster; "love," a giant cobra that raised its head, fanned its spectacle-marked hood, and hissed.

None of my creatures ever hurt me. It had been a while since I had produced so many poisonous ones at once, though. I called the zoo and they sent the usual handler over to pick up the animals. Because of the phone call, I had a good menagerie by the time Sheila arrived.

She shook her head the way she always did. She thought I bought exotic pets and didn't know how to care for them. I shrugged as I always did and appreciated her deft technique with the snake-catching stick. We nodded our farewells to each other.

I started a list of words that produced poisonous animals. I liked Newton and wanted him alive. If that changed, well, the list would still be a good thing to have.

When I had taken enough time to think it over, I said yes (a banded gecko) to his proposal.

"I do" produced a baby snapping turtle, and a small pit viper which I caught before it woke to its surroundings. I put the snake in the pocket of my wedding gown before Newton slipped a gold band onto my ring finger. Newton caught the turtle and slipped it into a pocket of his tuxedo. It didn't even bite him. We both smiled, and I felt effervescent.

I moved to the estate and gave up my library job, and for a time Newton and I were very happy, each in our own way. I had never had someone appreciate my words before. Heady wine.

One day I sat on a stool in the room with the saltwater tanks in it. Newton had been pestering me to tell him a story. I was tired just then and kept shaking my head. Finally I yelled "No!" and a marine toad the size of a basketball plopped into my lap.

"Beautiful," breathed Newton. "That's the biggest one yet! I've got to get the camera." He dashed out.

I touched the toad's moist, mottled back. It gazed up at me with huge golden keyhole-pupiled eyes. It looked wise and strange and wild. I lifted it until I stared straight into its eyes. Its pale throat fluttered.

My biggest "no" ever, I thought, and kissed its wide mouth.

It changed then.

In a moment between my legs stood a prince as beautiful as night, with eyes as dark as secrets and hair pale as sunlight. He was dressed all in burgundy velvet. He grasped my shoulders and kissed me again. I had never tasted anything so wicked or wonderful. "We've been waiting," he whispered, "all these years we've been waiting." He closed his arms around me. My nose bumped his chest. He smelled of violets. "Enchantments intersect," he said. "There aren't many doors into this world remaining, and for those of us trapped long ago and never loosed . . . we pray for you and await your every word."

The door slammed. "Who is this?" Newton demanded, behind me.

I felt a strange tightness in my chest. I thought of all the frogs, toads, snakes, lizards, efts, turtles, and crocodiles across the centuries. I remembered killing the first ones. How I had hated my mother for sending me to the well to meet the fairy who cursed me.

At first I killed them. Then my mother drove me from home, and everyone I met despised me and sent me anywhere so long as it was away from them.

When I had no one else left, I had learned to like my creatures, even as I learned not to make so many.

The prince's arms loosened and I pushed away. I stared up at his beautiful face, then glanced around the room, at tanks that hosted my words. I touched my lips. The prince smiled and nodded.

"Fanchon, who *is* this?" Newton asked me again.

I rose and went to a tank. An orange-eyed turtle stared at me through the glass. I lifted it from the tank and kissed its mouth, and it turned into a mermaid. She could not remain upright; she splashed and sprawled to the floor. Her tail fin spread wide and iridescent and damp across the cement. For a moment I stood, trapped in that resonance, the concrete and the fantastic.

She kissed my foot.

"Oh, man!" Newton started videotaping.

I wanted to tell him to stop that, but I wasn't ready to deal with another giant boa constrictor right now.

With the first prince at my shoulder, I went to each tank in the saltwater room, lifted each creature, kissed it. Toads and sea turtles, a few snakes, and then a wolf eel, which didn't change when I kissed it. The first prince put it back in the tank. I glanced at Newton, who said, "I had that before I met you."

I went through all the rooms of the Reptile and Amphibian wing, trailing more and more people behind me, leaving empty terrariums and tanks in my wake.

Transformed, my creatures were people of different sizes, shapes, and colors, and they wore clothes from all over the world and all through time. Most were princes. Some were kings. A few were princesses, and there were sheikhs, pashas, caliphs, sultans, sultanas, queens, emperors. The one cobra I had spoken since Newton and I married turned into a rajah.

My lips were sore. There were so many glittering people they couldn't fit into our wing of the mansion, and they opened windows and doors and went outside. They spoke in murmurs to each other. All gazed at me as though I were their savior.

Newton kept taping.

At last I sat down on a bench in the garden and studied these fantastically beautiful people. (One of the larger princes carried the mermaid out and put her in the fountain.) In clothes like that, with looks like that, what could they do in this day and age? Walk out into the world and get mugged? Get jobs as supermodels? Actors? Prostitutes?

I thought of all the creatures I had sent to the zoo with Sheila. All the ones I had let loose in the riverfront park while I worked at the library. All those who had lived out their aquatic or dirt-dwelling lives and died without ever being kissed.

My first prince sat beside me on the bench and stroked my cheek with the backs of his fingers.

How could I have known that locked inside my living words were such fabulous people?

"It's the nature of curses to crush things," he said. "We were all cursed, and you were, too. Nested in your curse was the blessing of our freedom."

"I don't know whether to ever speak again," I said, then looked down at a lapful of squirming lizards, snakes, and toads. Wearily I lifted a small spadefoot toad and kissed its mouth. It turned into a very comely girl in scanty Arabian Nights-style garments. She went behind the bench and massaged my shoulders.

Newton put down the video camera and seated himself at my other side. He leaned closer. "I liked them better before," he whispered in my ear.

If I kissed him, would he turn into a frog?

Of course not. I had kissed him on our wedding day, and since. He was the only stable person in sight.

We had a backyard full of strangers with no clear futures or destinations. Every word I spoke produced another stranger. What were we to do with them all?

I could lift their curses. Could they lift mine?

I kissed my last sentence from animals to people and leaned on my husband, who put his arm around my shoulder. "It's okay," he murmured. "It's okay. Better or worse, it's okay."

# PUCK IN BOOTS,
# THE TRUE STORY
## by Connie Hirsch

Connie Hirsch has written many excellent stories for various anthologies, including *100 Vicious Little Vampire Stories*, *The Shimmering Door*, *Wizard Fantastic*, and *Fantastic Alice*. She lives in Massachusetts.

Dumb as two sticks—no, make that three, all unequal lengths—that's how dumb he was. I've never had more unpromising material, and that's saying a lot. They should be *grateful*, I tell you, grateful that I did as well as I did, and look where it got me—it's to weep.

'Forty-seven was a bad year all around, what with the Plague and the downturn in guilder futures, and the tulip crisis on the horizon. Times were hard in the supernatural employment market, too—your little brown men and Tom-Tit-Toms and fairy godmothers are usually the professions they can't hire enough warm, qualified bodies to wear all the little green jerkins, pointed caps with feathers, and bejeweled tiaras, but that year they were only taking on unpaid interns. When I muffed up a little Bavarian job—

who'd have thought the maiden would have come up with the tongue-twisting secret name that I'd inscribed on a tiny scroll enclosed in a hazelnut swallowed by a donkey kept in a stable inside an impregnable castle? Not me, or my name isn't— Well, never mind what it isn't! Anyway, that was the end of my job, eighty years of seniority be damned, we'll take on a promising young sprite who will put some enthusiasm into his work.

Yes, I was—how shall I put this?—job-free. At leisure. Available to pursue other lines of work. And desperate. It was the desperation, I guess, that drove me to take a contract with the Starlight Agency, "Your Complete Supernatural Service Provider—No Quest Too Obscure or Too Difficult." It was widely considered the last resort of preternatural services—you'd go there last, because they'd never tell you no. They handled a lot of pro bono cases, too, just to keep their overall Balance in trim . . . but everybody in the business knows this means they've got a lot of Balance to trim, see?

I figured, hey, how bad can it be—a professional like me, who knows the ropes, the stuff they'll throw me can't be beyond *my* capabilities. I'm not like the burned-out hacks and wild-eyed ingenues they usually hire; *I'm a professional*. I figured this would keep my hand in, and maybe I'd get some of my enthusiasm back, take on some difficult challenges (or easy fixes that I could waltz through and thereby build up the ol' confidence).

Well, it worked like that at first. My first case was dead easy, a standard Helpful Stranger motif. I was the mysterious little old man by the side of the road: the three sisters passed me by, and I rewarded the one who stopped and shared her lunch. Left me feeling happier than I had in ages—virtue rewarded and all that. I even skimped on the punishment for the bad sisters, a couple of frogs and snails from their mouths, just a warning that things could have been much worse.

The next case was a bit more difficult. In hindsight, I know my Starlight coordinator softballed my first case. This next one turned out to be a nasty political assassination, that took out not only a redundant Prince, but a whole shipful of innocent sailors—I *did* go beyond the strict boundaries of my mission and gave Princey a strong hint that the magic salt machine *could not be turned off* once it got going. If the Prince had possessed a lick of sense, he'd have rushed onto the deck once the machine was started and tossed it overboard immediately, before the ship got so loaded down that it sank. The stupid machine is still churning away, I expect, having been magiced with a guarantee good for a hundred years and a day— for the budget I had to work within, I got good value!

I think I should get some credit for that, since the Law of Magical Consequences (what we in the trade call the Balance) says that if you, the Evil Vizier, employ magic to get rid of an inconvenient Prince, some balancing calamity has to take place. Adding salt to the *ocean* cleverly toes the line of acceptable damage, only *technically* harming anything. All things considered, the ocean isn't going to notice even a hundred years worth of extra salt! I figured the warning—really, just a hint—I gave the Prince could only have added to the Balance, squaring things nicely.

I was proud of the elegance of the salt-machine dodge, and I mentioned it prominently in my post-case report. In fact, I would have thought my coordinator would have appreciated it! I *didn't* mention the part about the warning—

didn't see any reason to, really—in retrospect, I suppose I should have expected that Starlight would have some-one checking up on me.

Yeah, spying on the new guy, seeing if he was just another job burnout on his way down the ladder—or somebody who was willing to bend a few rules, risk the Balance, to whom they could hand the sleazy jobs.

That's the only explanation I can come up with—that the coordinator weighed me in his own Balance, and found me wanting. What I wanted were some reasonable jobs . . . and what I got next was a job that no self-respecting supernatural entity could reasonably hope to bring off in good shape.

I tell you, I had a bad feeling before I even opened the dossier on my next case—maybe it was the smile on my coordinator's face that showed just a few too many pointed teeth, like a shark thinking about a midnight snack. I'd heard rumors that he was on a work-release program from the bad place, and I could believe them. "This one's a bit of a rush," he said, "you'll have to be in place before dawn, so I want you down in Wardrobe right away—you'll need to get outfitted." He paused. "You can read about it on your ride down," he said heartily. "We wouldn't give this job to just anyone."

Per orders, I marched right down to the Starch & Stitch Department, trying to riffle through the pages and not walk into a wall. "Not a Motif G211.1.7!" I said as I en-tered, having come to the pertinent paragraph.

The three ladies behind the counter looked up from spinning, weaving, and cutting cloth, respectively. "You the one for the Helping Animal job?" the eldest one said, looking over her half-glasses. She had an accent that I realized must be Greek. I guess I was not the only ex-deity (minor) that Starlight employed.

"He couldn't be anyone else at this hour, could he?" said the second lady. She was round and maternal, and flyaway hair straggled out of her bun. "You here for the fitting, right, honey?" she said.

"They call me *Mr.* Puck," I said, with perhaps a little more frost than was absolutely called for. The eldest one quirked an eyebrow, and the youngest one covered her mouth to not quite conceal a smile . . . and I counted to ten because I didn't want to antagonize Wardrobe. "Yes," I said, with what little heartiness I could muster, "the Miller's son's case, a Motif G211.1.7 as we classify these things."

"A scholar is our Mr. Puck," said the youngest lady. I felt a tiny trickle of sweat in the small of my back at the green coolness in her eyes. No, one really didn't want to antagonize these ladies, but it might be just a little late for the realization. They all drew out tape measures and circled around me, like lionesses sizing up an undersized warthog.

I'll draw a veil over the actual fitting, which was messy and uncomfortable—I don't know that they actually meant to jab me with those pins, or if that's an unfortunate (for me) byproduct of the process. Suffice it to say, I went into Wardrobe on two legs and left it on four, holding the dossier in my teeth, already late for my ride, but at least I knew they'd hold the horses and the chariot for me. That much I was certain of, and for about the last time, I was actually right.

They left me at the drop point just moments before dawn. I was scheduled to substitute for the family cat, a grumpy beast of advanced years who was all too grateful to take early retirement. Today was the day that a certain dying miller was due to leave his three sons a uniquely unequal inheritance. To his eldest son he left his mill; and to the middle son, a cow, some land, and a small house, not bad for a young man starting out in life. But to his feckless youngest son, he left the family cat, and a handful of ducats, nearly worthless since the devaluation of '46.

Maybe he *meant* the young man to starve, or—a theory that I cooked up once I'd read the full dossier—he meant to be so arrantly unfair that he would trigger the Law of Balances and call down pro bono preternatural assistance. However, now I've thought through the whole situation and come back to the starvation theory, and I'm quite ready to believe he had some justification, as the boy was not merely as dumb as a stump but as annoying as one, too.

Case in point: I made my entrance into the mill yard just as the miller's third son—his name was Steve, by the way—left the miller's house for the last time, carrying his worldly possessions in a rucksack, the door closing firmly behind him without so much as a good-bye. He was tall and fair-complected, with straw-yellow hair and watery blue eyes—now watering copiously. He took a few tottering steps and sat down in the dust, weeping uncontrollably.

I sprang into action—well, ambled—over to him. I'd barely had time to get used to my costume, a calico cat with a scruffy coat and oversized feet, too many toes on front and back, which caused me a little perambulation problem. No wonder the cat had been grumpy—her feet had hurt, I discovered. Oh yes, the cat had been *female,* to add insult to injury.

But I was a *professional,* so I stropped myself several times against his leg. Usually that draws attention, but Steve was wailing so hard that I might have knocked him over without it registering. Time for more direct means, so I put my front paws up on his knee, and said, "What distresses you, my Master?"

*That* should have gotten a response, but instead my putative Master just twisted his fingers in his hair and cried some more. I dug in with a plethora of claws. "O my Master," I said, "what distresses you? Tell me, your most obedient servant."

He left off his wailing to stare openmouthed. His expression was so gormlessly comical I had to sit down and quickly wash my furry ruff just to keep from laughing. A few licks, and I looked up, only to see that he was still staring.

I spit out a mouthful of fur. "What—distresses—you?" I said at last, enunciating every word as best I could around fangs. Dental appliances are hell.

Something moved behind those blue eyes, and at last Steve said in a regular voice, quite at odds with what I was expecting, "Puss, you never spoke before."

I was prepared for the question. "I never had reason to," I said. "We must leave, if we are going to seek your fortune."

For a moment I thought he comprehended, but the same confused look came back into his eyes. "You never spoke before!" he said again.

"Never had to," I said, trying not to huff. I butted his knee with my head, none too gently. "Come, my Master, we must be off to seek your fortune," I said, and walked a few paces, looked back over my shoulder. He was still sitting in the dust, his mouth open again.

I went back to him. "It's time to leave, *Buster*," I said. "Now, get up, or my sharp little teeth are going to get together with your butt."

It took several more exclamations of "You never spoke before!" from Steve, and some corporal persuasion—short of actual biting, which I wasn't too keen on—to get him moving. We were definitely going to have to work on his communication skills, I could see. I was having trouble getting across the concept of "seeking his fortune."

Maybe that was because I had not much in the way of plans myself. The mission objective was one that any preternatural professional runs away from: an open-ended quest, the goal being the subject's own criteria for "success." Get the wrong subject and you could be in for several years, even decades, of grief and hard work. Added to that, this was a pro bono case, so I had next to nothing in the way of a budget! What was Starlight thinking?

I chewed on that as I chivvied Steve along the road to fortune—or at least the road, anyway. I tried to lead my charge through the first market town we came to, but he kept getting distracted, standing with his mouth gaping, until I *meowed* and reminded him that he had a Fate awaiting him . . . as soon as I could figure out what it was.

Oh, another aspect of this case I didn't like—I was supposed to pretend to be an ordinary cat when other people were around. Suspiciously, that was added in pen to the page of restrictions, like a last-minute thought. It was okay if Steve talked to *me,* I'd explained to him on our walk, though he might want to keep it down in public or be thought stupid. (Though surely that was not a *nouvelle* experience for him.) Anyway, I'd meow, he'd get this solemn look on his face and follow me trustingly until something else distracted him.

While in town, I had Steve buy me a few little things from a secondhand clothes vendor—I was damned if I was going to wander around naked. It burned me to have to sit silent while Steve got the worst part of a bargain for a child's cap, a little cape (I couldn't see trying to put on a shirt, and forget pants with this darn tail!), and best of all, a pair of baby boots (please don't call them booties!) that would slip nicely over my rear paws.

Alas, there weren't many ducats left after that. Steve then went and blew them on sandwiches. I guess he was really certain I was going to provide him with a fortune. I only wished I had some idea of how I was going to do it.

Outside of the town we stopped for lunch. I'll give him this, Steve fairly divided what little he had. While I chewed, I sensed him tensing up, like he was going to either pass gas or share a thought. I had already learned in our unregrettably short acquaintance that it was much the same result. "When are you going to give me my fortune, Mis— er, Mr. Puck?" he said at last. (He was still tripping over my preferred form of address, since he knew Old Puss was nominally female.)

"I've been thinking on that, Steve," I said. I licked a back foot, my other back foot, my tail, then scratched behind my ear while he waited patiently and my mind raced fruitlessly. "Why don't you tell me what would make you happy?" I said.

Steve got the familiar glazed look back. "Just want to go on living at the mill," he said. "Working for my father, just like it was."

I sighed. "I'm not a miracle worker," I said—besides, resurrections were not only *way* beyond the budget, you have to get so many special permissions that it only got done twice that I know of. "Your father left me to you to provide for you," I added. "So what's the next best thing that you'd want—besides being back at the mill?"

"A good draft of ale down at the tavern?" he said artlessly. "And maybe a bowl of milk for you?"

"Well, it's a start," I said. I lashed my tail in frustration. "But the problem is, we haven't got enough cash to afford either one."

He got another of those "thoughts bubbling up from deep beneath" looks. "If he left you to me," he said, "maybe I could *sell* you. A talking cat is bound to bring a lot of money, maybe even a fortune?"

I sat stock-still and blinked slowly. It would never be allowed, of course, but the idea was tempting—he'd have his "fortune" and I'd be free to go. I remembered I was a professional, however, and steeled my resolve. "One doesn't trade magical animals," I said. "One inherits them, or one assists them and gets help in return. It just isn't done."

"I'd still like a beer, though," said Steve sadly.

"I bet you wo—" I nearly bit my tongue on my little sharp teeth, as I was having an Inspiration. "I think I know of a way to get you all the beer you could want, plus enough money to keep us put up at inns until we have found you your fortune. . . ."

My Inspiration did require a bit of coaching for Steve. Make that a *lot* of coaching, actually. He wasn't a natural, but I got him up to adequate. So it was that he approached the next tavern (The Squashed Toad, I believe it was called) with me perched on his shoulder, dressed up in my hat, cloak, and all—the boots on my rear feet made it impossible to cling with them, but as I was overequipped with claws on my front paws, I quite made up for it.

A man with a dressed-up cat excited more attention than Steve had ever had in his life. For a few rocky moments I thought he was going to blow it, when somebody asked him, "Is that your cat?" The mouth gaped, gaped, gaped—and then my fair-haired boy smiled. "My father left me this cat to make my fortune," he said, sounding not entirely like he was reading his lines. (He probably couldn't read anyway.)

He paused, trying to remember the next bit. I put my nose in his ear and whispered. "And I have taught him well," Steve said, as I prompted. "Does anyone want to wager—wager—" he was losing track of his line, but trying hard, "—whether he'll walk a tightrope strung between two chairs?"

Damn, he'd jumped right to the *second* wager I'd suggested, after we won the first, where I'd meow the number of times that somebody picked. But no problem—it wasn't the early bettors I intended for us to clean up on; these were to be friendly small wagers. It was getting the crowd to make outrageous bets that they would suggest their very own selves later on that I expected the majority of our profits to come from.

It was a good plan. Steve was not much of a bargainer, and certainly no patter artiste. He couldn't build a crowd's excitement even with the dynamite material I was so modestly providing. While we traveled for the next week, he got a bit better at hustling up bets, but there was no chance that we'd ever make enough from this game to qualify as even a small fortune. I contemplated taking up ventriloquism and performing the patter while

Steve silently flapped his lips, but after a few seconds I gave up on that idea.

In the meantime, I got inquiries into how things were going from my coordinator at Starlight. Had to borrow a fortune-teller's crystal ball to make the call—collect, of course. I immediately launched into my troubles, and we went a round or two over the no-talking restriction, but the coordinator said Agency policy always forbid it. "Always?" I said. "How come it was handwritten into the dossier, then?"

I thought I had him there, but he smiled. "New girl typed up the contract," he said, "and accidentally left it out. We let her go, of course—can't tolerate sloppy work in this business."

"Mmm-hhmmmm," I said. "If we can't do something about the talking, how about increasing the budget, so I can afford a decent magic widget for the subject? A little help would go a long way with this lad."

My coordinator got this soulful look. "You know what the bottom line is on these pro bono things," he said. "I know it's tough out there, but with a professional of your caliber, I'm sure you'll be able to improvise." He gave another one of those sharp-toothed smiles. "I'll expect to hear back from you next week with more progress." He cut the transmission, and I indulged in several minutes of spitting and hissing, I was so mad.

I resorted to doing something I'd sworn never to do— try dealing in the black market. There's enough illicit trading in magical widgets that a smart operator can get a bargain now and then. But most of the goods I saw weren't appropriate; a monkey's paw, for instance—can you just imagine Steve making three wishes, and what they'd be for? There were slightly used glass slippers (like they'd fit!), a singing golden harp (too loud), a magic mirror—the last had me intrigued, but when I looked into its background it turned out that nearly every possessor had come to a self-obsessed bad end, while somebody else got the Happily Ever After. Much as I might occasionally want to get Steve turned into a frog or other shape more in keeping with his mentality, I wasn't so desperate I'd risk completely muffing up my mission.

Another week dragged on; I'd never been in so many bars in my life. I still twitch a little when I see a beer nut, to tell you the truth. Even Steve was getting antsy, trying to be something he wasn't every night—and a cat upstaging him.

The next call from the coordinator was not the nicest conversation I've ever had. Let's just say that we had very opposite opinions on how this mission should have gone, and I wasn't getting a bit of give on the widget budget or the talking issue. "You don't think the Talking Animal Guild won't be down on Starlight like a ton of bricks, if we let our agents dress up as helper animals *and* talk?" said my coordinator. Aha, so that was the real issue!

I steamed for the next day, told Steve I needed the night off from doing forepaw stands and proving that a cat could always land on its feet. It was time to do some heavy thinking. If I didn't turn this mission around soon, I was going to go nuts in this damn fur suit. It didn't even have a zipper! Starlight wasn't backing me up one bit; they were, in fact, handicapping me, blocking the talents they had hired me for . . . unless they expected me to use those talents strictly against their orders, to give them deniability with the Guild? The more I thought about it, the more sense it made.

It was desperation. I know it now. In a hundred years—

maybe two hundred—I'd have never come up with a scheme as downright low as the Marquis de Calabash scam, but the pressure was on, and I had convinced myself I had the yellow light, if not the green light, from my agency.

How it went down was pretty much what you heard— I passed Steve off as the Marquis de Calabash. *I* did the talking whenever something really clever was needed, like getting Steve a nice set of clothes, and a place to stay. Just made him take a bath in the river, and hid away his miller's son's togs, then flagged down a passing nobleman's carriage, demanding help for my noble master, whose clothing had been stolen by bandits. All things considered, a talking cat in boots, cape, and hat goes a long way to establishing somebody's bona fides.

I'd pretty much gotten Steve under my paw in the past couple of weeks—in fact, you might say he had become the perfect cat's paw! I emphasized that he should give out as little information as possible, and follow my lead—I guess the lad wasn't as unteachable as I first thought. And what a relief it was to be able to talk and use my best weapon again!

I even set up a romance for poor Steve—bringing a young tender lass (of an impeccable family) little flowers, small fish I pawed out of ornamental ponds, and other tokens. (Out of this experience comes advice that I will give freely to all parents: beware of magic cats bearing gifts. Need I say more?) I tried my paw at some not-bad poetry, while I was at it. Of course, it was a complete success, though not before I had to cue Steve through stammering out a marriage proposal, with me hidden where the new fiancée couldn't see me. I might as well add, it wasn't just luck that made them fall in love at first sight, or I can't mix a love potion. . . .

Of course, the key to success in this hustle was to keep moving. I had to follow up that talk of nobility and lands with something more than a naked but charming Marquis. Free to move around, I scouted out the possibilities, and found an estate owned by an elderly gentlemen with only distant heirs. Please believe me when I saw that the old Marquis was an exceedingly nasty piece of work, and I did the Balance quite a favor, really, when I *hastened* his death. The servants were so relieved to be free of him that they unanimously agreed to go along with accepting Steve as the new Marquis, with the promise that he'd *really* be able to understand the plight of the common man—and how!

Within the week, Steve was in his new mansion on his new lands, with an adorable fiancée who adored him right back, with Steve's fiancée's family buying in on his reputation—they'd squash any rumors about how the Marquis had just sprung up from nowhere to safeguard their daughter, I thought. I felt pretty secure about abandoning Steve to a lifetime of near-brainless nobility, for which he was eminently suited. I called for a pickup, left Steve a nice little note wishing him luck, and started mentally composing a scorching exit report about the lack of support that I figured my mission had received from the Starlight Agency.

Instead I walked back into a pink slip. I had "engaged in morally dubious activities." I had "contravened direct orders about mission conduct." I had "associated with persons of low moral character"—I guess the last was my black market inquiries. In short, I was sacked for cause, despite all I'd done—that's gratitude for you. Even bringing their pro bono case in under budget didn't count for much.

I was better quit from them, anyway. I drifted for a while, decided that I'd be happier if I did keep my toes wet in the preternatural helper profession, which is how I ended up working as a Tooth Fairy. Okay, so it was that or end up under a bridge in Norway, trying to keep goats off the span. Anyway, it's solid 9-to-5 work—9 P.M. to 5 A.M., when the little kids are sound asleep. I don't have to convince anybody of anything, I don't have to dress up in a damn cat suit, do tricks in bars for drinks, or deal with the idiot sons of millers unless, of course, they've lost a tooth. Suits me fine.

# CASE #285B
## by Esther M. Friesner

Esther Friesner's latest novel is *Child of the Eagle.* She has
written over twenty novels and co-edited two fantasy collec-
tions. Other fiction of hers appears in *Excalibur, The Book of
Kings,* and numerous appearances in *Fantasy and Science
Fiction* and other prose magazines. She lives in Madison,
Connecticut.

*H*er Story:
   I don't know where to begin, Doctor. I guess
you've heard the same story about a million times: Our
relationship began *so* romantically. Well, of course they
all do. Why go on with a relationship that starts out in the
crapper, pardon my French?

   Ours started out in bed.

   Oh, it's not what you think. Well . . . all right, maybe it
is. I'd never met anyone like him, and the circumstances
weren't what anyone could call normal. For instance, I
don't *normally* hop in the sack with someone almost the

*instant* that I meet him; I was *never* that kind of girl, I don't care *what* people say about blondes.

Sure, I was young, I was a little wild. Maybe my parents should've kept closer tabs on me, been stricter, enforced curfews and stuff, I don't know. But I never really gave them any cause for alarm until that day, and *then* they hit the thatch! Of course, by that time the damage had been done—that's how *they* saw it, anyway—and it was too late.

I can't say that I blame them for reacting the way they did. *Over*reacting is what I used to call it until we had little ones of our own. Children change your whole perspective. Now I know just how Mom felt. Gee, I know how *I'd* feel if one of my babies brought home someone who was . . . well . . . who *wasn't* exactly what I'd had in mind for a son-in-law. But my babies are still *much* too young for me to start worrying about that kind of thing now. If they weren't so small and if I didn't believe that young children need their father, I wouldn't be here, talking to you. I'd have divorced that unspeakable beast long ago.

Yes, I know, but he used to be so *sweet!* I think having kids is what changed him. We never just cuddle any more. He's always growling and snapping at me over the teensiest little thing. He used to call me "Honey," but now. . . ? Don't ask. Do you have a tissue I could use? I'm sorry, but when I think of how perfect we were together, I can't help but cry.

I blame his parents. They were against us getting married from the start; they were against *me*. They hated me sight unseen! His mother is always saying how I don't keep a proper house. Well, let me tell you, I saw how she keeps *her* house! And I don't mean how she keeps it when she *knows* company's coming. I saw it the way it *really* is. I know what he's going to tell you, that I wrecked the place, but anything I did was one hundred percent accidental, and besides, it was pretty much trashed when I got there, and that's the truth.

And his *father!* He says I'm lazy, but do you know how long *he* sleeps? Don't get me started.

Look, Doctor, I know what they say about mixed marriages, but I *do* love my husband and I *do* want our babies to have a father. I'm willing to put in whatever effort it takes to make this work. But I need a clue so I can know where to begin. Can you help us?

*His Story:*

So did she tell you how we met? Yeah, that's right, in bed. My bed. I was young. You know how it is when you're young: All hormones and no brains.

Looking back, I know now it was a mistake, but right then, when I had my blood up, my adrenaline pumping like crazy, I wasn't exactly subscribing to *Common Sense Monthly,* if you get my drift. I've read a couple of pop-psych articles about how love works, and I bet you've written a few in your time, huh, Doc? You know, the ones about how when two people find themselves in a potentially dangerous situation, all of their senses are heightened, and they've got this whole fight-or-flee thing going on, and that makes it *real* easy for them to confuse what they're actually feeling with love.

Maybe I better give you a little background: I lived with my folks all my life. Our house isn't exactly within walking distance of shops and schools, if you know what I mean. It's out in the middle of the forest, isolated as all get-out. My Dad's kind of what you might like to call the original survivalist. He's seen too many of his relatives buy the ranch in hunting accidents, and he got it into his head that modern society's to blame. Mom just goes along with what he wants; it's easier that way.

I guess I should've left home and struck out on my own sooner, but you know how it is when you're the only one. Mom would give me one of *those* looks every time I even brought up the subject of getting my own digs. Then she'd start asking me what was wrong, wasn't I happy here, what could she do to make it better, was I running away because she was a bad mother, stuff like that. I didn't have the heart to leave.

So anyway, there we were, one big happy family, a pretty good life even if it was almost as interesting as watching paint dry, just going along, minding our own business, you know how it goes. A good life, calm and peaceful.

Calm and peaceful, yeah: That's always the way it is just before an earthquake hits. Right, Doc?

I guess just about every victim of a major crime goes along thinking, "It can't happen to me," until it does. We didn't live in a high-crime area. We didn't live in a high-*anything* area. Lock our doors? Against what? A hophead chipmunk? A serial-killer squirrel? I don't think so. Shit, our front door didn't even *have* a lock.

Doc, you ever been the victim of a burglary? The worst part's always the initial shock when you come into your home-sweet-home and realize that someone's been in there ahead of you, and I don't mean the cleaning lady. The sense of violation! The—the *contamination*! Just the bloody *nerve* of whoever broke in and made himself at home in *your* home—! I thought Mom was going to faint.

And then, the second stage: The fear. You know, it hits

you the moment you stop thinking, "Who could've done such a thing?" and "What do you think he stole?" That's always the exact same moment you start thinking, "What if he's *still here?*"

I won't lie to you, Doc: It's a scary thing when you start asking yourself that question. I know I'm big and tough and I can take care of myself pretty good, but I'll tell you honestly that I was scared. I'm not ashamed to admit it. And I wasn't the only one. I saw the look on Dad's face. I knew he'd just been hit right between the eyes by the same thought as me. He was frightened, too.

Of course we didn't let it show. We had to put on a brave front for Mom's sake. Man, I don't ever want to have to go through something like that again, acting brave when I'm shaking inside, and padding through my own house like *I* was the burglar! It was really weird and it got weirder. For starters, it looked like the creep hadn't actually *taken* anything. He'd made one hell of a mess in the kitchen, and my chair wasn't ever gonna be the same, but right about the time we discovered the pieces of it, I started figuring that maybe this wasn't a burglary after all. Maybe it was just some rotten kids doing a little hike-by vandalism. I'll tell you, I was so relieved I started to cry, and Mom thought it was on account of my chair! Like I said, she thinks I'm still her baby.

Then we all went upstairs. That was where I found her.

Doc, you saw her, how she looks now: Imagine what she looked like five years ago, before we started our family, back when she was living somewhere where she could get to the gym to work out on a regular basis, and to the beauty parlor before those dark roots of hers inched themselves halfway down to her ears!

Yeah, uh-huh, that's what I meant. What, you thought

she was a *natural* blonde? Oh, brother, *that's* a good one! Why don't you call me Nanook while you're at it?

So there she was, asleep in my bed. Mom and Dad were pretty mad by then. I guess they'd also gotten around to figuring out that we weren't dealing with a dangerous felon, so they weren't afraid anymore either. Even Mom was getting a good mad on, and the only time I've ever seen her lose her temper is when she thinks someone's trying to get between us.

I'll get back to *that* later.

I'm no Einstein, but standing there in the doorway to my room, staring in at that beautiful woman asleep in my bed, I knew I had to do something, and fast. If Mom and Dad got their paws on her when they were in *that* mood, there wouldn't be enough left for a casserole once they got through with her. Telling you about it this way, it sounds like it took a lot of time for me to take action. Really, it all happened in the blink of an eye. I saw her, I made up my mind to protect her, I turned to my parents and announced, "There's no one in here either. I guess they've been and gone. I'm tired; I'm going to bed," and I did.

Thank God we *do* have locks on our *bedroom* doors.

Stop looking at me that way, Doc: It was consensual. I'm not exactly a wild thing, you know, or how in hell would I be able to eat all that crappy porridge Mom keeps serving me and pretend I *like* it? And she wasn't some innocent little girly-girl, no matter how she's been telling you the story. She was a woman, adventurous, daring, open to new experiences. . . !

Not anymore, though. Marriage. Go fig'. It's like once you put the ring on their finger, they go from being Zorga the Amazon Love-Slave to Martha Stewart. *Not* what I'd call trading up.

I bet she's been complaining about how my parents treat her, huh? As if her parents were Lucy and Larry Liberal! It's a good thing for them that I'm patient and I don't believe in unnecessary violence, because if I hear one more so-called "joke" about the Chicago Cubs. . . !

And did she maybe *happen* to tell you what her father calls me when he thinks I can't hear him? Rugboy.

Sure, I admit that my parents are no picnic, Mom especially. She's got this crazy idea in her head that just because I'm a husband and father now, I don't love her anymore. I'm over at her house almost every day, just to prove to her that she's wrong, that I do still love her. I thought it'd help matters when we had the kids, but it only made things worse. Mom always criticized how my wife kept the house, and when the kids came, she started criticizing how she was raising our babies. I *do* love my mom—I know she'd kill for me—but she doesn't understand about how different it is raising kids these days. It's *really* different raising ours!

The last big blowup came this past Thanksgiving. Mom insisted we spend it with them, and I didn't mind: The Bears were in the bowl game that day, and no way was I gonna sit through *that* game with my father-in-law. He thinks he's soooo funny, but he's not, nuh-uh. Anyhow, there we were, sitting at the table, a nice dinner, turkey and all the fixings, and out of left field Mom says to my wife that if she wants to make an appointment at the beauty parlor pretty soon, she'd be happy to mind the kids for her.

That was it. That was when the porridge hit the fan. I mean, Mom *meant* well, she really did, but my wife took it the wrong way. I guess it was the last straw. She yelled something like, "Are you implying that there's something wrong with the way I look? Are you saying I *need* to go to the beauty parlor?" And then *Mom* said, "Certainly not, dear. I was just thinking that you look as if you haven't had the time you'd *like* to get yourself all tidied up. I remember how you looked the first time I saw you. Of course, your hair was a little . . . rumpled, but in the circumstances that was only natural. Still, rumpled or not, it was blonde." So my wife hollered, "It's *still* blonde!" and *Mom* said, "Maybe if you'd manage your budget better, you'd be able to buy some higher wattage lightbulbs to put over your mirrors, plus you'd be able to feed my grandchildren some decent hot porridge instead of that cold cereal slop," and then *both* of them turned to me and demanded that I tell the truth, was she still a blonde or wasn't she, and—and—and—!

—and I made the biggest mistake of my life: I *did* tell the truth. That's when she grabbed the kids and hiked home to her mother.

But I still love her, Doc. I married her, and if what I had to go through to arrange that wedding doesn't prove I love her, I don't know what does. Let me tell you, if you think it's hard finding a clergyman willing to perform a mixed *faith* ceremony, you ain't seen *nothing*.

Oh. A park ranger. Ha, ha, ha. Like we haven't heard *that* one about a million times before. You're almost as funny as my father-in-law. And here I thought you were a professional!

Okay, okay, apology accepted. You know, just because I'm gruff and grumpy sometimes, everyone seems to think I don't have any feelings, but I do. Underneath it all, I'm actually kind of sensitive. I miss my wife. I miss how we used to just be together and cuddle.

So . . . can you help us?

*Therapist's Analysis:*

Case #285B is interesting on several counts, one of which being its superficial similarities to certain other cases within my sphere of experience (See, for example, my monograph on Case #285A: *Snow White and Rose Red.*) In the latter, however, most of the couple's domestic problems were resolved when the husband came to understand that he was the one who had to change, to cast off and reject what I like to call the *wilder* aspect of his being, to become, if you will, more *human.*

In the instance of Case #285B, this was not an option.

Naturally enough, my first concern was for the welfare of the couple's offspring. In this case there were three, two boys and a girl, Arthur, Edward, and Ursula. They were still quite young, but one must not discount the subconscious impression parental strife can make on children of any age.

It was, in fact, while dealing with the couple's children that I discovered the key to their domestic problems. It is perhaps a cliché to lay the blame for marital disharmony at the feet of the mother-in-law, but in this case it was painfully accurate.

The husband's mother exhibited all the characteristics of a classic passive-aggressive. Her overprotective attitude toward her sole offspring could not have helped but strain normal marital relations between herself and her husband, which in turn caused her to focus her frustrated affections even more intensely on her own son. The need to control her child, even to the point of keeping him under her roof at an age by which he ought to have established his own home, was so great that even when he did—against all odds—find the mate of his dreams, his mother refused to step down from her role as the most important female in his life.

It will be my recommendation in this case to urge the couple to begin attending joint counseling sessions as soon as possible. I will also continue to meet with them on an individual basis. The wife must be encouraged to find capable child care help *outside of* the immediate family. She should then set aside a predetermined amount of time weekly to devote to pampering herself and regaining her premarital attractive appearance. I am by no means suggesting that she do this solely for the benefit of her husband, but rather on the basis of the fact that when a person feels physically attractive, his or her sense of self-esteem is automatically elevated, which in turn leads to a healthier, more productive attitude when it comes to confronting and dealing with domestic disagreements. Furthermore, since both parties have freely admitted that their relationship began on a purely sexual footing, it would do no harm to do whatever it takes to revive this aspect of their union.

As for the husband, I have already strongly suggested to him that he take a stand against his mother's manipulatory behavior and refuse to play a game he has no hope of winning. He should cut back on his visits to her house— her territory, if you will—until such time as she is willing to amend her attitude toward his wife and to accept him as an independent adult. He has expressed deep misgivings about this course of action. I fear that his mother's unhealthy influence over him runs so deep that, despite his professed love for his wife, he is mentally and emotionally unready or perhaps unable to make such a radical break with the past. Yet if this marriage is to survive, this is something that *must* be done.

I have, therefore, with my clients' consent, offered to initiate a dialogue with the mother, so as to make the son's eventual confrontation less traumatic. Sometimes, in difficult and sensitive cases such as this one, it is for the best if a detached third party interposes between mother and child.

*Epilogue:*

"Yeah, Chief, it's a mess in here. Blood everywhere, maybe a couple of pieces that might have been the doc; I dunno, that's for the boys in Forensics to say.

"The receptionist was on lunch break when it happened. She says the doc didn't have any enemies that *she* knew of. There wasn't any noon appointment down on the books either, but since when does a killer need an appointment? Maybe he got too close to a sensitive case or something, told someone to stop acting like a jerk and they took it personally. Yeah, *that* really narrows down the list of suspects.

"I'll tell you one thing, Chief: This one's gonna be a real bear to solve."

# THE BEANSTALK INCIDENT
## by Jane Lindskold

Fairy tales and mythology in general have long been among Jane Lindskold's most abiding loves. They have flavored writings as diverse as her doctoral dissertation (on the Persephone Myth in the works of D.H. Lawrence) and her forthcoming novel *Changer.* Her recent novels include *When the Gods Are Silent* and *Donnerjack* (in collaboration with the late Roger Zelazny). She resides in New Mexico with her husband, archeologist Jim Moore (who suggested which fairy tale to retell for this collection), and various small animals.

Little else had been talked about for a week in either the city or the surrounding towns or even in the woodlands all around. Sir John Aurelion, Knight of the Red Hen, Duke of the Singing Harp, the hero of a dozen tavern ballads and at least a couple more formal epics had been accused of being nothing more than a common thief!

The pre-trial investigation had been such that, even though Sir John was much beloved of the Crown and much honored by the court, King Paddock had been given no choice but to permit the trial to proceed.

Some whispered, especially the common folk who lived close to the Enchanted Forest, that King Paddock had been given no choice lest embarrassing incidents from his own past—and from that of Queen Flora—be brought forth and made public.

And so a judge was appointed, a somber old knight of some seventy years, called Adam. Sir John Aurelion announced that his defense would be handled by none other than Lord Conrad, the king's own counselor. Then a jury was selected. This last created no little difficulty, for the law of England requires a jury of one's peers and, despite the ballads, no one knew precisely from whence came the mysterious Sir John Aurelion.

Some argued that as Sir John was a knight and nobleman, the jury must be drawn only from the ranks of the nobility, but the attorney for the prosecution, a wily fox named Rufus Reynard, insisted that the jury pool be more diverse. Again he passed a neatly folded note to King Paddock. After reading it, the king whispered to Judge Adam and Lord Conrad, and Mr. Reynard had his way.

Thus the jury that sat in the bench consisted of six good English knights and true, each attired in the colors of his noble house, and six creatures never before seen in an English court.

There was a dwarf with a long beard and a dour countenance. There was a soft brown doe rabbit with a wiggling nose. There was a water nixie, who dripped on the floor until the bailiff brought her a basin in which to sit. There was a white hart, clean-limbed and bright of eye with a rack of antlers that made the knights of the jury, hunters one and all, murmur in envy. Finally, there were a red rosebush in full flower and a nightingale who watched the proceedings from disconcertingly bright, black eyes.

The twelve jury members listened most carefully as Lord Conrad and Mr. Reynard made their opening statements. Lord Conrad's was simple yet powerful:

"Everyone here knows Sir John Aurelion as a noble-born knight, one who earned King Paddock's favor after ridding the land of a terrible monster. His reputation is as sound and solid as the gold of his name. Let no one be swayed from what he knows to be true."

Mr. Reynard was equally brief: "My noble adversary says that this 'Sir John Aurelion' rid the land of a terrible monster. That is a lie. I say that the man who sits there in the defendant's chair, clad in cloth-of-gold, is nothing but a peasant boy named Jack, a thief, a simpleton, and—but for the grace of God above—a murderer. Do not let yourself be swayed by ballads and epics. Hear the true story and judge as the truth demands."

Now everyone knew that Sir John was accused as a thief, but only a few close to the royal court knew the identity of his accuser, so there was general consternation among those gathered in the courtroom when, after his opening statement, Counselor Reynard called his first witness.

"I call Mistress Cloudcroft to the stand," said the fox with a flourish of his white-tipped tail.

The great doors of the king's hall parted, and a shadow darkened the opening, blocking all the light. Then something far larger than any man or beast who sat in that high-ceilinged hall bent to come through the opening. There were stifled screams and Queen Flora paled and clutched at the arms of her gilded throne.

What entered was a giantess full twenty feet tall, horrid in her great size, but dressed much like any goodwife in a simple linen dress, clean white apron, and leather shoes. A ribbon broad enough to tie a ship fastened a modest bonnet over her graying hair.

Now everyone understood why the trial was being held in the king's own hall, rather than in the courthouse, for no other building in all the kingdom (save for the church, which could not be profaned with such matters) possessed a ceiling high enough for the giantess to stand beneath. Even so, her matronly bonnet brushed against the vaulted ceiling, loosening hidden cobwebs which drifted to the floor to the great embarrassment of Queen Flora and the greater consternation of the palace housekeeping staff.

Rufus Reynard had prepared for his client's needs. With a wave of his paw, he indicated that she should take her seat on a massive stone pedestal from which the statue (one of King Paddock in his heroic youth) had been temporarily removed. Once seated, the giantess became merely enormous rather than intimidating. She folded her hands into her lap and nodded politely, even with a trace of shyness, to the assembled company.

"Forgive me for not curtsying," she said, in a voice like summer thunder, "but I fear my skirts would disarrange the court."

King Paddock licked his broad lips and blinked eyes that were bulging a bit in astonishment, but he remained courtly and kind. When he spoke, there was only a slight croak in his voice:

"We shall accept the intention in place of the action, Mistress Cloudcroft. Pray, attend to the matter concerning this court."

"Thank you, Your Majesty." Mistress Cloudcroft turned eyes that truly were like deep blue pools upon her counselor and awaited his instructions.

Rufus Reynard, when certain that he had the court's attention, said to his client, "Mistress Cloudcroft, you have brought this complaint against Sir John Aurelion."

"I have."

"And of what do you accuse him?"

"Of theft and of causing grave bodily harm to my dear husband, Claus."

A murmur of consternation rippled through the court at these words. Many members of the audience looked over their shoulders as if expecting to see the looming form of this injured giant darkening the windows.

"Sir John," Rufus Reynard spoke the name with distaste, "claimed his place at court nearly a year ago. Why has it taken you so long to bring this complaint?"

The giantess lifted her hand to wipe away a tear that, had it fallen, would have thoroughly soaked the secretary of the court and ruined his careful records of the proceedings.

"It is only a month since my husband was judged to be out of danger," she explained. "Once I could leave the task of nursing him in the hands of our young children, I proceeded to make inquiries after his assailant. I did not find him at once, since I did not equate this new hero of the realm with the cowardly, thieving Jack."

Lord Conrad leaped to his feet. "Objection, Your Honor!"

Judge Adam nodded. "Sustained. Madam, kindly refrain from using such derogatory terms in reference to the defendant."

Mistress Cloudcroft nodded. Rufus Reynard turned to her, then and said, "Madam, perhaps you could tell us in your own words about the events leading up to the thefts and to the injury of your husband."

The giantess smiled nervously and asked for a pail of water to wet her suddenly dry throat. Then, with apologies for her lack of training as a public speaker, she began:

"To understand my story fully, I must take you back to before we ever met Jack, back to the days before my dear Claus was born."

Claus' parents farmed a small plot on the edge of the Enchanted Forest. Good, honest peasant folk, they were careful not to harm their magical neighbors. They put out milk for the brownies, avoided nixie-haunted springs, and never picked the roses that bloomed in winter.

Their one sorrow was that they didn't have a child of their own. One day, when the goodwife was picking beans in her vegetable garden, she looked sadly at a pod and said aloud:

"If only I had a little boy, one who would nestle up to me just as these beans nestle in their pod. Then I would be happy."

Oddly enough, soon after this, she developed a craving for beans. For nine months she would eat nothing else, and her husband was happy to indulge her in this fancy, for it was clear that she had conceived a child.

On the ninth day of the ninth month, a son was born to

this good couple. In every way but one, he was a perfect child, strong of limb, bright of eye, with rosy cheeks, and a hearty set of lungs. In only one way was he different . . . he never grew taller than a bean pod.

Still, the peasant couple loved their son and he loved them. As he grew older, when his chores were done, he would venture into the Enchanted Forest. One day, he spoke his secret sorrow aloud:

"If only I were not so very small, then I could be of greater help to my dear parents. As I am now, all I can do is sit in the plow horse's ear and guide him through the furrows or direct the cow to pasture. I would love to be as tall and strong as any hero of legend."

And the Enchanted Forest, which loved his parents for the simple honors they paid to it, caused one bean plant among those in the furrows to grow pods containing beans shaded brilliant blue, violet, red, and orange. When young Claus saw these beans, he understood them to be the answer to his plea.

Cracking open a pod, he ate one bean. It was a valiant effort, for the bean was nearly a quarter of his own size. After a moment, Claus realized that he was growing. When he was the size of two bean pods, the magical growth stopped.

With more enthusiasm than wisdom, Claus ate more of the beans. Soon he was the size of a boy, then that of a youth, then that of a small man, then that of a large man. At last he realized that he had eaten far too many beans. He had become a giant.

In his shock and horror, Claus let some of the remaining beans drop from his fingers. One of these fell into warm soil and sent forth a gigantic stalk. This grew until it stood taller than any of the trees in the Enchanted Forest and reached into the clouds beyond. Through the clouds, Claus glimpsed a land like that below, but on a larger scale and he knew that his patrons in the Forest were showing him one last mercy.

Saddened, he bid his parents farewell and went to seek his fortune. He had many adventures there in the cloud lands, winning renown, a fortune, and a princess for a bride.

(Here Mistress Cloudcroft colored prettily.)

In time, Claus and his wife had several children, all giants like their parents. He became fond of his life in the clouds, but he never forgot his parents. He sent them wealth to cushion their old age and gave them magical beans so that they could ascend to visit him whenever they wished.

If they planted a bean at night, by the next morning the bean put forth a stalk that would carry them to the clouds, but it withered by that night. When they stayed for a longer visit, Claus would lower them back to their farm on a long rope he kept for that purpose.

At last, at a ripe old age, these two good folk died. Claus brought their bodies to his estate in the clouds and buried them where he hoped someday to rest beside his wife and children.

Now that he had wealth, family, and estate, Claus turned his attention to bringing to others some of the kindness that he had been shown by the Enchanted Forest. He became a patron of the arts and a hero to the weak. Daily, he gave alms to the poor, doling out the gold and silver he had received as reward for his youthful feats of bravery.

He encouraged his wife and children to live simply

and enjoy the fruits of their own labors. Following his direction, they found happiness rarely known to mortal creatures.

Then tragedy struck.

(Here Mistress Cloudcroft paused to wipe fresh tears as they pooled in her blue eyes.)

After his parents' death, Claus let the Enchanted Forest reclaim his family farm, for he had no use for it. The Forest overgrew all but the cobblestone cottage. Even this was well concealed under flowering honeysuckle vines when an impoverished hedge wizard took shelter there.

Searching the ruin for something he might carry away and sell, the wizard found several old pots and a few cups. He also discovered a rotting leather bag containing the remaining magic beans. He was about to make them into a soup when he noticed their brilliant color.

The hedge wizard's training had not been for naught. He carried one bean outside and planted it. At first he was disappointed, but overnight, it put forth a stalk to the clouds.

The hedge wizard climbed up it and saw the cloud lands spread before him. He might have explored further, but he saw how the stalk withered away when evening came. As he was essentially a coward, the wizard resolved to sell the beans to the first fool who would trade him something worthwhile.

"Objection, Your Honor!" cried Lord Conrad.

"Sustained," said Judge Adam. "Mistress Cloudcroft, please refrain from alluding to the defendant as a fool."

"Yes, Your Honor."

The judge smiled with sudden kindness. "Pray, continue with your interesting account."

"Thank you, Your Honor," said the giantess. "Let me say before proceeding, that I learned the elements of the next part of the story from the hedge wizard, as well as from Jack himself."

The hedge wizard went to market the next day, bearing with him the pots and cups which he sold to a tinker for a few pennies. He had nearly given up hope that he would find anyone who could be convinced to trade for the beans when he saw a young man arrive late to market, leading a fine milk cow.

This youth was obviously poor, for his clothes were threadbare, and apparently credulous, for he was staring about him with a yokel's wide-eyed wonder. In bare moments, the hedge wizard was on him like a cat upon a mouse.

"Hello, young man. Is this your first visit to market?"

"Yes, sir," said the young man. "It is. What a huge and marvelous place it is! Certainly it contains all the wonders of the world."

The hedge wizard looked about the market, which at this late hour of the afternoon was reduced to a tinker, an apple seller, two bakery stalls, and a butcher. Taking the young man by the elbow, the hedge wizard steered him to one side.

"Hungry, my boy?"

"Very, sir," the youth said eagerly. "I've been walking since early morning, except for when I took a nap under a tree. A nap may rest the body, but it does little to fill the belly. My mother said there was neither bread nor soup for me in the house, not so much as a thin slice of bacon or an onion. I was to make my meal from what Bossy here would give me, but the elves must have milked the stubborn old thing, for she's been as dry as a stone."

The hedge wizard led the youth over to a baker's stall and for a penny bought the day's leavings of stale pasties and broken bread. The youth devoured the food as one might a fine feast.

"I've never had bread before," he confessed, "for my mother doesn't have an oven. It's far nicer than porridge."

"What's your name, lad?" the hedge wizard asked.

" 'Tis Jack," came the reply from around a mouthful of bread, "Jack the widow's son."

"And you've come to market to sell your cow?"

"That's right. She's a good cow, but we don't have the grazing for her." A sly look came into his brown eyes. "And neither does our neighbor."

The hedge wizard began then to suspect that Jack was a bit of a rogue as well as a bumpkin and felt better for the trade he meant to make with him.

"Come, lad," said he. "I'll take you to a tavern and buy you some beer. There's no way you can walk back to your mother's house before nightfall, and there are thieves and ruffians aplenty on the road at night."

Jack grinned. "I'm happy enough to bide here. Mother won't look for me until tomorrow, for she told me to walk to a market far from our home where the cow would bring a good price."

*And won't be recognized as a stolen beast,* thought the hedge wizard, but he kept such thoughts to himself.

The two men tied the cow to a post on the common where it could graze, leaving it in the care of the night watchman who was glad enough for the mug of beer they brought him.

Then the hedge wizard introduced Jack to those wonders that could be found in a tavern. A few pennies from the sale of the pots and cups bought them strong beer. They shared a meat pie thick with potatoes and brown gravy. By the time the tavern closed its doors, they were fast friends.

As the night was warm, the hedge wizard had no trouble convincing Jack to walk with him a short distance to where the town ended and a section of the King's Forest began. Once there, the hedge wizard made a great production of planting one of the beans.

"In the morning, Jack," he promised, "there will be a wonder for you to see."

Jack nodded, but full of beer and pie, he fell quickly asleep. The hedge wizard considered leaving then and there, claiming the cow, and thus escaping with both beans and beef. Remembering, though, how Jack had arm wrestled all comers in the tavern, how he had swept the prettiest of the wenches onto his knee, how his young muscles had bulged, the wizard decided that a fair trade would be best if he wished to keep his head unbroken.

In the morning, as promised, a wonder awaited, for a beanstalk had grown until it vanished into the clouds. Jack and the wizard climbed up it and saw a fine estate in the distance.

"Now that would be the place to be," said Jack. "Shall we sell the cow and then go see what is there?"

"I have a better idea," the hedge wizard replied. "See here. I have six more of these magical beans. I'll trade them to you for the cow. Then you can grow a stalk whenever you wish."

Jack looked interested, and the hedge wizard pressed his point. "I'm sure there's treasure up there, treasure beyond the worth of a mere cow if a man's bold enough to go after it. But this is not the place from which to make such a venture."

"Why?" asked simple Jack.

"Look down," said the wizard. "See how the people are gathering to look at this beanstalk? Soon others will climb up and claim what is your right. I am not a bold man—not as you are. Therefore, I'll take your cow and you take my beans. Hurry off with them to some lonely place . . ."

"My mother's cottage is lonely enough," interrupted Jack.

". . . and do your adventuring from there."

In a trice, the deal was made. Jack had the beans, the wizard had the cow. To seal the deal, they chopped down the beanstalk and sold it to the tavern keeper for firewood and horse feed.

Then, quite pleased with himself, a parting gift of bread and cheese in his pocket, Jack went home to his mother. Needless to say, the old widow was not happy to learn that her son had sold a valuable dairy cow for six oddly colored beans. Doubtless her temper was sharpened because the cow's owner had been making inquiries after his beast and hadn't been happy to find Jack gone to market.

In a fit of temper, the widow threw the beans out the window. Ignoring her scolding, Jack slipped outside. In the dim evening light, he managed to find five of the beans. The sixth was gone and he guessed that it had been eaten by the chickens.

But the next morning, there outside the cottage was a towering beanstalk. Seeming to forget her doubts of the night before, the widow urged her son up the stalk.

"And don't come back until you've found your fortune!" she cried.

So urged along his way, Jack made the climb. When his head poked above the clouds, he was pleased to see that the estate which he had seen the day before was much closer than he had thought.

"This is good," he said happily to himself. "Not only am I free from prying eyes, as my friend the wizard said I should be, but I won't have as far to go."

After he had been walking for a time, Jack realized that he was even closer than he had thought, for the estate was on a giant scale. The feathered tops of the carrots were as tall as shrubs in the world below and a single grain of wheat as big as a plum. Chickens the size of ponies scratched in the dirt. What he had first taken for a hunting dog proved to be a field mouse.

But the fortune Jack was seeking wasn't in grain or livestock. When she was younger, before life made her grim, his mother had told him tales of princes who ventured into golden mountains to seek gem-strewn caverns, and of the hoards kept by dragons and dwarves. In the tavern he had heard stories of misers' strongboxes and of merchants' warehouses. Now he was greedy for something more than a solid meal.

Carefully, ever so carefully, he crept across the fields. Stealthily, as if about to purloin another cow, he found his way into the giant's house. This was a sturdy structure, built of stone, with three bedrooms, a good kitchen, and a nursery for the little ones, as well as a library where the master and mistress read poetry or did the estate accounts. Finally, there was a large parlor where the family gathered after dinner to relate stories of their daily rounds.

Jack had spent most of the day inspecting the house, noting where the portable valuables were kept. At dinnertime, he had been forced into hiding, for the giant's cat—a creature the size of a warhorse—had been too much about. Now, however, Puss was sleeping under the stove and he felt safe to take his leave. First, however, he wanted to collect a nice gold thimble—about the size of a knight's helmet—from the parlor.

Nimbly he climbed to the top of the sewing basket and was about to claim his prize when, to his horror, he heard the giant family trooping into the room. He hunkered down among the spools of thread, seizing a small darning needle to use as a sword, and vowing that, if he couldn't run, he would sell his life bravely.

Peeking out through the basket's weave, he watched the giant lord romp with his little ones (the smallest of whom was still far larger than Jack). When the children wearied and wanted a quieter game, the giant called to his eldest son.

"Bring me my little red hen!"

The giant boy did so, bringing a hen that, to Jack's surprise, was the size of a normal hen, not of a horse. The giant stroked the red hen with a fingertip, then declaimed:

"Little hen, once again, lay an egg for me!"

The hen obliged and a gold egg rolled out. Jack watched as the golden oval, so small against the giant's palm, but worth a tidy bit nonetheless, was placed on a table and the hen, lavishly praised, was returned to its coop.

There followed a long discussion as to where the gold would best be put to use. Finally, the giant family agreed to trade the egg for blankets and warm winter clothes for a poor family.

This, then, led to a discussion of other charitable projects in which the giant family was involved. In short order, Jack learned where the giant's strongbox (a box as large as a room to a human) was and noted that he was small enough to slip through the keyhole.

Then, obviously as a special treat, the giant family listened to music played by a wonderful golden harp—this again built on a human scale, not a gigantic one—that strummed itself and sung in a voice sweet and mellow of the heroic deeds of the giant Claus.

Here Mistress Cloudcroft cleared her throat and turned to face the judge and jury.

"The next part of my story," she said, "is mine to tell, for I was there."

"Proceed, Madam," said Judge Adam, though Sir John stirred uneasily at this, as indeed he had been stirring ever since the tale had come to focus on the adventures of Jack. "But bear in mind that you are not to malign the defendant."

Mistress Cloudcroft bowed her head graciously and, after sipping delicately from her bucket of water, continued:

"I found Jack in my sewing basket that night, when my dear Claus had gone to tuck the children into bed. The tiny creature fenced at me wildly with my own darning needle, but I could see fear in the whiteness of his eyes. I spoke to him softly, then, as softly as I could, for I understood the fear a trapped creature feels. I myself had once been held captive until my dear Claus rescued me from the cold claws of Nightwing the . . ."

"Objection, Your Honor!" shouted Lord Conrad. "Immaterial!"

"Sustained," sighed Judge Adam, for he would have like to hear the story of the giantess princess and Nightwing. "Mistress Cloudcroft, please restrict your comments to the matter at hand. Clerk, enter into the record only that Mistress Cloudcroft spoke as gently as she could to the youth Jack, for she understood his fear."

After politely waiting while the clerk changed his records, the giantess went on:

" 'Be easy, little man,' I said. 'How did you come here?'

" 'I climbed the beanstalk,' said he, 'and I will climb down again if you but let me go.'

"In a few short words, I told him that the beanstalk would have withered with the setting sun. Jack's terror was great then, but I offered him an acorn cup of wine, such as we keep for the woodland elves who sometimes visit."

"Objection!"

"Sustained."

"I offered him wine and that calmed him some. Then Jack told me his tale, much of which I have just related. I suspected that the wine loosened his tongue a bit, or he would not so freely have admitted to stealing his neighbor's cow.

"By this time I felt pity for him and, when he begged

me to hide his existence from my husband, I agreed to do so, for I feared that else Jack would die of fright."

Sir John Aurelion, seated at the defendant's table, looked as if he would protest these words, but his attorney laid a firm hand on his arm and he kept his peace.

"The next day," Mistress Cloudcroft continued, "I myself lowered Jack to the ground, using the rope we had from the days when my sweet Claus' parents would visit. I gave him a satchel full of food, a skin of sweet wine, and a purse filled with gold and silver coins, for Jack's stories of the poverty in which he and his mother lived had touched me to the heart.

"But Jack had not told me that he had five more magical beans. (I learned this later to my dismay.) When the food I had given him was gone and the money squandered, he again planted a bean and climbed up the stalk. This time he had the good fortune to find us away, visiting my cousins at the court of King . . ."

"Objection!"

"Sustained," sighed Judge Adam deeply, for he did love a good story.

"He carried away the little red hen who laid the eggs of gold and left a dead hen, similar in appearance, in her coop. He also carried away several sacks of gold from my husband's strongbox."

"Objection!" shouted good Conrad. "If she was not there, how could she know that Jack carried these things away?"

"Denied," said the judge sternly. "You will have ample opportunity for cross-examination. Indeed, let me warn you, Counselor Conrad, that your frequent objections may force the jury to draw conclusions that you might not care for at all regarding the identity of this 'Jack.' "

Lord Conrad paled at this and sat down immediately. Indeed, his lips remained sealed for the rest of the giantess' tale.

"We did not know what to think about the missing gold," she continued, "and, indeed believed our poor hen dead. Still, we moved the strongbox, buried the little red imposter, and went on with our lives.

"A time or two, I sensed someone skulking about, but I dismissed this as the natural nervousness of one whose home and hearth had been invaded. When a few small items went missing—the silver counters from one of the children's games, the topaz ring my mother had given me, several teaspoons from the good silver service, I resolved to be more strict about reminding the children to pick up after themselves. However, since material goods were not our family's main concern, we left this by the way and went about our simple lives.

"Then Jack returned once more. Although he had the money from the little red hen's golden eggs and from the small items he had pilfered, he was greedy for the rest of the gold in the strongbox and for the singing harp.

"He lurked about the estate for some days until he learned where the gold was now kept. I admit this was a brave enough act, for Puss was alert to his presence. However, since he was as small as a mouse (only somewhat smarter), she had trouble catching him. Though Jack's beanstalk had shriveled after his first night in the cloud lands, he had made contingencies for his retreat. At last, he learned we were to dine at the home of Prince . . ."

Mistress Cloudcroft blushed and corrected herself.

"We were called away to dine, and Jack took his chance. He signaled his mother and told her to plant a bean so that his ladder would be ready in the morning. Then, all that night, while we were away from home and the servants given holiday, he carried away those things he desired and piled them where the beanstalk would emerge. Last of all, he took the singing harp, leaving the empty case to fool our casual inspection.

"Early that morning, when the first green leaves of the beanstalk peeked above the clouds, Jack began ferrying down his take. First went the gold, then some of my best jewelry, then a few of the children's trinkets. He took his time, for he knew we had been out late and he did not think we would rise very early.

"However, he did not count on my dear Claus' sense of duty. Soon after dawn, Claus rose and went to tend the horses and cattle (the servants, you recall, had been given a holiday). He was coming out of the barn when he heard a little voice calling: 'Master, save me! Master, save me!'

"Claus saw the leaves of the beanstalk peeking above the clouds and knew what that portended. He ran across the fields, but Jack was nimble, Jack was quick, and he was halfway down the beanstalk before Claus even had his feet on the first part. But Claus had climbed many a beanstalk since he was a tiny boy, and he followed rapidly.

"Still, Jack reached the ground first, and, seizing an ax, he chopped away at the beanstalk. Trapped between the clouds and the ground, Claus could not escape. The wicked youth cut the stalk in two and Claus plummeted to the earth. Jack must have believed him dead, for, taking his mother and his goods in a wagon he had bought some time before, he whipped up the horses and traveled to a kingdom on the other side of the Enchanted Forest. There he established himself as a hero.

"Claus, meanwhile, was not slain, only sorely wounded. The bones in both legs were broken, as were those in his arms, and several of his ribs. Only the aid of the many little creatures he had helped in their days of need brought him home to where we could care for him."

The giantess took a shuddering breath that felt like a gale to those gathered in the king's hall. "I will spare you the details of those terrible months during which we struggled for his life. Doubtless, that is 'immaterial,' but when his life was no longer in immediate danger, I resolved to find Jack and make certain that he did not profit from his wicked ways. My search was not as difficult as I had feared, for in his arrogance, Jack had not gone far."

Rufus Reynard rose then and crossed to his client.

"Mistress Cloudcroft," said he, looking up to where the blue eyes were once again threatening to flood with tears, "can you identify this man who you have called 'Jack'?"

"I can," she answered, a great throb in her voice.

"And is he anywhere in this court?"

"Yes," she cried, forgetting to speak softly in her fervor, so that the very stones of the king's hall vibrated. "He is there, seated at the defense table. He is the man who now calls himself Sir John Aurelion, Knight of the Red Hen, Duke of the Singing Harp!"

There really wasn't much the defense could do after that, for in his pride, Jack had named himself after two of the items that he had stolen from the giants' estate.

In vain did Sir Conrad question Mistress Cloudcroft about the well-known words: "Fee, Fie, Foe, Fum, I smell the blood of an Englishman. Be he alive or be he dead, I'll grind his bones to make my bread!" Mild as any good-wife, Mistress Cloudcroft took oath that these words had never passed her Claus' lips.

In vain did he raise the question of whether one hen could truly be told from another. (Yes, for only one hen laid golden eggs.) In vain did Sir Conrad protest permitting a singing harp to give evidence. (Yet it did, and damning was that testimony. Not only did the harp relate how Jack had stolen it. It admitted to composing the ballads that had brought Sir John such fame.)

Rufus Reynard had an easier time of it. From the Enchanted Forest came elves to testify that they had given the singing harp to the giant Claus in return for his kindness to them after the rainbow crash some years before.

From beneath the Misty Mountains came dwarves to testify that they had coined the gold that Sir John had spent so freely. Finally, from a small dairy farm came a former hedge wizard to testify that he had indeed found magic beans in a ruined cottage at the fringe of the Enchanted Forest and traded them to Jack in return for Bossy the cow.

Yet, when the jury retired to discuss the verdict, Sir John Aurelion looked amazingly cheerful, a thing that Rufus Reynard noted with deep concern.

"The jury is half made up of humans, after all," the fox explained to Mistress Cloudcroft, speaking low-voiced from where she had set him on her shoulder. "And the actions of nixies and dwarves are hard to predict. That rose bush may be a problem, too. I forgot that she's likely a relative of the queen's. No wonder Lord Conrad admitted her."

"Do you think the jury might find against us, even with all the evidence we've provided against Jack?" said the giantess, worry creasing her features.

"They might. Jack looks mighty smug, and he's not as much a simpleton as he was—if he ever was one."

"But the evidence!"

"Forget the evidence, my lady. It's all against *Jack*. You know that Sir John and Jack are one and the same. I know that Sir John and Jack are one and the same, but some of those brave knights and true might be convinced to think otherwise, especially if they are given incentive."

"Incentive?" asked the honest giantess.

"Gold, perhaps," sighed the wily fox, who had resisted some flashed his way. "Or maybe a ballad or two composed on the singing harp. Look what those did for Jack's reputation. Without them, he'd never have convinced people he was a nobleman. Don't think that's escaped the jury's eye—especially the part of the jury that's made up of knights who want to be thought heroes."

"Surely King Paddock won't permit such injustice!" Mistress Cloudcroft protested indignantly, forgetting once more to keep her voice soft. This time, however, they were waiting in the empty hall, everyone else having gone out to escape the looming presence of the giantess.

"He might, and he might not," Reynard answered, swishing his tail as he paced on her shoulder. "Not every man respects his roots—and since the king's are in a pond, he's got good reason to want them forgotten."

The giantess raised a thumb the size of a sapling to her mouth and chewed unhappily on the nail. "So our home may be robbed and my dear Claus be injured almost to death, yet this rascal could continue to profit?"

"That's the long and short of it, Mistress," the fox admitted. "We've put on a good show. Now it's up to the jury to decide the question."

"Hmm." The giantess thought deeply for a moment. "I'm certain that the rabbit, the hart, and the nightingale will decide in our favor. That leaves only the dwarf, the nixie, and the rosebush—for you seem certain that the humans will side with Jack."

"Not certain," the fox said, "but fairly so."

"Then all we can do is wait, but I can't promise not to break something if they decide against us—the roof perhaps."

"Quite understandable," Reynard agreed. "Just give me a chance to get to the woods first."

After being sequestered for some hours, the jury emerged and the foreman (the most senior of the knights) announced that they could not reach a decision. The vote was tied, six to six.

Oddly enough, the split was not as Rufus Reynard had predicted. One of the knights, the youngest and most idealistic, had voted against Jack. The white hart, perhaps in fear for his antlers, had voted with the knights.

"A hung jury," mused King Paddock aloud. "The decision, then, is up to you, Judge Adam. What will you rule?"

The judge adjusted his wig, looking as if he had been considering this matter for a long time, as indeed he had, though like Rufus Reynard he had expected a different split.

"Have you any advice to offer, Your Majesty?"

King Paddock shook his head, as if too regal to interfere. In reality, Jack's promise to give him the little red hen was what stayed the king's wide-lipped mouth from recommending a finding in favor of the giantess.

"No. You are the judge. Proceed."

Judge Adam considered the defendant, the jury, and, lastly, the giantess and her red-furred counselor. He also considered the three solid gold eggs rolling against each other in the deep pockets of his robe and the bag of coins resting in his coach. Then he smiled at Sir John Aurelion.

"You, sir, have given me one of the greatest gifts of my life. I am certain you are capable of giving many more."

A thin, high wail, like the shrilling of a winter wind came from the giantess, but otherwise she held her peace until the verdict be given. Sir John, for his part, looked smug.

"Thank you, Your Honor."

"Ah, but wait. The gift to which I refer is not the one you may be thinking of, Jack."

At the sound of his peasant name, the defendant's face lost its smile and became grim.

"Without you, Jack," Judge Adam continued, "I would have missed an opportunity to hear some marvelous stories. Sadly for you, you are not the hero of these tales."

The judge straightened, twitching his robe into order, then gaveling to silence the murmuring spectators. When he spoke, his voice was nearly as thunderous as a giant's.

"Sir John Aurelion, alias Jack the Widow's Son, Simple Jack, Cattle Thief Jack, Jack of the Beanstalk, Jack the

Would-be Giant Killer, I find against you. You are sentenced to return this lady's property to her at once. I also order you to cease using titles that are not yours by birth or deed. If you can apologize to Mistress Cloudcroft, you might prove yourself a noble soul after all, but I suspect such courtesy is beyond you."

Jack, no longer ever to be called Sir John Aurelion, pushed back his chair and rose to his feet.

"Bugger all. Take the junk," he growled and stalked from the room.

As the judge had already made arrangements for Sir John's property to be confiscated, he let Jack depart unimpeded. He thumped his gavel once more.

"This concludes the hearing of the case of Mistress Cloudcroft versus Sir John Aurelion."

"All rise," called the bailiff and all, even the giantess, did so. The judge left the bench, but rather than departing the king's hall, he crossed to speak with the lady.

Mistress Cloudcroft mopped at her tears with a handkerchief the size of a tall ship's sail.

"Thank you, Your Honor," she said at last, managing to squeeze the words out between her sobs.

"My pleasure, Mistress Cloudcroft. Tell me," said Judge Adam, raising his voice to be heard above the departing spectators, "I don't suppose you would have time to tell me the rest of those stories?"

"Stories?"

"About the giant princess and Nightwing of the cold claws, or what happened when you visited your cousin the prince."

A smile like daybreak banished Mistress Cloudcroft's tears. "I should be delighted. Come home with me for dinner, if you'd like. As soon as I collect my property and reward Counselor Reynard, I'm departing by beanstalk."

"That sounds wonderful," said the judge, draping his wig and robe over the bailiff's arm. "I do love a good fairy tale."

# GILLY THE GOOSE GIRL
## *by Nancy Springer*

Nancy Springer is a lifelong fiction writer, author of thirty-one volumes of mythic fantasy, children's literature, mystery, suspense, short stories, and poetry. Her latest novel is *I Am Mordred,* a young-adult Arthurian fantasy from the point of view of Arthur's unacknowledged son. A longtime Pennsylvania resident, she teaches creative writing at York College of Pennsylvania. In her spare time she is an enthusiastic, although not expert, horseback rider, and a volunteer for the Wind Ridge Farm Equine Sanctuary, a home for horses that have been rescued from neglect or abuse. She lives in Dallastown with too many brainless animals.

A true princess can be distinguished from other people almost like a subspecies by the following attributes: she is highly decorative, pallid, exquisitely prone to bruising both physical and emotional, has hair like spun gold, is innocent to the point of stupidity, is weepy, has a few charmingly harmless magical abilities, is irrefutably virginal, has no name (being known simply as the Princess), and has no mind of her own.

Princess Gillianna knew herself to be lacking in some of these attributes. She had the decorative appearance and the requisite golden hair, along with the usual sky-blue eyes; she was virginal, having been raised in the usual secluded tower; she had a few magical abilities suitable to parlor entertainments—but she was not weepy or prone to bruising. She had a name—Gillianna. And she had a mind of her own.

Her mother the queen, however, didn't know what else to do for her other than arrange the requisite marriage to a prince in a distant kingdom, a young man Gillianna had never met.

Therefore, upon a sunny day in her fifteenth summer, Gillianna left her tower and, richly gowned in garments appropriate to a princess, bade a tearful good-bye to her poor old widowed mother and mounted her white horse, Falada. Accompanied by a chambermaid, she set forth for the distant kingdom of her betrothed.

Even though her horse, the chambermaid's horse, and their packhorses were loaded with gold and jewels, and even though Princess Gillianna presented every appearance of a royal princess with a rich dowry on her way to be married, it was not necessary to provide her with more escort than the single chambermaid, because this particular chambermaid was known to be the psychological equal of any dozen armed men.

Also there was the additional safeguard of the white horse, Falada, who could talk—although, being exceedingly well-bred, a palfrey with the mane upon her highly arched neck trailing as fine as a maiden's hair, Falada

spoke only when appropriate or necessary. Horses should
be seen and not heard.

There was no chatting, therefore, as Princess Gillianna
and her party jogged along. Falada had nothing to say, the
chambermaid had nothing to say to the princess, and certainly Gillianna had nothing to say to the chambermaid.

Until she got thirsty. When they came to a stream,
Gillianna told the chambermaid, "Get me a cup of water
to drink."

"Get it yourself," said the chambermaid.

"Huh," said Gillianna, and she dismounted and did so.
It felt good to get off the horse for a minute. The fresh,
cold stream water tasted very good. Gillianna took a cup
of it to the chambermaid while she was at it. The pleasure
of performing that simple act gave her thoughts that
tasted even better than the water. Gillianna had a mind of
her own, as aforementioned, and she made it up quickly.
"Tell you what," she said to the chambermaid as the latter drank, "let's trade places."

The chambermaid (who had no name, as befitted her
imminent position) nearly choked on the water. *"Huh?"*

"Get down and let's swap clothes and horses."

The chambermaid, being the chambermaid, knew it
had to be a trick. She did not move. Eyes wide, she demanded, "Why?"

"Because I want you to marry the prince."

The chambermaid nearly fell off her horse. *"HUH?"*

"You think I'm going to marry some keister I've never
met? You can have him. If you don't like him, a few years
with you will kill him."

Falada spoke for the first time, her voice issuing long
and morose from her long, morose white-horse face.
Cassandra-like, she intoned, "Oh, if your poor old mother

knew, her heart would break in two." Falada always spoke in rhyme, another consideration which kept her from speaking too frequently. If she couldn't find a rhyme, forget it. In her fillyhood, Falada had once been silent for an entire year because she couldn't think of a rhyme for "orange."

"Shut up, Falada," Gillianna said. If her mother knew, indeed. Hypothetical reasoning always annoyed Gillianna. Mama didn't know, and likely Mama never would know, and what Mama didn't know wouldn't hurt her.

"Shut up, Falada," echoed the chambermaid with greed in her voice. She hopped down from her mount and said to Gillianna, "You have to swear you're not going to change your mind when you see him."

"I won't." No matter how princely the prince was, Gillianna did not want to marry him. Or anyone. Not for years and years. She was only fifteen, for God's sake.

"Swear under the open sky that you'll never betray me to anyone."

So under the open sky, by firmament, welkin, and all forms of celestial judgment, Gillianna swore. Then she and the chambermaid exchanged clothing. Dressed in the chambermaid's simple and blessedly lightweight frock, Gillianna mounted the chambermaid's honest and blessedly silent brown horse, and she and the now-princess rode on.

The journey grew trying, because the ersatz princess practiced her princess skills and ordered Gillianna to do this and that. She also starved herself in order to look pallid and ethereal by the time the prince saw her, and starvation made her testy. But Gillianna ate heartily, smiled demurely, hid her golden hair under her humble muslin cap, and looked forward to the end of the journey.

At last the day came when they rode into the castle courtyard.

The watchmen had seen them approaching, and everyone had turned out to welcome them; the prince stood on the steps of the keep for his first look at his bride. He was, of course, as befit a prince, instantly distinguishable from all the other people. He had golden hair, blue eyes, and an air of aristocratic élan. When Gillianna saw him helping the now-princess down from her white palfrey, she almost regretted her promise. The prince was very handsome. Very handsome indeed.

Gillianna stood and held the horses and said nothing. Arm in arm with the prince, the quondam chambermaid gave Gillianna a triumphant grin.

"Who's that?" the prince asked his bride, jerking his head toward Gillianna.

"My servant. But I don't want her as a chambermaid anymore. Just find something for her to do, would you?"

Gillianna took the horses to the stable, ate supper in the kitchen, and found that she was to be the new goose girl.

At dawn, therefore, she yawned, got up from her bed of straw in the back pantry of the scullery, and stumbled forth, rubbing her eyes, to make the acquaintance of the geese.

And the goose boy, who stood waiting for her at the postern gate. "Sleepyhead," he greeted her with a smile.

"You're the goose boy?" She was a bit surprised, for he was no boy, but a young man taller than she. A pleasant-looking young man with a wide, droll mouth, a pug nose and high, freckled cheekbones, over all of which he wore a droopy-brimmed felt hat dignified with a curling flourish of cockfeathers; it seemed to be his prized possession, for he touched it as he spoke.

"That I be. Name's Conrad. What's yours?"

"Gilly."

"Gilly? That's a pretty name." Gillyflowers bloomed tall by the sunny cottage walls everywhere at this time of year. "Lavender blue, Gilly, Gilly," sang Conrad in a true tenor voice as he headed the geese out the gate.

"Am not," Gilly said.

"Are too blue. Blue eyes, anyway."

"Are not. Gray." She bickered with him just for the fun of it. "How come you're a goose boy? You don't look like a goose."

"Don't I? You do."

"Thank you so much. Why aren't you in the king's service? You're tall enough."

"I like tending the geese," Conrad said.

"Why?"

"You'll see."

At first she did not see why, not at all. Geese were not much nicer than snakes on stilts, she found within a few minutes. They bit without warning or provocation. And when they bit, they grabbed a fleshy portion of thigh in their horny bills and twisted it hard before letting go.

"Take your stick to them when they do that," said Conrad serenely when Gilly shrieked.

"I did! He bit me again anyway!"

"She. It's the wimmin that bite worst."

She let that pass, because she had noticed that he himself did not strike the geese, just shooed them along with his stick. "I'd think being a soldier might be easier!"

"Nah. Once we get them up to the meadow, you'll see."

Then she did see. These geese grazed, and all there was to do was sit on a grassy lea in the sun and gaze around at golden hills and green dells and a cataract singing its way down to a winding stream and the castle standing peaceful below it all. To Gillianna, who had spent most of her life looking at the inside of her tower, the wild wide-sky freedom of the place was heavenly. She held her breath, watching an eagle fly. She saw deer standing at the edge of the upland forest, a fox running like a spark along a rift of rock. Conrad lay on his back in the sun, eyes closed under the tilted brim of his hat, humming to himself, while Gillianna gazed and gazed until all her seeing filled her so that she could no longer sit still. The geese honked and nipped at her as she darted away to explore. Where the cataract made a silver pool she washed her face in the flowing water. On a boulder in the sun she sat again, took off her cap and undid her golden flow of hair, which she had not cared for that morning. She had remembered to tuck a comb in her apron pocket, and with it she combed—

"Your hair is the color of a king's crown!" exclaimed Conrad.

Where had he come from? Gillianna frowned but continued to comb her golden tresses curling almost to the ground.

Kneeling close by, staring, Conrad reached for a single hair falling loose from the others. Gillianna snatched it away.

"Let me have one," Conrad begged. "Just a single strand."

Gillianna tilted her head toward the wide sky where fat, slow clouds flocked like sheep. "Wind," she sang, "blow Conrad's cap away and make him chase it half the day!"

All had been sunny calm till then, but at once a puff of breeze lifted Conrad's hat from his head and carried it off like a bird, far down the hillside. Conrad swore and chased after it. Gillianna smiled and set about braiding her hair. When Conrad returned, panting, carrying his hat in both hands, she had her hair all tucked up under her muslin cap again.

"How'd you do that?" he asked.

"Strength of virtue."

"Virtue? You're supposed to be tending the geese, goose. They've strayed down toward the woods."

They bickered as they rounded up the geese. They ate bread and cheese from Conrad's knapsack. They watched the slow growing and fading of the clouds. At day's end they drove the geese back to the castle, and the next day they did it all again. Days passed that way. Every day Gilly combed her hair, and Conrad chased his cap.

"Are you never bored?" Gillianna asked Conrad as they lay in the grass and watched sunset coming on. She herself loved every moment, but then, it was all new to her.

"No," Conrad said. "Other folk get bored, maybe. Not I."

"You like watching and dreaming."

"Yes."

"You like the geese." She had noticed that he was always gentle with them, although they obeyed him no better than they did her.

"Yes. Don't you?"

"No." Gillianna considered that a man who could be kind to geese would be kind to anything and anyone.

"I like creatures in general," he said. "I'd rather be with beasts than with most people."

After a spell of silence, he added, "The castle folk, they think I am stupid, you know. When they try to make me learn weapons, I act stupid."

Gilly laughed. "You're smarter than they are, then."

"Maybe. They're probably thinking of trying again. Letting you tend the geese."

"I hope not! I mean—I wouldn't mind tending the geese . . ." Gilly faltered to a confused halt, but Conrad turned to her with happy eyes.

"You like it, too? Being out here?"

"Yes." Gillianna thought of being a princess again, sitting all the livelong day embroidering kerchiefs. She wondered whether the chambermaid was enjoying herself. She smiled.

That day, when Gilly combed her hair, Conrad knelt by her side and begged once more, "Let me have a strand. Just a single strand." And when she called up the wind to take his cap away, he did not run after it. He stayed by her side. "Let it go," he said.

And she gave him a strand of her golden hair.

That evening when they took the geese home, in the dusky shadow of the postern gate, she let him kiss her.

That night she could barely sleep for happiness.

But the next dawn, when she met Conrad at the gate, something white hanging above the dark arch caught her eye. She looked, gasped, and cried out. With her white mane streaming down as fine as a lady's sorrow, Falada's head hung there.

"What's the matter?" Conrad asked.

Gillianna pointed. She could not speak. Tears trembled in her eyes.

Conrad nodded. "It's a shame," he said quietly. "A pretty palfrey she was, and no harm to her. But the prince sent her to the knackers because his new bride told him to."

Then anger took away Gillianna's tears. Because Falada could speak to reveal the secret, that selfish wench had ordered her killed? "And told him to hang her head where I could see it?"

Conrad gave her a puzzled glance. "I don't know what the head's doing up there."

"Falada," Gilly told the head of the dead horse, her voice breaking, "I'm sorry."

As if the voice of her princess gave her power to reply, Falada spoke. There was no life in those sunken eyes, horrible to look upon, but from the sagging mouth speech issued forth. "My princess, is that you? Oh, if your mother knew, her heart would break in two."

Conrad staggered as if he had been struck, and his mouth felt at the air. He babbled, "Bu-bu-bu—"

"Oh!" Gilly cried. "Quickly! Hurry!" She grabbed Conrad by the hand and ran, leaving the geese hissing and squabbling by the gate. "Falada can still speak," she told him as if that explained everything.

Conrad did not ask where they were going in such a hurry. Instead, he gasped, *"Princess?"*

"Not anymore."

"But—"

"Hush." They had reached the slaughterhouse, and Gilly ran in, although the smell squeezed her chest. "Is there any of her left?" she cried.

Several large, bloodied men regarded her round-eyed.

"Falada!" Gillianna saw the snow-white hide and seized it. "Is there anything more? Her bones?"

Without questioning her, without a word, they gave her a few bones boiled clean of meat and four sunset-colored hooves. Conrad helped her carry the things back toward the postern gate.

"Who is the vixen wedding the prince?" he whispered.

"My chambermaid."

"But—but you should be his bride."

"Wedded to a man who would send Falada to slaughter? No, thank you." At the gate, Gilly lowered her burden gently to the cobbled ground. "Help me get her head down. Please."

He lifted her to his shoulder—he was strong.

Cradling Falada's head between her hands, Gillianna lifted it from the spike that impaled it. Conrad set her down.

On the cobbles Gilly arranged head, bones, hide, and hooves so that with a little imagination—no, a lot of imagination—Falada could have been lying there on her side asleep. She knelt and stroked Falada's mane, silver threads as find as her own golden hair.

Conrad's humble voice sounded behind her and above her head. Halting and awkward, he said, "We could take her out—you know, out there. Give her a decent burial."

Without looking at him, eyes on her mare, Gillianna shook her head. It was no ordinary parlor magic she contemplated, but she hoped she could do it. She had to do it. "Falada," she whispered, "help me out. What rhymes with 'alive'?"

Falada did not speak.

"All right, then, why rhymes with 'living'?"

Falada said, "Loving."

And in that moment, as Falada spoke and Gillianna stroked her mane, Falada's eyes bloomed alive and alight, and she lifted her head and neighed like sunrise. Gilly cried out for joy; in that moment all the wretched dead parts of Falada had knitted together and filled with life, and what had been taken away was restored. Nickering, Falada scrambled to her feet, her white mane lifting like wings in the shadow of the castle gate, her white tail trailing to the cobbles like a bridal veil. Gillianna hugged her around her neck, wetting her silky hide with her tears.

"Gilly," said Conrad. "Um, I mean, Milady—"

She turned and saw how miserable he looked; she put out her hand to him. A small crowd of curious folk had gathered; there was not much time. Soon word would reach the prince.

"I must go," she whispered to Conrad. "Will you come with me?"

His face lighted with that wide, kind smile she loved. He nodded. Leaving the geese behind, they walked through the gate together.

Out in the sunshine, he lifted her onto Falada, seeming to know that Gilly would not need bridle or saddle. Arching her lovely neck, the white palfrey paced along at a gentle lady-gait, and Conrad walked by her side.

"Where are we going?" he asked Gilly, his eyes alight.

"Anywhere."

Falada said, "In these fairy tales, the one who is kind to animals always wins."

"Falada," Gilly chided, "that didn't rhyme."

In a severe, lecturing tone Falada said, " 'Loving' doesn't really rhyme with 'living' either. And don't you know the animal guide is supposed to be killed, usually by cutting off its head?"

"Falada! Are you going to turn into a nag?"

Falada droned, "Oh, if your poor old mother knew, her heart would break in two."

Gillianna said, "I don't think so. Actually, I think we should go see her. I think she'll have a cow because of all that dowry, but after she gets over it, I think she'll love Conrad almost as much as I do. And I think she'll be happy not to be lonely anymore. If we live near her, I think she'll be a dear."

And as it turned out, all of the above came true, because in fairy tales, good wishes always do. Especially when there's a rhyme involved.

# FIFI'S TAIL
## by *Alan Rodgers*

Alan Rodgers' short fiction has appeared in such anthologies as *Miskatonic University*, *Tales from the Great Turtle*, *Masques #3*, and *The Conspiracy Files*. His first published short story, "The Boy Who Came Back from the Dead" won the Horror Writer Association's Stoker Award for Best Novelette. He lives in Hollywood, California.

The wolf caught scent of the huntsman long before he heard the girl-child plead for mercy.

He *knew* that scent. *Knew* it. That was the huntsman who'd ambushed him just as he'd been about to devour the riding-hood girl. The wolf would have known his foul stink anywhere. He tracked it quietly through the brush, stalking, savoring . . . the huntsman would pay for his crimes. Hideously! He would pay for his crimes against the wolf, against *all* wolves; he would pay for all hunters for all time!

The forest opened out into a clearing. And there in the center of the clearing stood the huntsman and the *girl*.

The big oaf had a knife in hand, drawn and raised as if he were about to pierce the girl's *innocent* heart, and then the little witch began to weep!

"Oh, dear huntsman," she said, "leave me my life. I will run away into the wild forest, and never come home again."

The wolf would have laughed if he could have. But wolves of his blood never laugh, for there is no mirth inside them.

"The queen will take my life," the huntsman said. "I dare not leave you alive."

The girl gave him a look that could have melted stone.

"But I am so small and so weak! If I ever should survive this wood, how could I find my way back to the castle? The queen need never know you spared my life!"

The girl looked downright pensive. *Well, she ought to be,* the wolf thought.

*All right,* he growled. *Enough of this.*

And leaped through the air to devour the huntsman in a single gulp.

The girl swore when she saw him.

"What took you so long?" she shouted as the huntsman's left boot vanished down the wolf's vast maw. "He could have *killed* me!"

The wolf smiled at her hungrily.

*Would've,* he said, licking his chops.

And then said nothing more.

The wolf had known the girl was trouble from the moment he first set eyes on her. He knew it when he first saw her, and every solitary thing she did confirmed it, bit by bit by bit.

White skin, red lips, hair shimmery and black as coal. The girl was trouble. Trouble!

He was still in the chain-link pen that had been his prison for three long weeks (since the pathetic business with the pigs) when he first saw her. He was in the pen, and she was in the corridor outside, strolling toward him with that hapless oaf of a dogcatcher. She approached him purposely, directly, staring at him as though she knew who and what he was and exactly where he'd be.

She caught his eye and *smiled* at him.

"That's the one I want," she said, kneeling close before the prison, *smiling* as she looked him in the eye. "Call me Snow White," she said to the wolf. "You won't need my other names."

She spoke her words sweetly, and carried herself like a princess of all things innocent and pure, but the wolf saw through that clearly as all canae see into the hearts of men and women: there was an evil in that child that was deeper than the blackness of the wolf's own heart.

If the wolf had had a choice, he would have turned tail and run from her.

He surely would.

But he had no choice.

He stood chained and imprisoned in that fateful place, utterly unable to object: the dogcatcher didn't care about the wolf's feelings in the matter, and it wouldn't have mattered if he *had* cared, because that man was deaf to the language of wolves and dogs, and thought that the wolf's speech was nothing but the yipping of a cur.

How he would pay, the wolf swore! But he'd sworn that a thousand times, now, in the three weeks since the dogcatcher had caught him unawares as he howled mournfully outside the bricked fortress that was the house of the great pig, the brick sanctuary of the three pigs, stronghold of the third. And no matter how he swore he would revenge himself for the dogcatcher's indignities, the dogcatcher persisted, blithe, dim, hapless, and unafraid.

"*This* dog? Big, ugly, bad-tempered Fido? You're sure?"

"Yes," the girl said. "I'm certain he's the dog I want."

"You're out of your mind, young lady! What would a pretty girl like you want with a mutt like that?"

*I am not Fido!* the wolf shrieked. *And my blood is the pure true blood of the great war-wolves of the Iron Mountains! Slander me and die!*

The dogcatcher hardly took notice of this. He kicked the wolf's cage and threatened him with the prod, but he did not deign to take his leering eyes off the girl.

"I'm going to call him Fifi, not Fido," the girl said. "I think it suits him."

And the wolf screamed mournfully to Diana, Goddess of the Moon, who is the secret patron of all wolves.

She left his prayer unanswered.

"I hope you have a muzzle for him," the dogcatcher said. "That mutt is *loud*."

The girl had neither muzzle, the way it happened, nor any interest in acquiring one. The dogcatcher had equipped her with a leash and a choke collar for the wolf before he'd let the girl take him from the pound, but even these she used reluctantly. When they were out of sight of the pound, she knelt before the wolf and removed the leash. Oh, how he savored that! The hunger, the slavering, the promise of her dainty bones crushing in his jaws . . . ! She put her hand to his throat, unfastening the leash; in a moment the collar would go, too.

And then the child did the thing he should have anticipated, but did not:

She pressed her fingers through the thick fur of his
coat. Found his skin and pressed something small and
sharp and cruel into his flesh.

And then she cast her spell upon him.

> *Bear me bind me obey me*

she chanted,

> *Defy me at your peril,*
> *monster from the night.*

And the wolf's heart froze.

He wanted to scream in rage, frustration, and fear. He
knew what was to come, for he'd been bound to necro-
mancy more than once before.

*You will suffer for that, child,* the wolf said. *I promise
you, you will.*

The girl frowned.

"And I promise you I'll slap your nose with a newspaper if you threaten me again!" she said.

The wolf tried to lunge at her, but his muscles defied
him. They could not move against the charm she'd put
upon him.

*Why, girl-child, why? Why have you bound me? Why
have you sought me out?*

The girl smiled hungrily. "My stepmom's up to no
good," she said. "You know, the Wicked Queen? I don't
trust her. And *you* are going to be my ace in the hole."

The wolf howled mournfully, but his goddess still did
not answer.

* * *

Fifi licked his chops again. *So greasy!* he complained. *And smelly, too. Next time you make me eat something, make sure it takes a bath first!*

Snow White gave him a cross look.

"Mind your manners, Fifi, or it's back to the pound for you! Didn't you learn your lesson in that story with the three pigs? Oh, never mind. If you didn't learn following that blonde with the red hat, you aren't ever going to learn."

*Stop calling me Fifi!* the wolf demanded.

Snow White smiled ruefully. "The name suits you," she said.

The girl brushed the dust off her dress and started deeper into the woods.

"Shouldn't we be going back to the castle?"

Snow White rolled her eyes. "And let that old bat try to poison me or something? No thanks! We'll find someplace else to stay."

The wolf didn't care much for this, since he'd grown fond of the table scraps available from the castle's kitchen. But he had no more choice about following the girl into the woods than he'd had about following her from the pound.

And so the girl and Fifi wandered deeper and deeper into the woods till they came upon the ruins of a straw house.

The wolf growled resentfully at the sight, for the memory was still fresh in him, and it enraged him.

But it did not enrage him as much as the ruins just beyond the next hillock for those were the ruins of the wood house, and the events that had befallen him in that place were even farther beneath his dignity.

The wolf shuddered with rage as they passed the wooden ruin.

"I always thought you had bad breath," Snow White said. "Now I know."

Beyond the bend was a brick house, intact and occupied. Inside it there were three well-dressed pigs, watching television contentedly.

As Fifi edged up toward the brick house, the rage and hunger began to overcome his best judgment, for he had an awful and unquenchable impulse to jump through the window and devour the pigs, and in a moment the impulse would consume him.

"Don't get any ideas," Snow White said. "Those pigs are armed and dangerous."

The largest of the pigs opened the window and leaned out, leveling a shotgun at the wolf.

"You'd better put a leash on that thing, lady," the great pig said. It was a vast, hungry, feral-looking pig, a pig that even the wolf could fear.

Snow White snorted indignantly. "Don't you pick on my Fifi," she said.

The wolf slunk away with his tail between his legs, muttering.

As the afternoon wore on, the Wicked Queen grew anxious.

She had instructed the huntsman explicitly; he was to return to her directly with Snow White's heart and liver, so that she could cook and eat them. Not even the Wicked Queen herself was entirely sure why she wanted to eat the poor girl's heart; it could be that she was hungry, and unwilling to waste a meal; it could also be that she was just plain mean, which she certainly was.

"Where's my huntsman?" she muttered. "He should have come back by now! He's got my heart and liver, and I'm hungry!"

At last she turned to the mirror which she kept in a compact in her purse.

"Mirror, mirror in my hand, who's the fairest in this land?"

An ugly and loathsome countenance appeared in the mirror, a face as hideously ugly as the Wicked Queen was beautiful; a face as ugly as the shadow of her heart.

"Snow White. Next question?"

"Where is she?" the Wicked Queen demanded. "And where's my huntsman? Where are my heart and liver?"

"She's wandering around the enchanted woods, looking for a place to stay. A wolf ate your huntsman. And your heart and liver are inside you, where they've always been."

"Oh!!!" cried the Wicked Queen. "You just can't get good help these days. You want something done, you have to do it yourself."

"I could have told you that a long time ago, if you'd bothered to ask," the mirror said.

"Enough from you," the Wicked Queen said, closing her compact and secreting it in her purse.

And so she dressed up as a peasant woman, so that she could avoid public scrutiny, and stomped out into the enchanted woods.

That wasn't the smartest thing that the Wicked Queen ever did. By a lot! They didn't call the Enchanted Forest an enchanted forest for nothing, after all. No sooner had she stepped into the forest than she found herself utterly lost and alone, completely confused, and unable to get her bearings.

At great length she came to a small house made of gingerbread. As she approached it, an Anthropophagous Witch came out to greet her, more as a matter of professional courtesy than out of any personal affection.

"Have you seen my huntsman?" the Wicked Queen asked. "He was supposed to bring me back a heart and liver. I just love those hearts!"

The Anthropophagous Witch frowned. Even if professional courtesy obliged her to greet the Wicked Queen politely, she didn't like to see competition working her territory.

"Haven't seen him," the Anthropophagous Witch said. "But I could offer you some gingerbread."

The Wicked Queen, who knew exactly what that gingerbread was for, scowled. "I don't think so, deary," she said. "I'm hungry, but not hungry enough to end up on the wrong end of the food chain."

"Darn," the Anthropophagous Witch said. "Some days I just can't win."

And with that the Wicked Queen turned and stomped off into the forest, leaving the Anthropophagous Witch to her just desserts.

"She could've stayed for tea. It isn't like I bite. Er. Hmm. Well, it isn't like I chew! Oh. Well. Maybe *some*times. . . ."

Something loud and clumsy stumbled through the brush at the edge of the forest, and Hansel emerged from the woods, followed by his sister Gretel.

The Anthropophagous Witch's eyes grew wide and bright with anticipation and delight, and she chortled quietly. "There they are!" she said. "And right on time."

With that the Anthropophagous Witch hurriedly ducked into her house, hoping to remain unobserved.

"Oh, Gretel," Hansel exclaimed. "Look, look, a gingerbread house the size of a cottage!"

"Hansel, I think it *is* a cottage. Look, there's somebody in there, by the window. Nobody lives in a real gingerbread house!"

But Hansel, hungry and impetuous young lad that he was, had already snapped off a shutter and begun to nosh on it. And the shutter was indeed made of gingerbread!

"You ought to try some, Gretel," he said, stuffing his face with a wide lump of iced windowsill. "It's awfully tasty!"

"Mark my word, Hansel," Gretel said, "No good will come of this." But she was starving, just as Hansel was, so Gretel elbowed her brother aside and set to work eating her way through the cottage wall.

In no time at all the two children had managed to eat their way through the cottage's living room wall, and now they began to grow logy from having overeaten.

"I'm tired, Gretel," Hansel said, looking not entirely unlike the pop'n'fresh doughboy. "I want to take a nap."

"Me, too, Hansel," Gretel replied.

In a moment the two were snoring noisily just outside the ruptured living room of the gingerbread house.

"I've got them now," the Anthropophagous Witch said, rubbing her hands as she emerged from her hiding place inside the living room closet. "I'll be eating roast peasant tonight!"

And, indeed, she would have eaten well that night if Snow White and her pet wolf Fifi had not chosen that exact moment to emerge from the woods themselves.

"Oh," the Anthropophagous Witch said, catching Snow White's attention, "visitors! I *love* visitors!"

Fifi gave the Anthropophagous Witch a wary glance.

*With gravy and dumplings,* he muttered.

"We were looking for a place to stay," Snow White said. "Can you direct us to a hotel? We're travel-weary and very tired."

"Hotels," the Anthropophagous Witch said. "Hmmmm. Hotels, hotels. I don't know of any . . . say! I could put you up, you know!"

*In salt and vinegar, with your vegetable preserves,* the wolf said, *sotto voce.*

The Anthropophagous Witch turned a deaf ear to Fifi's comments. Snow White heard them clearly enough, but before she could react, the entire moment slipped from everyone's grasp as Gretel stirred enough in her sleep to open her eyes and see the Anthropophagous Witch, the wolf, and Snow White.

"Hansel!" she screamed. "Hansel, wake up. It's a monster!"

"No!" the Anthropophagous Witch shouted. "No, no, no, no!"

Hansel woke, tubby and sputtering. "An *Anthropophagous Witch* and a monster!" he shouted, grabbing his sister's hand and dragging her away into the woods.

In a moment Hansel and Gretel had vanished into the woods, and the Anthropophagous Witch began to weep in frustration.

"I'll always be hungry again," she wept. *"Always!"*

"Your name isn't Scarlett, is it?" Snow White asked her.

The Anthropophagous Witch favored her with an indignant glance. "My name is Abigail," she said. "And don't you forget it."

Hansel and Gretel ran wildly through the woods for most of twenty minutes before they came across the

Wicked Queen, who sat on a large rock near a small, noisy stream, looking exhausted and confused.

"Kids," the Wicked Queen said, "I hate 'em."

"Gee," Hansel said, wild-eyed and breathless, "we don't hate you."

The Wicked Queen regarded him suspiciously.

"That's what my stepdaughter always said. I gave her the best years of my life! Well, her governess did, anyway. And what did the little witch give me in return? She tried to eclipse me! Made herself prettier and prettier, till she started turning heads all over the kingdom! I was *born* to be a Beautiful Queen, not second fiddle to some little starlet!"

Gretel, who'd only then caught up with her brother, looked querulously at the beautifully Wicked Queen. "Surely the girl has no control over how beautiful she is? I mean, beauty is as beauty does, or something like that. I'm sure she doesn't mean to be prettier than you."

The Wicked Queen shook her head woefully. "You could never be more wrong, child," she said at last. "That girl's taken the mail-order course from the Enchantress Guild. She knows exactly what she's doing!"

"Oh," said Gretel.

Hansel pried a stone loose from the meadow dirt with the toe of his left shoe. "I'm sure she doesn't mean anything by it," he said. "I mean, it isn't like she's trying to kill *you* or anything."

The Wicked Queen sneered at him. "You really think so? Ha! That nasty husband of mine, her father the king, is a real piece of work. How do you think the girl's mother died? You really believe that died-in-childbirth story? Ha! Ha again! He likes 'em young and pretty. And when I'm no longer the fairest in the land, I'll have an *accident,* too."

With that the Wicked Queen began to weep dolefully as self-pity consumed her.

Gretel crept up to the Wicked Queen and gave her a hug. "There, there," she said.

"Have you considered hiring a good divorce lawyer?" Hansel asked. "I hear that they can do amazing things with restraining orders nowadays."

And the Wicked Queen's piteous weeping suddenly metamorphosed into a piercing, keening wail, and she began to go to pieces.


The wolf began to grow impatient with the conversation between the girl and the Anthropophagous Witch the third time it looped around to start where it had begun. *Oh,* the girl would say, *you never told me where I might find an inn!* And the Anthropophagous Witch would dissemble and obfuscate till the subject wandered to something else entirely.

*She's leading you on,* the wolf said at last. *You might as well just leave.*

"Hush, Fifi!" the girl said. "One more interruption from you and I *will* swat your nose with that newspaper!"

The Anthropophagous Witch favored him with an especially cross look. "One more from you," the witch said in unaccented High Canae, "and I'll cook your carcass beside hers."

This was a terrible mistake on the part of the Anthropophagous Witch, for she assumed that the princess Snow White had no ear for doggerel. And that was far from the truth! The princess spoke the tongue of wolves and dogs, and understood it well.

"Now you wait just a second, Little Mrs. Cannibal!" she said. "I won't have my dog speaking to you rudely, but I'm not about to let you threaten either of us."

"Well," said the witch, "I never!" and then, after a moment's reflection, "and what exactly are you threatening to do to *me,* child?"

*"Fifi!"* Snow White shouted.

And Fifi lunged.

And swallowed the witch whole.

After a long while, the Wicked Queen's sobs began to ease, and now she wiped her tears into her kerchief and stopped crying.

"Oh, dear me, children," she said. "You're so right! And here all this time I thought divorce was out of the question!"

Gretel shook her head. "Of course it isn't," she said. "You need a women's shelter, that's all."

"And a lawyer," Hansel chimed in.

"A *good* lawyer," the Wicked Queen insisted, for no matter how sad and bereaved she might be, she was also a practical woman with an eye toward the future.

And so Hansel, Gretel, and the Wicked Queen set out across the Enchanted Forest in search of a women's shelter and a telephone that the Wicked Queen could use to call a lawyer.

"Well," Snow White said, "Now that Little Mrs. Cannibal is out of the way, we might as well stay here."

The wolf growled.

*I don't like it,* he said. *This place stinks of her. It promises a trap.*

"Oh, don't be silly," Snow White said. "What can she do to us now? She's dead!"

The wolf had no argument for her, but he knew how wrong she was, all the same.

*As you wish,* he said. *But I have warned you.*

Snow White went to the larder of the gingerbread house, fixed herself a big and satisfying meal, and took a nap on the witch's couch. After a long while, the wolf fell asleep on the floor beside her.

And that was his undoing, just as it had been during the episode with the seven kids, just as it had been when he'd ingested the Riding Hood girl's grandmother.

For he had swallowed both the huntsman and the Anthropophagous Witch whole, and without chewing either of them properly.

Worse, and more to the point, the huntsman had been holding a knife when the wolf devoured him. And no sooner had the wolf drifted off to sleep than the huntsman set about cutting his way out of the wolf's belly!

It wasn't easy going, for Fifi had a cast-iron stomach, but soon enough the huntsman managed to open up an aperture large enough to crawl through.

The Anthropophagous Witch followed him out, and when she was clear seven large stones fell out behind her, which in the long run was no small relief to the wolf, since he'd carried those rocks in his gullet for three years and a day, ever since the episode with the seven kids.

"Ick!" said the Anthropophagous Witch. "So messy!"

The huntsman gave her a sidelong glance. "Just count yourself lucky that the wolf wasn't listening when his mother told him to chew all his food completely," he said.

"Lucky, schmucky," said the Anthropophagous Witch.

"When I'm done with these two, they won't have the time to wish they knew how to chew their food."

She said this in something of a voluble tone of voice, which was her second terrible mistake, since it woke Snow White, who screamed, mostly because the huntsman and the Anthropophagous Witch looked absolutely disgusting, covered as they were in stomach juice and bits of chewed-up grass and all the other odd and repellent things one is liable to find inside the stomach of a wolf.

Screamed, and screamed, and screamed again. And finally shouted, *Fifi!* which woke the wolf and sent him charging at the recently disgorged pair. He'd have eaten them again, in fact, if his small intestine hadn't slipped out through the hole in his gullet and gotten caught up in his hind legs, causing the wolf to trip all over himself.

As it were.

Being practical and sensible folks, the huntsman and the Anthropophagous Witch took the opportunity before them to run for their lives.

While they still could.


Hansel, Gretel, and the Wicked Queen wandered through the forest for hours, over sharp stones and through cruel thorns and worse things, too, not so much for want of decent clear paths to walk upon as because none of them had the woods sense to stay on the path.

Finally, toward late afternoon, they came upon a little house in the deep woods that was surrounded by forest flowers and shady gardens. The house belonged to the seven dwarfs, who were at that hour still working in their mine on the far side of the Enchanted Forest. It was a nice little place, considering that it was a bachelor pad, and it was very empty.

"I bet there's a phone in there," Hansel said, jimmying the window.

"Hansel!" the Wicked Queen shouted, scolding him, for no matter how wicked she was, she was also a law-abiding citizen.

But law-abiding or not, she was also a woman in a terrible position. When Hansel slipped in through the living room window and came back out to let her and Gretel in through the front door, she walked into the dwarfs' cottage, thereby reducing herself to a common burglar, or at least a burglar's apprentice, for the breaking-and-entering laws apply as much in the Enchanted Forest as they do in town.

They found no telephone in the cottage, but they did find lots of small but neat and orderly furniture.

There was a little table with seven little plates, seven little spoons, seven little knives and forks, seven little mugs, and against the wall there were seven little beds, all freshly made.

The Wicked Queen was hungry and thirsty, and so were Hansel and Gretel, so they ate a few vegetables and a little bread from each little plate, and from each little glass they drank a drop of wine.

Well, maybe more than a drop.

After all that food and wine, the three where all exhausted, and none too eager to wander out into the sunset in search of a telephone.

"If we wait, the folks who live here will come home and tell us where we can find a phone," Gretel said.

"Sure," Hansel said, yawning. "I'll wait."

He sat down on one of the small beds, and tried to make himself comfortable.

"Why not?" said the Wicked Queen, plonking herself down on the bed beside Hansel's.

In a moment all three of them were asleep on the little dwarf-beds, snoring like a trio of chainsaws.

Three and a half hours later, the dwarfs came home late from work in the mine, overtired and more than a little grouchy. They lit their seven little candles, and saw that strangers had been in their house.

The first one said, "Who's been sitting in my chair?"

The second one said, "Who's been eating from my plate?"

The third one said, "Who ate my bread?"

The fourth one said, "They didn't finish my vegetables!"

The fifth one said, "They got something icky all over my fork!"

The sixth one said, "It's on my knife, too!"

The seventh one said, "And in my mug!"

*Ewwww!* they cried in unison.

Which prompted the first dwarf to examine his bed. "Who stepped on my bed?" he demanded.

The second one chimed in, "And someone has been lying in my bed."

And so on until the fifth one, who found Gretel snoring loudly away in his bed, fast asleep.

Beside her was the beautiful and Wicked Queen.

Beside the queen was Hansel.

The seven dwarfs all came running, and they cried out with amazement. They fetched their seven candles and looked at the trio of fellow travelers.

"My God! My God!" they cried. "Will you look at that! Three of them!"

None of them liked having strangers in their beds, but they weren't the sort to chase off guests, even uninvited guests like these. So they ate what was left of their dinners quietly, and when the Wicked (but beautiful) Queen woke, they spoke to her politely and with great interest.

"I've got to call my lawyer," the Wicked Queen told the seven little men. "Can you direct us to a telephone?"

The senior dwarf (whose name, contrary to what you may have heard, was *not* Stinky, and if you doubt me I suggest you try calling him that name to his face) scratched his head.

"Us dwarfs don't have much use for telephones," he said. "Some people say we're still living in the Middle Ages! But I think I saw a pay phone down by the truck stop on the far side of the mine."

"We can take you there in the morning, said the dwarf whose name really *was* Greasy, and for a good cause. "Would you like me to show you the way? Huh huh huh?"

"Uhm," the Wicked Queen said. "Can I get back to you on that?"

It took Snow White most of three whole hours to untangle Fifi's guts from his legs, and most of another two to sew everything back together again. The wolf, fortunately, was made of Tougher Stuff Than Most, and Not Afraid of a Little Dirt, so he survived it well enough. But he certainly didn't enjoy it!

*Ouch,* the wolf said. *Ouch ouch ouch.*

"Stop your bellyaching, Fifi," said Snow White. "You aren't making this any easier."

*Gee,* said the wolf, *I thought my part was hard enough.*

Snow White scowled. "Not as hard as it could be!" she

said, deliberately jabbing him in the rear with her sewing needle.

*Yow!* cried the wolf.

"See, I told you!"


Meanwhile, the huntsman and the Anthropophagous Witch were running for their lives, and running in a very straight line. After a while the huntsman realized that they were getting near the castle, and shouted to the witch:

"Follow me!" he shouted. "I think I know a way to get us out of here."

Whereupon he led the Anthropophagous Witch out of the Enchanted Forest, into the capital of the kingdom.

Now it had been a long long time since the Anthropophagous Witch had been to town. She was the sort of cannibal who can't abide crowds, or, more exactly, can't wander through a crowd without feeling and acting like a kid in a candy store, and no one takes it well when you drool over them cannibalistically in public.

Well, almost nobody. And those few who do enjoy that sort of thing were all in therapy that year.

"O huntsman," the Anthropophagous Witch said, just barely controlling herself, "What on earth have you led me into?"

"This is just the town, Mrs., um, Abigail," he told her. "We'll go to the castle in a moment and seek an audience with the king."

"The king? Whatever for?"

"Why, to tell him our tale. And to make sure the Wicked Queen doesn't return and try to seek revenge on us."

The Anthropophagous Witch sneered. "I wouldn't worry about her, deary," she said. "But keep your eye on that little girl. *She* is dangerous."

* * *

When the dwarfs were in their cups, the one who wasn't Stinky had an idea that delighted him to no end. "You don't have to go to the women's shelter," he told the Wicked Queen. "After you come back from calling your lawyer, you can come back here. We can put you up as long as need be. If you keep the place tidy for us, you'll more than pull your own weight."

"Um," said the Wicked Queen, for she wasn't much on housework, and foresaw herself, on the King's Alimony, continuing to live a life in the style to which she'd become accustomed.

"You'd have the place to yourself most of the time," not-Stinky said. "We come home in the evening, and supper must be ready by then, but we spend the days digging for gold in the mine. You will be alone then. Watch out for the king! Don't let anybody in when we aren't here!"

"Um again," the Queen said, looking furtively to Hansel and Gretel for support or half a clue.

But they were both still fast asleep.


The huntsman and the Anthropophagous Witch didn't manage to get an audience with the king until well after dinner, and they only managed that because the huntsman promised the Royal Steward that he had seriously nasty gossip about the queen.

"The queen is trying to kill your beloved daughter, O King," the huntsman said when they stood at last before the throne.

The king favored the huntsman with a jaundiced look. "My daughter is a dangerous little minx herself," he said. "She can handle herself, I wager."

"It's worse than that," the witch chimed in. "A little bird told me that the queen is calling her lawyer and plans to take you to the cleaners."

"What?" cried the king, rising to his feet. "She's calling *who?*"

In the morning The Wicked Queen (who'd grown a good deal less wicked by then) traveled with the dwarves to the Enchanted Forest Exit Truck Stop. Hansel and Gretel went with her, hoping to use the same phone to call their dad to come pick them up.

The calls went well enough for the Wicked Queen anyway. She managed to contact the law offices of Dewey, Cheatam, and Howe, and engage the services of Dick Cheatam, the firm's most senior divorce specialist.

"Don't you worry, Queenie baby," said the Dick (as he was affectionately known throughout the kingdom). "We'll take His Highness right to the cleaners for you."

"Can you recommend a good women's shelter?" she asked.

The Dick considered this for a moment. "You'd be better off with friends," he said at last. Every shelter in the kingdom operates under the king's protection and his seal. In your particular case, that might not be much help."

"Hmm," said the Wicked Queen, uncomfortably considering the proposition that the dwarf who was not Stinky had made to her.

"Can you do it?"

"Well," she said, "I guess. . . ."

Hansel's call to his dad was another matter altogether. For it was his nasty stepmother who picked up the phone on the other end, and the last thing she was about to do

was send his father halfway across the kingdom to re-
trieve him.

"You mean to tell me you're *still* alive, you little
wretch?" she fumed. "What's it going to take to kill you?
Do I have to get out the ax and cut you up myself?"

"Gee," Hansel said. "That doesn't sound like fun."

The truth about Hansel was that he was a pretty dim
bulb, when you get right down to it.

"That's strange," said his nasty stepmother, "it sounds
like an *awful* lot of fun to me!"

And with that she gave an evil, bone-chilling, cackling
laugh, and slammed the phone into its cradle, hanging up
on poor Hansel.

"I wonder if the dwarfs could use a couple of extra
gardeners?" he said, stunned and altogether taken aback.


At sunrise the king called for his ministers.

"I'm calling a war party," he said, rising from his
throne to pace the length of the throne room. "The queen
has left the castle and called the best divorce lawyers in
the land. This outrage will not stand!"

The Minister of War was the first to make the mistake
of raising his objections. "But Sire," he began, "knights
and foot soldiers are for taking hills, not, ahm, tracts of
land."

The king motioned to one of his guards, drew a finger
across his throat, and pointed at the Minister of War. The
guard advanced; the minister screamed. The guard drew
his sword, and the minister's head went flying across the
room as his body tumbled to the floor.

"Do I have any other objections to answer?" the king
asked. "I assure you all, I am eager to address them."

"Not a one, Sire," said the Minister of Education.

"Great plan, Chief," said the Minister of Welfare.

"You Da Man," said the Minister of Justice.

"Brilliant, Sire," said the Minister of State.

And so the king called his vast war party into existence: every knight in the land, every soldier in the realm, every blackguard, barbarian, and sell-sword for hire gathered in the forecourt of the castle keep to march off and do battle with the lawyers of the enemy.

The king brought his own Justice, too, of course, including his entire personal and executive legal staff, seven consulting attorneys, three hanging judges, and a pair of headsmen.

And when they had all gathered in the keep, the king led his war party into the Enchanted Forest, intending to be done with the queen once and for all.


Hansel, Gretel, and the Wicked Queen got back to the dwarfs' house a little after ten in the morning. Not-Stinky had had them at the truck stop right up against the Crack of Dawn, and maybe even inside it. They would have gotten back a lot earlier, but Hansel had gotten hold of the map not-Stinky had drawn for them, and read it at right angles (and even upside down!) till he had them lost, lost again, and now turned utterly around.

"No great wonder this kid's stepmom was trying to murder him by getting him lost in a forest," the Wicked Queen muttered, having half a mind to kill him herself. And letting him navigate was as sure a recipe for devastation as any she could imagine.

In the end she had lost patience, seized the map, and led them back to the cottage herself. It didn't take long, once she had the reins.

"I'm tired," Hansel said as they stumbled into the dwarfs' house.

"I'm hungry," Gretel added.

"I told you, you should have eaten at the truck stop while you could," the Wicked Queen told them.

Gretel made a face. "Who could eat in *that* greasy spoon? Even the roaches in that place were sick with food poisoning!"

"Pshaw, young lady! I'll have you know that that is the single finest Enchanted Truck Stop Dining Area in the entire kingdom!"

Hansel rolled his eyes. "It's the *only* Enchanted Truck Stop Dining Area in the kingdom," he said. "Heck, it's the only truck stop in the kingdom. We don't have many highways here in the Middle Ages."

"Well, yeah," said the Wicked Queen. "But you're confusing the truth with facts! You'll make a mess of things that way."

Hansel sputtered three times, and was about to reply almost as senselessly as the Queen had, when suddenly a wren, or maybe it was a sparrow (neither Hansel nor the Wicked Queen knew their ornithology) appeared on the windowsill and began to speak to him.

"The king has gathered a vast army," the little bird said, "and is leading it through the Enchanted Forest to capture you."

"Goodness," Hansel said. "What'd we do this time?"

The bird squawked. "Not *you*, you little fool! The queen! The queen! He's going to make her dance in shoes as hot as branding irons!"

"Oh, no," the Wicked Queen said, looking quietly scared out of her mind. "I have to run," she said.

"There's no time to run," Gretel pointed out.

"Then we'll have to hide her," Hansel said.

And they spent most of ten long minutes looking around the dwarfs' house and the surrounding woods, but there was no hiding place anywhere that would shelter anything larger than a dwarf.

And probably for cause.

At length Hansel made room for the Wicked Queen inside the closet; which was no mean task, since the closet was about as full of skeletons as you can imagine.

It was terribly uncomfortable in that closet, small and cramped, and the skeletons, bony as they were, poked her like a dozen dozen elbows. Worse, she could have sworn there were *live* dwarfs in there with her, as if they hadn't heard that things were cool nowadays and *every*body was supposed to come out of the closet and make an appearance on the *Jerry Springer Show,* if appropriate.

When the little bird had spoken its peace to Hansel, Gretel, and the Wicked Queen, it flew off directly to the royal assemblage, intent on telling its tale directly to the king.

"The queen is in the closet," the bird said. "In the dwarfs' house? You know the place where all seven of those little guys live? She's in there with all the other skeletons the little guys have in their closet."

"I knew it," the king said. "Living in a state of ill repute with seven men."

"I wouldn't call them men," the bird replied, but by then the king was no longer listening. He was off among his knights, shouting orders and demanding fealty.

"We're going to storm that hill," the king shouted. "And then we'll demolish the cottage on the far side of it."

"Demolish . . . ?" asked the Silver Knight. "I don't understand. We're going to war against a cottage?"

The king made the neck-and-pointing signs at the Silver Knight, and in a moment he was in pieces, scattered across the forest floor.

"Anyone else here have trouble following simple instructions?" he asked.

"Not me, Sire!"

"No sir!"

"Not a bit. You point, we storm."

"You direct, we wreck!"

"You Da Man, Kingy Baby!"

And the king and his minions stormed the hill and descended on the cottage, shredding it. Walls, furniture, pots, pans, and, most especially, skeletons went flying everywhere, literally and figuratively.

Hansel, brave lad that he was, tried to warn them off. But he was only one brave lad, and anyway he wasn't armed; when he stood up to the charging knights and warned them away, they ignored him.

And kept ignoring him, as he told them to go pick on something that could fight back, instead of tearing up the poor dwarfs' house.

Not that the knights (or the king) listened. They reduced the dwarfs' house to so much litter and debris, and when they were done, the Wicked Queen stood alone in the center of a great pile of skeletons, looking scared out of her mind.

"Men!" she cried. "Can't you all just go away and leave a poor woman alone?"

"That's enough from you, trollop," said the king, who grabbed his wife by the wrist and proceeded to lead her up onto the hilltop. "Light a bonfire," he commanded, "and warm up her iron dancing shoes!"

"Robert!" she shouted. "Do you know what my lawyer

is going to do with this? Can you say spousal abuse? I knew you could."

"Silence, Darla! I am Justice in this land! You will do as my court commands!"

"Just *wait* till my lawyer gets ahold of you, Robert. Just *wait!* You're going to be sooooo sorry, I promise you."

"Silence, woman!" the King demanded. He gestured at his knights. "Assemble the courtroom! Bring on the jury!"

"And the witnesses," a small voice said from somewhere a thousand times closer than anyone expected.

The Wicked Queen gasped.

"Snow White," she said, in a voice even smaller than the girl's. "You've come for your revenge."

The girl smiled.

"Maybe," she said. "Maybe not."

"Snow White," said the king, "what are you doing here, child? This court is no place for a beautiful young lady like you."

The girl bit her lip.

"Somebody's got to stop you, Daddy," she said. "It just isn't right, is all."

"You tell him!" shouted the Wicked Queen.

"What do you mean, child?" asked the king, looking genuinely wounded.

"I mean, she's just afraid, is all," said the girl. "And who wouldn't be, after you killed my mother when she got middle-aged and dumpy and *pregnant!*"

The Wicked Queen gasped. So did most of the knights within earshot.

The king had a look on his face like he'd been hit with a mallet.

"What an awful thing to say," the king said at last.

"Your mother died in childbirth, child. I'd never have harmed a hair on her head."

"Yeah, right," Snow White said. "Just like you'd have said you'd never hurt *this* wife if I'd asked you a week ago. But look at you! Dragging her up the hill, manhandling her! And where did you get those branding shoes? They look *used*, Daddy. Who did you use those shoes on the last time? Huh?"

"You men are all the same," the Wicked Queen said.

"Through and through," the Anthropophagous Witch chimed in. "And I ought to know, tee hee, tee hee."

"Goodness," the king said. He looked genuinely hurt, mortified, in fact.

"Ahem," said the hanging judge, who'd taken his position before the court. "If the litigants are prepared, I believe we can proceed. . . ."

"We are, indeed," said the Dick, who'd appeared out of nowhere (as greasy lawyers are wont to do) only moments before. "If your honor will examine my brief. . . ."

The king blinked twice, then clapped his hands. Three dozen of the kingdom's finest lawyers, anthropomorphized sharks, every last one of them, appeared immediately at his side. He led them aside to huddle.

"What's all this about?" the king asked. "Who's this man with the briefs? I'd just as soon prefer boxers, myself, but in his case I don't honestly want to know!"

The lead shark shook his head. "No, Sire," he said. "He has a legal brief in hand. Methinks he means to take you to the cleaners."

The king let out an exasperated sigh. "We have our own cleaners in the palace," he said. "And when they fail to do their work, we behead them as often we must. I have no need for this lawyer's out-sourced cleansing."

The shark shook his great sandpapery head. "No, Sire," he repeated. "I mean to say she wants to take you for every penny you've got."

The king sighed. "I could have told you that," he said. "Women! They're all the same."

"What a thing to say!" said Snow White, his daughter, who'd somehow wormed her way into the legalistic conclave.

The king threw up his hands. "Not you, child! You're my *daughter,* for God's sake!"

"And a woman, too."

"I'd say that you were still a girl," the king allowed. "But even so, I take your point. What's behind it? Do you have a case to make, or are you here simply to bedevil me in my moment of forensic extremis?"

The girl shook her head. "You aren't a bad man, Daddy. I love you very much. But your judgment isn't always what it should be; you don't belong in charge of things."

"Child!" the king said, "You wound me!"

"You wound a lot of people, Daddy. Look at the sharks you have working for you!"

And the lawyers were indeed sharks, and sharks of the hungriest and most fearsome breeds.

"My legal team is the finest in the land," the king insisted. "There are none better."

"You need to retire, Daddy."

"Retire?"

"Abdicate, Daddy. Pass the crown on, take a nice comfy cottage in the woods, and enjoy the pleasures that the world affords."

The king gaped, and kept gaping; he stood stunned and silent for the longest time.

"But what about your stepmother, the Wicked Queen?" he said at last. "What of her?"

Snow White rolled her luminous eyes.

"Offer her a decent settlement. She'll go away quietly."

And the queen did indeed accept the king's settlement. She took her money, bought a nice little cottage a few blocks from the House of the Great Pig, and made a comfortable and happy retirement for herself.

Hansel and Gretel stayed with her for a few weeks before they tried to find their way home to their dad and evil stepmom, but always got lost no matter how they tried. Eventually they found their way back to the queen's cottage, and she took them on as servants. They're still there, tending the gardens, cooking, tidying up around the house; their mistress is quite fond of them.

The seven dwarfs were thoroughly insured. When they got home and found their home in tatters, they immediately called their State Forest insurance agent, and he got them a check before sunrise.

With the insurance money in hand, they rebuilt their comfortable little house, this time with All Modern Conveniences, including a skylight and a dishwasher and a garbage disposal.

The king did indeed abdicate his throne. But he didn't go quietly into retirement! Far from it. When last seen, he was in Monte Carlo, living it up and dating all the pretty girls. It's a natural fact that he's a happy man.

Snow White, who inherited the Kingdom? She rules well enough, but there are those who say she's a little overbearing.

The real winner in all of this, though, is Fifi.

Fifi the wolf is Top Dog in the castle, and eats whatever he pleases.

Mostly he likes pork: ribs, bacon, butt roasts. Country sausage! Pork chops! And he's very choosy about which pigs the butcher slaughters for him.

# THY GOLDEN STAIR
## by Richard Parks

Richard Parks lives in Mississippi, works with computers, and writes. Other short fiction by him appears in *Wizard Fantastic, Elf Magic,* and *Robert Bloch's Psychos.* He has a wife named Carol, whose first date with him was a campus screening of *Psycho.* As for other details of his personal existence, well, the less said the better. He firmly believes that his stories are much more interesting than he is. Humor him.

"**W**icked, wicked child!"

Threeteeth grabbed Rapunzel by the arm and dragged her away from the balcony. Rapunzel protested, trying to see what had befallen the young man, but Threeteeth was too strong. She took another grip on the girl, this time around her long braid of red-gold hair, and pulled her along, though Rapunzel made the witch work for every bit of distance covered.

"What have I done?" she said. "Why are you so angry?"

Her beloved Threeteeth acted as if she hadn't even heard. "Wicked!" the witch repeated, like a clockwork parrot. In another moment she had reached the sewing trunk. She released Rapunzel's arm and rummaged around among the patch cloth and skeins of yarn. Rapunzel took advantage of Threeteeth's distraction to try and pry the witch's fingers out of her hair, but Threeteeth merely reached up from her rummaging and, almost without even looking at her, slapped Rapunzel hard across the face. Rapunzel sat down, as much from surprise as the force of the blow. Threeteeth had never raised a hand against her before, never once. It was too much. Rapunzel felt the tears flow, and she had no strength to fight them.

"What have I *done?*" Rapunzel wailed again.

"Done? You've obeyed your compulsions, child. As we all must do. As I am about to do . . . ah!" Threeteeth held up the iron shears in triumph. In Threeteeth's familiar, kindly face all Rapunzel could see now was madness, and in the witch's gentle eyes nothing but rage and pain. Rapunzel's own eyes were open wide in horror and she tried to crawl away, but Threeteeth's grip on the girl's hair was like iron itself. Another moment and it was done. Threeteeth gathered up the shorn lock, folded it like yarn, and put it in the sewing box. Then she produced another lock, this one of iron, from one of the many pockets of her apron and sealed the box tight.

"You shall lack for nothing, girl, except company. You will need neither food nor sleep, and indeed you shall have neither. This is my curse on you, and my punishment." The witch hesitated then, as if bringing forth the last few words took a great struggle. "And my duty," she finished at last.

In a flash, Threeteeth was gone.

* * *

Rapunzel thought losing her hair was the worst of it, but after about a year she knew she was wrong. The absolute worst part of her imprisonment was the boredom. She didn't even have the luxury of wishing that her prince would come. He had, and gone, thanks to Threeteeth. Now the golden stair was closed, the ship of her prince had metaphorically sailed, and the worst part of any day was filling the time.

"Is it supposed to be like this?"

She wasn't really clear on what "it" was. Her life had been predictable enough before the prince. Threeteeth was the only friend, indeed the only other person she had ever known. Threeteeth brought food, Threeteeth brought conversation, Threeteeth brought anything Rapunzel could imagine she ever needed. If it was true her world was confined, then what of it? Rapunzel knew no other. She could see the forest below her tower, but that was for deer and birds and the other small creatures she saw living there. They to the wood and she to the tower, and that was the way it was supposed to be, so far as she knew.

Then *he* came.

Even the word "he" was strange. Something that was and yet was not of the same flesh as Rapunzel and Threeteeth. She wasn't sure yet what that part meant, but just now that difference was the least of what the prince meant to her. What mattered were the stories he told of grand palaces and endless kingdoms, dragons and maidens, knights and ladies. Of love—something else to do with that difference in flesh, and something she did not understand at all. The only love she'd known before was of Threeteeth, at once mother and sole companion. Now everything was changed, especially Threeteeth; Rapunzel's shorn hair was enough proof of that. She still didn't know what it meant, though it seemed she might have the rest of eternity to figure it out.

Rapunzel looked in her mirror, noting how much her hair had grown in the preceding year. Threeteeth had taught Rapunzel much about needle and thread, weaving and cloth, but not so much in the way of figures. Still, it was clear to see that the hair that had taken nineteen years to grow so long would take as long again, or more. Even if the prince hadn't died in the fall—and Rapunzel took the fact that there were no bones at the base of the tower as a good sign for that—he would not be able to reach her. The sides of the tower were like glass.

Not that she was even sure that she *wanted* him to return. Her life had been content before he came; now everything was ruined.

"He owes me for this," she said aloud, surprised at the thought, but knowing the rightness of it once spoken. He owed her. For her hair, for Threeteeth's madness, and, most of all, for her shattered happiness. He owed her, yes, and she would be damned if she'd wait twenty years to collect.

The lock on the sewing chest was stubborn, but Rapunzel had nothing but time. Threeteeth in her madness had spoken the truth: Rapunzel needed neither food nor sleep, though there was nothing to eat anyway and even when she tried to sleep she could not. Still, she did need to rest now and then and did so. The rest of the time she worked on the lock and tried not to think about her loss of dreams.

She used a hairpin she'd found on the floor to imitate the key, tricking the mechanism bit by bit, listening, experimenting through the long hours, days, weeks.

The effort took most of a month, but she finally mastered the lock and the hinge popped open. Rapunzel pulled out her shorn locks, almost weeping but not quite. There was plenty of time, yes, but not for grief. Rapunzel had a purpose now. It might have been all that she had but it was enough. She laid out the long strands of her hair, noting where Threeteeth had repeated the cuts at each turn of her winding, so that no one lock was as long as the entire red-gold stair had been. She was disappointed but not defeated.

"It's still hair. It can be braided."

Rapunzel got to work.

"This isn't right." The small bird sitting on the balcony rail had a high, chirpy voice with odd echoes. Rapunzel stood on the edge of the balcony, the rope she had braided from her own shorn hair tied now to the loop of iron on the railing she'd once used to brace her hair for Threeteeth—and later the prince—to climb when her hair had still been attached to her head. The end of the hair rope dangled far below as the whole length of the rope swayed and quivered in the breeze. Reduced now to one stout cord, it seemed even longer than before.

"What isn't right?" Rapunzel asked, as she steadied herself against the rail. It was a long way down and, when it came to climbing, she found she was in no hurry.

"None of it, and now here you are trying to make it worse! Tying your hair, climbing down instead of awaiting rescue like a good and proper lady. Accepting the fact that a bird is talking to you with human speech as if it were the most natural thing in the world. It's not, you know."

The maiden blinked. "It isn't?" She leaned close and

the bird bore her inspection calmly. It was a finch with russet head and breast, quite lovely but otherwise unremarkable. Rapunzel addressed it directly. "I've seen birds all my life, and I never assumed that, just because none had chosen to speak to me before, they couldn't speak. Why should I? And how should *I* know what is proper for me to do?"

"The same way Threeteeth knew what was proper for *her* to do when she caught you and that prince fellow together. Did she hesitate? Did she consider the matter at all that you could tell? Did she let her love for you—honest and deep, I assure you—interfere in anything that she did? No. Maybe she was right to call you wicked."

"Maybe," Rapunzel said agreeably, "since I've always heard 'wicked' applied to witches and, knowing only Threeteeth, I thought being wicked was a grand and lovely thing indeed."

The finch just glared at her. "Drop that rope to the ground and forget this nonsense right now. You must!"

"Why? And who are you, bird, to tell me what I must do?"

Silence. Then: "Consider this warning, Rapunzel," the bird said at last. "I am who made you, and you *will* follow your compulsion. And you will do what you must."

Rapunzel put one long leg over the edge of the balcony. "You're just a bird, but I *am* following my compulsion," she said, "This is it."

"Remember what I said."

Without another word the finch flitted away from the balcony and disappeared into the trees. Rapunzel began to lower herself down. It wasn't easy. The sides of the tower were every bit as glassy as they looked.

Rapunzel had wondered now and again why the prince

pulled himself with the strength of his arms and legs alone rather than bracing his feet against the tower, and now she understood. Her cloth shoes slipped against the strange stone every time she tried to push against it, once banging her shoulder painfully against the stone. Her bare feet didn't fare much better when she kicked off her shoes to try that way. She finally gave up and wrapped her legs around the rope as best she could as she lowered herself hand over hand.

About halfway down Rapunzel began to understand why the prince panted and sweated so after a climb. After she had come three quarters of the way, she stopped understanding how and why he had made the climb at all.

"Was it . . . just for me?" she said aloud, laboring to get the words out with her failing breath. She mostly fell the last several feet and landed with a thump on the grass. "Just for me?" she repeated, when the pain of landing on her rear and the effort of her descent had both faded a little.

When the prince had appeared the first time, it had seemed no more out of the ordinary than anything else about her life. She was a maiden. She lived in a tower with an old crone she thought of as her mother, if she thought of their relationship at all. This was her life and she knew no other, until now. The thought came that, maybe, her world had not been so ordinary as it had appeared. Perhaps, to some degree, the bird was correct about that, for all the other nonsense it had spouted. This seemed the perfect opportunity to find out. Rapunzel retrieved her shoes and set out into the forest.

"Are you ready to return to your tower now?" asked the snake. "I imagine you would be."

It was the third day after Rapunzel's escape though, truth to tell, she hadn't gotten very far. To the north she could see the towers of a distant city like the one the prince described, but all Rapunzel's walking had not brought it one jot closer for all that she could tell. Her poor cloth shoes had long since turned to rags and fallen off. She had stopped to bathe her feet in a little gurgling stream when the snake suddenly appeared, coiled and glistening, on the other end of the fallen tree where she sat.

The snake's head was red as rubies, the scales of its long body yellow and gold, its tail tipped with a short horny barb. It nibbled the barb, absently, as if it might decide to take the tip in its mouth, turn into a hoop, and roll away at any second. Instead it dropped its tail and looked at Rapunzel intently. It seemed to be waiting. Rapunzel continued to bathe her feet in silence. When she was finished, she made as if to rise again.

"Where are you going?"

"To the city. To find the prince."

"That is not possible. Surely you can see that now?"

"I can see that it will be harder than I thought," replied Rapunzel, calmly. "But I see little alternative."

"The alternative is to forget this nonsense and go back to your tower," the snake said, sounding somewhat annoyed.

"You sound like the finch," Rapunzel said.

"I *am* the finch," the snake replied. "Or rather, he is me. We are all each other." The snake seemed to think that was all the explanation required, but to Rapunzel it was just sounds of different pitch and tone, signifying nothing.

"You certainly make no more sense than the finch did,"

she observed. "If you're not going to be more useful, you can go away."

The snake gave out a low, hissing chuckle. "I made you. *We* made you. What you want doesn't matter, or rather, you want what we want. You have to, sooner or later. You will understand that in time."

"In time, but not now. I have to find the prince."

"He's not there."

That was something new. Something she did not know before then. "Where is he, then?"

"In his place, of course. As you should be."

Rapunzel glared at the creature. "If I should be there, I would be there. If I had not decided to leave, I would still be there. If I had no *choice,* I would be there. And yet I am not. Why is that, snake?"

The snake was annoyed again. Annoyed and something else besides. Rapunzel tried to read the snake's expression, hard as that was since snakes don't really *have* much expression, but what there was spoke volumes. "You're afraid of me!"

The snake shook its head, side to side. "Of you? No. Of what you represent . . . ?" It sounded like a question, and when the snake spoke again, its voice was different. It was as if many voices had been twisted together like the strands of Rapunzel's braided hair, and given the form "snake." It finally spoke again. "We were once all the same. We made you. Now there is confusion, now the story is under attack."

"What story? What are you talking about?"

"Our story. Your story. All the stories!" The voice was a multitude, and then it fell silent. Now the snake did take its tail in its mouth and roll away quickly as if all the devils a nightmare could summon were chasing it.

*     *     *

The city came no closer, despite Rapunzel's best effort, and when she finally allowed herself to look back behind her, the tower prison was still visible just beyond the treetops.

*It's their doing.*

She knew it was true. She still didn't understand who "they" were, the voices given shape and form in bird and snake, but she had thought about what they said and decided that she'd been wrong to call it nonsense. She just didn't understand what it meant, and, Rapunzel was beginning to suspect, that was not the same thing at all. Now Rapunzel almost wished for another of the creatures to appear, so she could question it—them?—further but no other scold had appeared to her for days now, in any form. Worse, she wasn't getting anywhere.

Rapunzel finally got tired and frustrated enough to consider her situation. "I can't go forward, and I refuse to go back. Which leaves?"

Right and left, of course. Neither "toward" nor "away" either of the two key destinations, the one she couldn't reach and the one "they" wanted her to accept. Rapunzel plucked a few strands of dried glass and released them into the wind. The wind carried them to the right. Rapunzel made an abrupt turn and the world changed.

"My . . ."

She couldn't finish at first. She didn't know what to add to make the expletive complete; what she saw was so out of her experience that none of the few swear words she knew seemed adequate. In the end it was not a swear word at all that came to her, but one of a number of toys and wonders that Threeteeth—in her friendlier days—had brought to the tower for Rapunzel's diversion.

". . . kaleidoscope."

The world was fractured like the image in the kaleidoscope. The pieces turned past one another in a jumble that was at once confused and yet followed a very precise pattern. For a while Rapunzel treated it like the kaleidoscope she knew, letting the images turn, form, then separate again and again as she watched with some of the same awe and delight she knew from the toy. In time some of the sense of it impinged, the way the vibrant crystalline images created a *pattern* in an actual kaleidoscope. Rapunzel saw bits of what looked like a forest, then a palace, then an ocean, and then more trees and the pieces of a cottage. As the image broke apart and re-formed, Rapunzel found herself looking hard into the face of a woman standing in the doorway.

*It's Threeteeth!*

Only it was, and it wasn't, and both at the same time and far more besides. The woman standing in the doorway was Threeteeth, and then the pattern changed and there was a woman with beaked nose and chin stirring a cauldron and that, too, was at once Threeteeth and not, and again a woman locking a door set in a wall in a dark cave, and that was and was not Threeteeth as well. Even the figure in the pattern that revealed her own prison tower, and herself, and the prince, was at once Threeteeth and not. No matter how familiar the image, there was something strange, no matter how strange there was something familiar. Just as the image of the tower started to fade, Rapunzel reached out, touched nothing, and as the image fell apart she called out her friend's name.

"Threeteeth!"

The kaleidoscope froze in mid-swirl, leaving images fragmented. Rapunzel glanced backward, saw the forest as it had always been. She looked down at herself and saw no change there. She looked back to the right and saw the same confusion as the pieces of the world shivered and shimmered, trying to turn and re-form yet still held, though by what Rapunzel did not know.

"Who calls us?" The voice came suddenly out of the confusion, and it was almost confusion itself. It was like the multiple echoes Rapunzel heard in the voice of the bird and the snake, only worse.

"Who are you?"

"I am Threeteeth," said a multitude of voices, each trailing away into echoes of voices that were not Threeteeth at all. "I am Baba Yaga," they said. "I am the Wicked Queen . . . Circe . . . the Witch of the Wood." Those, and hundreds more beside. Rapunzel strained to listen to only one voice, and after a while she finally made it out again.

". . . should not be here."

"Who?" Rapunzel asked.

"You. Me. It isn't time." Then: "You should have waited. You were supposed to wait." The voice was clearer now, as if, by speaking to and listening for the owner of one voice, the rest had begun to fade. Fade, but not disappear. The broken voices echoed faintly whenever Rapunzel's guard dropped.

Rapunzel had long since surmised how the story was supposed to turn out, at least in broad terms. Yet she couldn't help asking the question. "Why?"

"I don't know. There was a reason. There used to be, anyway."

Rapunzel could almost see the witch now. She was a fragmented form standing next to a fragmented tower, both like pieces of a poorly-assembled puzzle.

"I don't understand. Where are you? Why did you punish me?"

"Because I had to, just as you had to wait for the prince to return and find you. It's how the story goes . . . how it used to go."

"It's not a story. It's my *life*."

"Everyone's life is a story, lambkin, always to themselves, but sometimes to others as well. Told and retold as long as there are ones who remember. Once upon a time. And how the story goes depends on who's doing the remembering. Eventually the people doing the remembering change. Their *idea* of what your life was changes. The idea of what a life *should* be changes. It takes time, but eventually it happens. The story changes. That's why you were able to leave the tower. Those who remember are out of agreement. They're fighting over you now, though they don't really know that. Can't you hear them?"

"I hear many voices," Rapunzel admitted. It was true. There was always a faint murmur in the air now, often drowned out by the birds of the forest or a faint breeze, but always there.

"Just so." Threeteeth sighed a broken sigh. "You would have been happy, sooner or later. Now, who can say? Those who remember will make up their minds again, and then you are what they say you are. Until then . . ."

The image was in motion again. Threeteeth's form fragmented like broken crystal. Rapunzel found herself sobbing, though she was not sure why.

"What should I do?" she asked.

". . . live."

\* \* \*

"It doesn't matter."

The voice was the hum of a bee, many sounds blended into one. It even came from a bee, a big yellow-and-black bumble bee that circled around Rapunzel's head. She had left the kaleidoscope worldview behind and walked into the forest on the leftward path.

"It does," said Rapunzel grimly. Her feet were bleeding and her limbs ached, but as long as she was drawn to neither palace nor tower she didn't care.

"We've decided," said the bee.

"Not quite," said Rapunzel. She could feel the weight of events crushing down on her, of guilt and compulsion. Now she understood what Threeteeth had meant about doing what she was compelled to do. There had been no compulsion on Rapunzel's part before. Talking to the prince was just curiosity. Remaining in the tower would have been simple necessity. Or laziness. Rapunzel hadn't quite decided about that yet. Perhaps it was just the weakening of consensus that had allowed her to leave the tower, but she didn't think so. Now that she recognized compulsion for what it was, it was easy enough to see that compulsion had been at work all along. Her own compulsion, and she wasn't ready to give it up just yet.

"Tell me what was supposed to happen," she said, "before it all changed."

The bee told her. Rapunzel shrugged, "It wasn't such a bad resolution, but I think we can do better."

The bee ignored that. "Go back to the tower; you'll see what we've decided now."

"No," said Rapunzel.

"You must," said the bee. "This obstinacy serves no purpose."

"It serves mine."

Humming laughter. "Threeteeth was like you once. Not young—never that—but with a will of her own. Now one witch is pretty much like another. Call them 'Threeteeth' or one of a hundred names, they're all the same. Surely you noticed?"

"Should one maiden be just like another? Made to suffer and be rescued? To wait patiently while everyone acts and *does* except her?"

"You are what we decide. Your life may be worthless. Your suffering may be in vain. Your beauty may be a curse."

"I may be what you decide," Rapunzel said. "But I am you, too."

The hum faltered. For an instant the individual voices could be heard. "Lies," said the bee.

"I am what you make me, but I'm more than that. Whatever you see in me, you see in yourselves. Or else how can any consensus exist?"

"It's not true," said the bee.

"Say it again," said Rapunzel, smiling. "Say it three times and try to make it true. But I know. How can I not know you? Whether you drink joy or despair, am I not the cup? If you see yourselves, am I not the mirror? Do what you will, in the end I am all that you are. Maybe more."

"We are the Creators!"

Rapunzel smiled. "Perhaps. But not the Masters. Try as you might."

A multitude of voices. DAMN YOU! The bee dove at her in a straight line and stabbed her neck. Rapunzel did not dodge, or cry out. She merely grimaced slightly as the bee tried to jab repeatedly.

"Temper," she said.

The bee just hummed, straining to fly. Its stinger, of course, was stuck.

"Shall I free you?" she asked.

WE WILL DIE.

Rapunzel nodded. "For a while. I have no doubt you'll be back." She reached up and pulled the bee apart. It flew into a multitude like a swarm of gnats that quickly faded. The pain in Rapunzel's neck was fading, too.

"Not much longer," she said, thoughtfully.

Soon after Rapunzel found the prince in a clearing, by a pool. He was a sorry sight. His once fine clothes were spattered and torn. His eyes were caked with dried mud that he pawed at, uselessly.

"Wash your face," she said.

He turned his blind eyes toward her voice. "Rapunzel? How did you find me? What happened to the witch?"

"It doesn't matter. Wash your face," she repeated. "I want to talk to you."

"I can't," he said. "It's not time."

She took his hand and slowly pulled him down to the water. "No, it isn't time. But you can," she said. "And you will."


Some things changed, some things didn't. Neither Rapunzel nor the prince ever reached the grand city, but that no longer seemed to matter. Rapunzel began to understand what the prince was and what it had meant, once upon a time, to be a prince. She was still very fond of him. The prince regained his sight with a little scrubbing and together they made a life for themselves in the wood while they came to know each other better. They made a farm, and a marriage, and two fine sons. It wasn't a happy ending because it wasn't an ending at all, but still a great deal more than they would have had, for all that time the story says they should have waited.

Rapunzel still could not sleep. After a time she found herself standing by the bedroom window every night while her farmer prince snored and slumbered. Now and then she would turn, and smile at him, but her eyes kept going back to the shadows of the wood.

Rapunzel didn't know how much time had passed before she finally saw the fox. She only got a glimpse of it. There was none of the boldness she expected about it, and none of the mistaken confidence; the creature skulked from one shadow to the next, little more than a shadow itself. That didn't matter. She knew what it was beyond doubt or question. Rapunzel left her prince sleeping and stepped out into the moonlight.

"I've been waiting for you," she said. "Come out."

She only saw its eyes, gleaming at her from the forest.

NO, it said, and it spoke with all the voices.

"Why not?" she asked. "You still want me or you wouldn't be here."

WE DON'T KNOW WHAT YOU ARE NOW. WE'VE TRIED, FOR SO LONG. WE CAN'T FORGET, BUT WE'RE NOT SURE WHAT WE REMEMBER. EVERYTHING HAS CHANGED. WE'RE AFRAID.

Rapunzel nodded. "Me, too," she said, knowing that for truth. "But we have to do this, don't we?"

WE NEED YOU, they said grudgingly. YOU AND ALL LIKE YOU.

She put her hands on her hips. "Then let me finish the new story. Let me *find* the new story, the one that makes sense for all of us now. That's all I ever wanted. It's time."

The fox finally stepped into the full moonlight. It was hesitant and fearful. It did not say anything. It didn't need to. It smiled tentatively at her with bared teeth and, to her own surprise, Rapunzel smiled back.

"What about the prince? And Threeteeth?"

WE THINK . . . THAT IS UP TO YOU.

"You're learning. That's a change by itself." She followed the fox into the wood and it brought her back to the tower in no time at all. At first it was as dark as a tomb, but suddenly there was a light on the balcony above, and Rapunzel saw Threeteeth there, waiting for her. The fox was gone, and Rapunzel could barely remember it being there at all. Off in the woods Rapunzel heard the clatter of hooves, and the snorting of a noble stallion. She looked up at her friend, who smiled down at her with every tooth she had.

Threeteeth shouted down from the balcony. "What happens now?"

"I don't know. Isn't it marvelous?"

Rapunzel took the rope of hair in her own strong hands and began to climb.

# TRUE LOVE
# (or THE MANY BRIDES OF
# PRINCE CHARMING)
## by Todd Fahnestock and Giles Custer

Giles Custer and Todd Fahnestock met in high school eleven years ago. Within an hour of meeting, they started a philosophical conversation they haven't been able to finish yet. Their nomadic lifepaths have crisscrossed over the years, and they have managed to collaborate on four novels and a smattering of short stories. They currently live on opposite sides of California and hope to solve that problem shortly.

Some people blame poor Prince Charming for throwing Cinderella into the dungeon. They call him heartless for having little Snow White beheaded. Few know the real reasons Sleeping Beauty had to be burned at the stake. But that is because they have only heard one side of the story.

It is time the truth came to light.

Prince Charming—or Evil King Chuck, as he came to be known—was hardly the merciless and maniacal madman many would like to believe. He was a big-hearted man, a man of strength and compassion, a man who did his duty. The prince married for love, and fought for justice. In the end, he was forced to battle to save his wounded heart.

The tale of Prince Charming began, as all romances should, in the Enchanted Forest. Magic sparkled in the air. Zephyr breezes swayed through the trees. Birds sang their sweet songs into the amorous ears of all who would listen. . . .

Have you ever noticed that fairy tales never continue past the last dance at the royal ball, the sumptuous palace wedding banquet, or true love's first kiss? There's a reason for that.

That first kiss eventually twists itself into a wedding, and marriage can bring out the worst in a person. Even the Enchanted Forest doesn't change that. Magical enchantments tarnish into nothing but lust. Those zephyr breezes can turn shrill and howl through the castle halls. And those birds—those damn birds!—can chatter loudly enough to drive a man insane!

Certainly, Prince Charming blames the birds for many of his own matrimonial disasters. Charming's lot was a sad one. His choices were difficult, but he made them with a stiff upper lip. And his thanks for all his sacrifices? A cold throne. The hatred of his subjects. Tales of his legendary cruelty spread throughout the land. A mockery made of his name. So how did it all come about?

Let me tell you the tale of the sadly misunderstood Evil King Chuck.

Back in the Enchanted Forest, down there among the breezes and singing birds, a handsome young prince named Charming stood to inherit a fabulous kingdom. He considered himself the luckiest among men, and why should he not? He was much loved by his people, and he took to the business of being prince as naturally as though he'd been born to it—actually he *had* been born to it, come to think of it. Among his princely attributes, he was a superb host, no matter how ill-assorted the gathering was. Conversation never lagged before Charming filled it with a witty jest or a fanciful tale. People flocked to spend time in his presence.

Charming was also a natural athlete. A strapping lad, he excelled at all the manly activities. By age eighteen, he'd outjousted his father's strongest knights, outfought the most experienced men-at-arms. His physical endurance was without equal. He could run through the woods for days without tiring. On the hunt, Charming always killed twice as many beasts as any other man.

In politics, Charming was a fast study. From the time he was a boy, he spoke freely and wisely during his father's royal councils. Charming had an uncanny ability to understand men's hearts and what forces moved them. Ambassadors and ministers sought his advice. The nobles of the court all whispered that he was everything they could hope for in a man, a friend, or a king. They knew a golden future lay before him.

Charming could have done anything, but there was only one direction his heart ever led him in. Charming was a true romantic.

He loved jousting with the knights. He loved matching swords with the men-at-arms. He loved outthinking the generals. He loved making people smile and laugh, but he craved one thing above all: he wished to find his True Love.

Surely there must be some woman out there to share his life with, a lovely, sensible woman with wise eyes and gentle hands. Someone to rule by his side through the years, faithful and loyal to him and to his future kingdom.

Charming had seen into the hearts of the women at court. He heard their petty gossip. He saw them sing a man's praises to his face and then speak poison of him behind his back. He wanted none of that. In their eyes he was nothing but a husband to be won. Charming wanted to be loved for himself, not for the attached position and real estate. He wanted the kind of love that no one in the kingdom had seen in ages. He wanted True Love.

Charming searched far and wide. Sometimes he would leave the palace using the pretext of a long hunting trip, sometimes with the excuse of visiting relatives in other kingdoms, but always he searched for the perfect woman he just knew was out there, waiting, ready to love him and only him.

All his looking was to no avail. No matter how hard he searched, he could not find his True Love. Charming began to despair, to feel that perhaps he was setting his sights too high. Perhaps True Love was just a myth.

With the death of his dream, he began to sink into an unaccountable melancholy.

The king worried over his son and asked what was wrong. Charming did not want to alarm his father, but he could not hide the sadness in his heart.

"Surely you have not met with every woman in the kingdom?" the king asked his son.

"Father, I have traveled far and wide. Everywhere I go, it is the same. I speak with women. I laugh with them. We tell each other stories. They do that strange thing with their eyelashes. I wait for the spark that will warm the deepest corner of my heart, but there is nothing. . . ."

"Surely you have not knocked upon every door in the kingdom and asked to meet the daughters of the house?" the king asked his son.

"No, Father," Charming admitted. "I have adventured high and low, but not door to door."

"Well, then," the king said, "so we shall."

The next day the king issued a proclamation. There would be a royal ball. All the eligible ladies in the kingdom were invited to spend a night dancing at the palace. The king sent his messengers door to door, presenting the invitation.

Charming could hardly wait for the night. The ball seemed to be the answer to his dreams. Surely he would find the woman he searched for.

The night of the ball came and the palace was filled to capacity with women of every sort. Prince Charming danced with tall women, with short women. He danced with golden-haired women, with red-haired women, with dark-haired women. He danced chest to chest with heaving breasts, gut to gut with bursting girdles. He danced with women who could glide silently across the floor, with women who trod painfully upon his feet. He danced with silent women. With boisterous women. With demure women. Fiery women. Beautiful women. Ugly women.

He danced until the soles of his shoes wore through.

Charming's outlook was grim indeed that night. Was there not a single woman in the entire kingdom that he could love? As he pulled his tortured feet out of the scraps of leather that had been his shoes, he knew that True Love could not be found in such a manner.

Then *she* walked through the ballroom doors.

Charming's jaw dropped. She had hair of shining gold, ruby red lips, and milky white breasts. His eyes traveled the length of that pearl-studded blue-on-blue gown which hugged and emphasized her wonderful curves. He lost his heart in an instant. Cinderella turned toward him and met his gaze with a lovely blush that tinted her cheeks the color of rose petals.

As the prince stood there watching her, he realized he was not truly alone.

For a short time, it was wonderful. In fact, it was the memories of that first night that kept Charming from insanity or even suicide in later years.

But that was the future. On that night, Prince Charming forgot there were any other women in the palace. Arm in arm with Cinderella, he swept about the dance floor for hours. The blisters on his feet were forgotten. The bruises on his shins were a memory. Everything was perfect, or so it seemed, until, at the stroke of midnight, Cinderella suddenly screamed and ran for the doors.

Charming stood in shock as True Love fled from his arms. Too late he tried to give chase, sprinting across the dance floor and onto the grand staircase. Nothing was left of the woman of his dreams, save for a glass slipper on the steps and an enormous pumpkin rolling away into the night.

The glass slipper should have tipped him off. Cinderella's odd carriage should have nailed the coffin shut on her chances of marriage. There were hints all along of trouble to come, but Charming was smitten. He could see nothing beyond her beauty, her soft skin, her fine figure. Her dulcimer voice haunted his memories.

But what kind of a woman owns glass shoes? Shoes in which the slightest misstep meant severe lacerations? What kind of a woman shuttled herself around in a squash?

From the moment she stepped out of the coach, Charming should have realized she was out of her gourd.

With that damn slipper, Charming managed to find Cinderella. He and his entourage went door to door, searching for the owner of the glass slipper. When he found it fit upon the delicate foot of a servant girl, he could not have been happier. Two days later he was married.

No one truly knows what occurred on the honeymoon. As honeymoons should be, it was an affair between the young lovers alone, but Charming returned with a smile on his lips and light in his eyes.

Things went downhill after that.

Perhaps he had begun to learn of his new bride's eccentricities. Perhaps the fire of his idealism had dimmed. It is possible that Charming, with his keen insight, had seen where his relationship with his wife must certainly lead. If so, he blocked it out and continued on in the most noble manner.

He did not question his dear wife when she brought all of her pets into the palace. When the nobles fled the city due to the singing rodents in the west wing, Charming was concerned. Still, he had nothing in particular against mice and pacified his father. When the seamstress complained that the little rodents were stealing her best fabric and thread to make hideous dresses, Charming hushed it up, bought new materials, and set the seamstress up on the other side of the palace.

Then the royal stables became infested with rodents and lizards, lounging in the mangers of the matched teams, draped across the ornate handles of the state coaches. The pests could not be chased off. Like quicksilver, they would zip out of sight when the royal cats went after them, then resume their positions the moment no one was looking. The entire stable staff resigned after the first month.

By all rights, Charming should have immediately dealt with his wife's hobbies. When Charming discovered his mother's twelve prized Persian cats dead beneath the west tower window—a window filled with singing mice— he should have staged a mass rodent execution.

But Charming was a romantic. He was a man of honor, and he loved his wife above all else. He cleaned up these messes and covered for her. Charming held onto his illusions to the bitter end.

Then Cinderella invited that woman into the palace. Charming checked his sigh when she introduced the old hag as her Fairy Godmother. But the prince loved his wife and put on his most charming smile. The old woman was given her own rooms and whatever she might require to make Cinderella happy.

The old woman was plump and jovial. She sang silly songs, but that did little to hide the truth that she was the most criminally expensive dressmaker of all time. And after long years of making due with the dregs from her stepsisters, Cinderella had some serious shopping to get out of her system. That sweet-smiling, rosy-cheeked Fairy Godmother inflated Cinderella's wardrobe to epic proportions. Charming's new bride ordered the finest fabrics from the ends of the Earth. Diamonds from the far Southlands, pearls from the West Coast, even rubies from the East. Even Cinderella's undergarments glittered, shone, and could cut glass.

Then came the interior decorating. No chair satisfied Cinderella until it was worked by a master carver and upholstered in silk. No bed was fit to sleep in unless the headboard was inlaid with precious metals and mother-of-pearl. Even the royal castle was not up to the standards of this ex-scullery maid.

"The fixtures are too dull," she said, "Replace them in gold."

Perhaps the old king should have done something before it got out of hand. He should have told Charming he was letting his wife run all over him, but just as Charming could deny his wife nothing, so the king denied nothing to his only son. They both waited in painful anticipation for Cinderella's next request.

The expensive balls began shortly thereafter, as Cinderella decided it was time to show off her new clothes. Money flew out of the treasury. Taxes were raised, slowly at first, then faster and faster, until the peasants began grumbling. Discontent among the people grew as quickly as Cinderella's wardrobe.

Within a year, the kingdom reached the edge of revolt. The peasants were taking up arms. Curses, and worse, were flung at the king when he rode through town. The peasants were starving, and Princess Cinderella had five thousand pairs of shoes. Charming knew he had to do something. Balance had to be restored before an angry peasant mob attacked the palace gates.

Every man has his breaking point, and Prince Charming's came late one night when he went to his father for counsel on these brewing matters. When he walked into the king's room and found the mice taking down the drapes to make yet another dress for Cinderella, Charming snapped.

He ordered every hungry cat in the kingdom to be set upon the mice. He trapped them, poisoned them, burned them out of their holes. The lizards became belts. The thieving Fairy Godmother was sent back to her Enchanted

Forest, wearing a new gown of tar and feathers. Cinderella was finally thrown into the dungeons after psychiatric counseling and a series of expensive twelve-step programs failed to curb her spending.

Prince Charming then began to restore the kingdom he'd nearly brought to its knees by his foolishness. He had Cinderella's dresses and shoes sold off, the rich furnishings and rugs returned or auctioned to the highest bidder. The palace's golden door handles were melted down, replaced by more serviceable brass ones. Soon, both the bellies of the peasants and the chests of the royal treasury were full again.

Life in the dungeon was not too bad for Cinderella. She made friends with the rats down there. She sang them songs and they wove her petticoats out of garbage and the remains of corpses. . . .

Poor Prince Charming, however, was devastated by what had happened. Once the kingdom had been righted and riots no longer ravaged the streets, he went off to live alone in the woods. He hoped a little solitude would salve his badly wounded, too-trusting heart.

He lived a month alone in a small cottage, hunting for his supper, and chopping his own wood for the fire. In the evenings, with his belly full of venison, Charming would watch the sun set and marvel at the beauty of nature. Slowly, he put the insanity of Cinderella and her entourage behind him. He began to take long walks deep into the woods. He would choose a different direction, walk a different route every time.

And so it was he stumbled across the crystal casket lying alone in the woods. When Charming peered inside, he was amazed. The prince had never seen a more devastatingly beautiful young woman. She was so radiant as she lay there sleeping. She had raven dark hair, ruby red lips, not to mention those milky white breasts barely concealed by a velvet gown.

Charming shook his head. He nodded gruffly and looked at her in what he hoped was a clinical fashion. She was beautiful, but the prince had just had his fill of beauty. Still, his curiosity was piqued by her predicament. Why was this woman asleep in a crystal box out in the middle of nowhere? He considered tapping on the glass to ask her, but wasn't certain what would be polite in a situation like this.

As the prince stood there watching her, he realized he was not alone.

Charming's acute ears heard them scuffling. His hunter's eyes spotted the tiny men hidden in the trees.

Charming unsheathed his sword. "You may as well show yourselves!" he called, "If it's gold you're after, you'll find your work difficult enough this night! I've given up enough gold lately, and, frankly, I'm in the mood for a fight!"

The little men came out of hiding, hands out and open in a pacifying gesture. There were seven of them, and each was stumpier and uglier than the one before. They swore they were not thieves and had no wish to fight the strapping young prince. Instead, they told him of a horrible curse that had been put upon their friend in the casket, the beautiful Snow White. Only the kiss of a real prince could break the spell.

Charming almost turned on his heel and marched out of the glade. He knew that would be a very unprincely thing to do, however. With power came responsibility, and he knew that princes didn't come by this neck of the woods every day. If he didn't help the girl, who would? Besides, the little men seemed so sad. They obviously thought of the girl as a daughter and cared very deeply for her.

Smiling a little, Charming announced that he was a prince. The dwarfs cheered. Flipping open the casket's lid, he leaned over and kissed the girl. Her lips became instantly warm. Her soft arms wrapped snugly about Charming's neck, and he found himself in the midst of a deep kiss.

No, it was a legendary kiss.

Fire spread throughout his body as he kissed those ruby red lips and she pressed those heaving, milky white breasts to his chest. Finally, the kiss subsided like the tide receding from a beach.

Charming's breath came in short gasps as he looked down into the young woman's dark, sultry eyes. Those eyes beckoned him for more. He tried to think of sunsets alone by his cottage, of roasting venison over a fire. All of these memories blurred like watercolors in the rain and vanished.

Two days later, Prince Charming was married again.

No one truly knows what occurred on the honeymoon. As honeymoons should be, it was an affair between the young lovers alone, but Charming returned with a smile on his lips and light in his eyes.

Things went downhill after that.

Charming felt like he was revisiting a bad nightmare when Snow White moved her pets into the palace. He could not turn his head without seeing a bluebird twittering. He could not walk down the stairs without being passed by a pack of rushing squirrels.

But Charming was a patient man, and he had seen far worse. He let these things go by.

Then the dwarfs moved in. They were loud and annoying. Charming tolerated it at the behest of his new wife, whom he could deny nothing. After all, the gnarled old men had taken care of her in her youth.

After the first day, Charming began to wonder if he had made a grievous error. He tried to take an interest in his wife's friends, but it was impossible to tell the little buggers apart. Some of them were chronically grumpy, others were manic. One of them went around sneezing on everyone. A few days after the dwarfs moved in, half the staff came down with the flu.

The dwarfs were horrible houseguests. On top of being ugly as sin, they had no table manners whatsoever. Burping, snorting, farting at the table! After the conclusion of the Cinderella debacle, the local nobles had slowly begun to sift back into the palace. They were still skittish, and it didn't take long for them to start sifting politely back out. One dinner with a dwarf was enough for anyone to lose his appetite.

The dwarfs dug up the basement. They dug up the yard. They would have dug up the ballroom floor if Charming had not physically disarmed them.

"It's just in their nature," Snow White would say sweetly and give him one of those deep kisses. Thoroughly pacified, Charming would nod and smile his charming smile. And so it went. . . .

Perhaps things would have smoothed out after a while if those pacifying kisses had continued. Who can say how long a man can stay lost in the eyes of a lovely and willing woman?

But the kisses came less frequently, then stopped altogether. In the beginning, it would have been an understatement to say that Snow White enjoyed her wifely duties. As the months went on, however, she became less and less interested in poor Prince Charming. If she did not suffer from a headache, then she was simply too exhausted to muster more than a passing greeting to her husband before she slipped into slumber.

Every man has his breaking point, although Charming was a more patient, compassionate man than most. He wanted nothing more than his beloved wife's happiness, but when he found the long, gray hairs in his bed one morning, his blood began to boil. But Charming had no proof, so he held his tongue. Every day after that he suffered when he saw the smug little smiles on their wizened little faces, that rosy tinge to their wrinkled little cheeks.

Charming was a hunter, and began to hunt his wife. He found little muddy footprints in Snow White's private bath. He noticed extra lumps in the feather mattress on her bed. It was only a matter of time before he caught her.

Charming could actually hear his heart split in two that night he walked into the apple orchard and found all eight of them together. Really together.

Though it made him sick at heart, Charming had no choice. The law is the law. He called the axman and had the lot of them put to death.

Charming fell into a deep depression. The squirrel hunt he arranged in the palace made him feel better for a few hours, but it didn't last. All he could think about was Snow White's betrayal. What did those little bastards have that he did not?

Soon after, the executioner brought him the answer. Not every part of those dwarfs was little.

* * *

Enraged, driven by the need to release his anger, Charming went on a quest, seeking out good deeds that needed doing. He hoped some adventuring would take his mind off his troubles. He scuttled a pirate ship and rousted a pack of bandits, but they were only passing fancies. Then Charming heard tales of an evil witch who was keeping an entire kingdom encased in a spell of eternal slumber. It was rumored that the witch could metamorphose into a dragon with black fangs and burning yellow eyes. Charming's budding misogynist streak flared. He took it upon himself to rid the world of this evil bitch.

Prince Charming and the sorceress-dragon met upon a battlefield of thorns. The fight was long and bloody, but Charming emerged victorious. He stabbed the dead dragon body numerous times once she had fallen. He stomped on her head, chopped off her claws, made a necklace of them as he laughed into the wind.

Finally he tired and stood there empty and alone staring at the dead witch.

As the prince stood there watching her, he realized he was not alone.

Struggling through the remains of the thorns was a skinny, officious man. Charming had not had so much fun in almost a year, and he nearly lopped off the offending man's head for interrupting. The prince stayed his hand long enough to listen to the man. He was a messenger from the kingdom that the evil sorceress had enchanted. He had been sent to report that the spell had not been broken with the sorceress' death. In order to truly free the kingdom, a prince must kiss Sleeping Beauty in the high tower.

"Oh, God," Charming spat, "I'm not going through

that again. I'm just here to kill things. Find yourself another prince!"

Why the stupid girl had to go and get herself cursed in the first place, Charming didn't even want to know. The messenger cajoled and bribed. In the end, Charming had to admit that an entire kingdom shouldn't have to suffer just because he didn't want to kiss some sleeping tart stuck in a tower. Finally, after great deliberation, Charming swore to go into the high tower and break the spell.

Charming climbed the tower, threw the cover off of Sleeping Beauty and kissed her. He made certain to jump back before she could get her tentacles around him. She awoke slowly. Charming turned his head, not wanting to even look at her. He wanted to run, afraid of what would happen next. His damned curiosity caused him to pause.

Instead of igniting the fires of his passion, however, she began to sing. The melody of her voice filled the room and wrapped Charming up in its power. She sang of a daring prince who faced the horrible dragon of her nightmares. She sang of how he risked his very life to come to her aid, of how sweet and kind his lips were against hers. She sang of how she owed him everything.

Charming, poised to flee, slowly turned and looked into her eyes, which were brimming with tears. He smiled hesitantly, and her song turned joyous. He looked down at her honey-colored hair, her ruby red lips, her milky white breasts. . . .

Two days later, Prince Charming was married yet again.

No one truly knows what occurred on the honeymoon. As honeymoons should be, it was an affair between the young lovers alone, but Charming returned with a smile on his lips and light in his eyes.

Things went downhill after that.

More pets. Getting dressed in the morning was tantamount to a full-fledged hunt. If it wasn't the damned owl stealing his shirts, it was the bunnies running off with his boots! Soon, even his own horse started laughing at him! But Charming bore it in smoldering silence because he was determined to be such a fucking good husband.

Charming soon noticed an even more frightening trend in his new wife. Beauty had spent her entire life being told that if she pricked her finger she'd die. She'd never even been allowed close to anything sharp until the moment she entered Charming's castle.

Perhaps it was the curse, or perhaps she had been warped long before because of being raised by fairies, but Beauty began to develop an obsession with sharp objects.

"Charming, be sure to bring the needles to bed with you."

"Charming, what a lovely new dagger you have."

"Charming, if you love me, you'll use that sword on me like a man, not a boy."

"Charming, meet me at the ballista again at midnight, you chicken-shit bastard!"

Hushed rumors began spreading throughout the servants' quarters. Blood on the bedsheets. Strange rituals in the prince's rooms at midnight. Perhaps they were sacrificing chickens . . . goats . . . newborn babies!

This time, Charming wasn't going to wait until things became intolerable. He wasn't going to wait until he woke up, impaled with a fence stake by his wife's latest gesture of affection. Charming didn't want to do it, but he had no choice. He had to get rid of her and he couldn't be merciful about it. The headsman's ax would have excited the girl far too much. It would have been indecent. Instead, he had her burned at the stake.

\*    \*    \*

Charming never left the palace again. He wouldn't risk it. He spent the rest of his days locked away from all women. When his father died, the once charming prince became the Evil King Chuck, the king who outlawed marriage. He had any passing love poets put to a painful death. Minstrels who strayed from strict battle hymns into softer songs of the heart soon found themselves swinging from the gallows.

Much as Chuck wanted to ignore it, he knew the inky smoke from Beauty's pyre lingered in the air. Snow White's little gasp at the falling ax still echoed in King Chuck's memory. Sometimes, late at night, he could still hear Cinderella talking with the mice. Slowly but surely, the memories of his past weighed him down. As the dark years passed, Chuck developed a crick in his walk. His hair and beard grew wild and unkempt. His once broad shoulders curled over into a hunchback's lump. The few servants and nobles who had survived the first three brides of Prince Charming quietly fled the palace, and it became a dark, dank place. The peasants abandoned their fields and went in search of richer kingdoms.

It was said that Evil King Chuck was cursed.

Soon the king was all alone in his dismal castle. His fingernails grew into claws. He took to talking with the clocks and candlesticks to keep himself sane. But Chuck was not completely unhappy. Never did his yellow eyes look upon a woman. Never did his hairy ears hear the words: True Love.

But one day a stranger snuck into his castle. Chuck was up in the farthest reach of the west tower when he caught the scent of her perfume. He flew into an immediate rage. Grabbing two knives, he raced down the stairs, charged through the long hall and threw himself over the banister that led into the grand foyer. With a maniacal snarl, he fell upon the foul creature.

"Please, please!" she cried out, "Don't hurt me! My name is Beauty. I mean you no harm!"

The young beauty looked up into the Chuck's bestial eyes. Fear marked her face, but courage held her fast. Chuck watched as compassion for him slowly entered her features.

No! He would not be swayed! Evil King Chuck grabbed his knives tighter and prepared to make supper of the girl.

And yet . . .

Chocolate-colored hair . . . ruby red lips . . . milky white breasts . . .

"You don't have any pets?" he asked. His grip on the knives relaxed.

"Ah, just a horse," she said, keeping her composure despite the flashing knives.

Chuck paused.

"He doesn't sing, does he?" he growled.

"Uh, not so far."

He paused.

"I think this could be True Love," he said.

# SAVIOR
## by John Helfers

John Helfers is a writer and editor currently living in Green Bay, Wisconsin. His fiction has appeared in anthologies such as *Sword of Ice and Other Tales of Valdemar, The UFO Files,* and *Warrior Princesses,* among others. He is also the editor of the anthology *Black Cats and Broken Mirrors.* Other projects include co-authoring a fantasy trilogy and editing a second anthology. In his spare time, what there is of it, he enjoys disc golf, inline skating, and role-playing games.

High in a tree I wait, motionless. My green jerkin and brown breeches blend perfectly with the leaves and branches. The yew bow at my side, with an arrow already nocked, waits with me. It waits for a target. I wait for vengeance.

I've been here for hours. My waterskin is empty, my jerky long gone. It doesn't matter, the hunger, the thirst. Nothing matters except finding it, killing it. If I can, there's the barest chance I can save her.

The merest thought of her makes me think of the last time we were together. Could it have been only yesterday? The touch of her lips, the softness of her under my hands. Her gentle yet urgent gasp as I held her, her lithe body rising to meet me. All grown up, little in nothing but name.

My free hand drops to the crimson velvet hood that hangs from my belt. A gift from me, now it is spotted with her blood and ripped where its fangs had torn it to get at the soft meat underneath. The flesh that, just hours before, I had nipped with my own teeth.

Touching the hood again, I remember discovering the cabin. The overturned chairs, torn bedding, smashed clay jars. What was left of her grandmother was in a closet. Of my love there was no sign, save for the hood my hand is constantly reaching for. I remember how she looked wearing it. I remember her wearing it, the red silk cloak, and nothing else. I remember sliding it off her raven hair. . . .

A rustle in the bushes snaps my attention back to the present. I raise the bow and aim at the brush where I heard the noise. It's coming toward the clearing, near the tree I'm hiding in. I choose where it is most likely to appear and aim, drawing the bowstring back and waiting.

A form appears, I see a flash of gray fur. Without conscious thought, I release the arrow. A moment later, a howl of agony splits the afternoon air, rising quickly and just as quickly being choked off as if by a hand. Or by blood.

Leaping from my perch, in my haste I land wrong, feeling a sharp pain in my leg. Uncaring, I limp to where the wolf has fallen. He's there all right, a huge monster, as tall at the shoulder as I am. His stomach still bulges from his meal this morning. The shaft of my arrow juts from his neck. On seeing me, his golden eyes widen, as if he knows who I am. Not just that I am his killer, but his gaze tells me he knows what he has taken from me.

He tries to rise, spraying a mouthful of blood as his legs buckle underneath him. I walk over, careful to avoid his fangs that are as long as my fingers. He snaps at me weakly, almost as an afterthought. Our eyes meet again, and he knows it is over.

My bone-handled hunting knife is in my hand, but I wait, watching. I can see movement in his stomach, something pressing against his side, trying to escape. Yet still I wait. I wait for him to die. Somewhere deep inside me, I know this is wrong.

The wolf collapses on his side, and I move. Leaning down, I plunge my dagger into his belly. Two quick slits and I see her, squirming helplessly. Tossing my blade aside, I take her groping hand and pull her out. Then the smell hits me.

In the waning sunlight, she writhes in agony. Turning, the dried beef I ate this morning slides back up my throat. I can hear her mewling, her reddened arms flailing, groping for help that came too late. I see the ruin of her once-beautiful face. I see the empty sockets where her beautiful blue eyes had been. I could not let anyone I love live like this.

Picking up the knife again, I bend to the task at hand. A moment later, it is done.

Untying the red hood from my belt, I drape it over

what's left of her face. Uncertain for a moment as to what to do with her, I wrap her in my cloak, pick her up and slowly walk back to the cottage. I think she would have liked to be buried in the garden.

# WOLF AT THE DOOR
## by Lupita Shepard

Lupita Shepard lives and writes on the West Coast. This is her first published story.

His business card said "Joe Wolferman, Collections Technologist, Houston, San Antonio, Austin, Dallas, and Santa Fe." It was followed by a graphic of a stag wearing a big rack of antlers and a dollar sign in its middle with the motto, "We always get your bucks." Some of Joe's clients would have said that motto was way too modest. Hell, Joe was the best in the business. Satisfied customers claimed that Joe actually *could* get blood out of a turnip. Joe admitted privately that blood was occasionally involved.

For that reason, among others, he declined to teach seminars and workshops to people just entering the field of collections technology. While this disappointed some of his clients, it did not by any means discourage them from using his services. He contributed to his chosen field in other ways. For instance, he was the one who had come up with the idea of the creditor taking out a "free" death and dismemberment policy on the debtor.

Joe was on the phone, working a deadbeat account now. Sharon Bacon, self-employed graphic artist, divorced for two years, five foot two, one hundred and five pounds, size five dress, size two panties, size 36DD bra, no criminal record, two driving violations, $100 in her checking account and $16,000 in debt to his client. It wasn't that much, not even in Joe's own bank account, but a lot of little $16,000 amounts could add up to big money if you let the deadbeats get away with it. The problem was, most collectors didn't know their prey, had no class, went in there with both barrels blazing and got nowhere. Joe was a hell of a lot smoother than that and, with his background in police work and his own private methods, could also get a hell of a lot rougher.

He had been talking to her for several minutes, his mouth on the phone, his eyes on the computer screen where her life was scrolling in front of him. Her purchases: jewelry, cosmetics, perfume, boutique clothing, shoes—she must have more shoes than Imelda Marcos in her heyday. Even a case of gourmet steaks. These people were always such pigs, greedily buying everything up till their credit was all gone, then not wanting to pay because they had even more stuff they wanted to buy with the money they should use to pay their bills.

He had had a hard time getting through to her. She had not been answering her calls or his messages, which was not unusual. Joe only took cases within driving distance unless the client paid his airfare. Caller ID had made getting through by phone much more difficult, even when you disguised your voice. The collectee saw that "unavailable" number pop up on their box and let it ring. Joe had been about to go to her home and knock on the door. The first time, he always knocked on the door.

Then all of a sudden she answered.

"Hello? Who is this? Hello?" Her voice was fast, nasal, clipped—a Yankee transplant probably. She didn't sound like a Texas girl.

"Sharon? Is that you?" he asked, trying to sound like a friend.

"Yeah, sure. Who's this?" He listened to her voice again, carefully, from the few words hearing that she sounded frightened, edgy, excited, breathless. Good. Fear was good. Whatever the reason, it made a collectee more receptive to persuasion.

"It's Joe. Joe Wolferman."

"Huh? Do I know you?"

"Listen, are you okay? You sound a little funny," he said. The longer he could duck the real purpose of his call, the more personal he made it sound, the longer he could keep her talking, the better chance he had of finding out what he needed to know to nail her.

"I've—had some problems recently. Sorry. I really can't talk right now."

"It'll only take a little while if you'll work with me on this, Sharon. Say, did you enjoy those steaks you ordered?"

"What? Steaks? Oh, yeah. They were great! Didn't last long, though."

"That must have been some big barbecue you had. There were eighteen of those steaks, four pounds each," he said, looking at his screen. Her picture was there now, big brown eyes, dark brown hair with lighter bits around her thin little face. That expensive beauty salon that charged $75 per visit must have done the light streaks.

"I—yeah, they were good. Is that where I met you?"

"No, I couldn't make it," he said. He could have lied directly but he was already making up the party. He didn't know what she'd done with the steaks, but a little babe like her couldn't have eaten them all. "So what's got you all upset, Sharon?" he asked in his best sexy baritone drawl, oozing heartfelt sincerity. Knowing what upset her was part of his job. If he knew what upset her, he could use it, and she would pay to make it stop.

Her voice was tearful when she answered, "Oh, just everything! I haven't got caught up on work since I was in the hospital last month, I still have all these funny aches and pains, wake up in the morning just complet- edly disoriented and exhausted. And you know, it's get- ting to be that time of the month."

He wanted to make a lewd remark, but he kept it to himself. Later, maybe. "All those bills piling up must be gettin' on your nerves, too, huh?" he asked, finally cut- ting to the chase, at least a little. Next he could offer to "help" her, reduce her payments, take something for col- lateral, start collecting.

"All the people dunning me for money sure do. I'll get the bills paid or I won't. Frankly, that's the least of my worries."

"It's bound to have affected your credit, though?" he said, keeping just this side of the concerned friend, maybe one-night-stand boyfriend she couldn't remem- ber and was too embarrassed to say so but not too embar- rassed to tell her problems to.

"Credit schmedit! That's shot already. What I most need is a good night's sleep, a good meal, and to get back to normal." She was whining now, almost crying, repeating, "I just haven't been able to get back to normal. I want everything to be normal again."

This sounded important. "Isn't it normal? Since when?"

"Ever since the attack. I just can't get over it."

He couldn't ask, "What attack?" He wanted to. Attacked made her vulnerable and him—excited. He could show her "attacked," too. The thing about these victim types was they whined about it, complained about it, but they invited it, they liked it really. This could be more than business. She sounded like his type. He couldn't ask more right now, however, couldn't go too fast. Obviously, if he was whoever she was assuming he was, he knew about it. Or she thought he did. "Look, maybe you need some company," he said soothingly. "Maybe you need to talk to someone about it."

"Maybe," she said doubtfully. If she was the kind who called the cops and took things to court, she wouldn't go for it. Who in their right mind would invite a strange guy in when they didn't even know who he was? But some of these gals weren't exactly rational. They kidded themselves that it had happened once but wouldn't happen again—that everyone else was going to sympathize, hold them, comfort them. Anyhow, the victim types told themselves that's what they wanted. Really, they just wanted a little more excitement. He could relate to that—and provide it.

"Look, I've got a couple of things I have to finish up here, but I'll be over as soon as I can," he said, just the way a friend would. "You'll be home, right?"

"I—I think so. Try to come before dark, though. It—gets scary after dark."

"Now, now, don't worry. I'll be there as quick as I can. And there's a full moon. It'll be bright enough. Just stay calm, okay?" And he hung up before she could think about it anymore.

He took his time. He'd get there just before dark. Dark came late this time of year. He didn't mind the overtime when he could taste success once more like this. He'd check out her place, see what could be repossessed, sold, or returned. Half the time these compulsive shopping types never took the price tags off things. He'd check her out, too. He was a workaholic. Didn't get a lot of time for recreation. Dedicated to his job. But this looked like one where he could collect a little interest.

He showered and brushed his teeth. Dressed carefully, casually enough not to scare her, well enough to look respectable—someone she'd let in without thinking. Jeans with a crease in the front, black western-cut shirt. Combed his hair over the thin spot and placed his black stetson just so over his brow. Black boots with silver tips. Not unusual dress for Houston this time of year. A business suit would be a little too formal—tip his hand. The cowboy look was more appealing, the black made him look as lean and mean as he felt, and, he grinned—she had only herself to blame if she opened her door to the guy in the black hat.

He wondered if she'd be wearing any of that expensive lingerie she'd bought—and what the shoes looked like.

He'd find out soon enough. His old black magic was working again; he could feel it.

He was so pleased with himself as he drove to within a couple of blocks of her place, walked the rest of the way. A little research, a little insight into human nature, that's all it took. Basically, in this line of work, you herded grasshoppers. Not the ants, the tight-ass types who compulsively took care of business, never let a payment date slip. No, these people fiddled and fooled around and kidded themselves that they hadn't spent money because the money they spent was not yet their own. Then when the time to pay came, they had excuses. Like life didn't happen to everybody.

He never had to waste his breath huffing and puffing in front of the brick house built by the smart little pig. All his little pigs lived in places made of straw or twigs, and all he had to do was breathe to bring the whole place down around their ears, repossess the stuff, and take what he could find as interest. This particular interest looked—interesting.

She lived in a medium-priced condo, paid for, in a medium-high high-rise. One of those things where you give your name to a speaking tube. He pushed the bell and said, "Hey, Sharon. I made it."

"Oh," she said. She sounded quavery and uncertain again.

"Look, have you eaten recently? What say I come up and take you out for something to eat, okay?" He remembered she'd said she was missing meals. If she was having second thoughts about letting a stranger in, that ought to do it. It did.

"Oh, okay," she said. "Just a minute." The buzzer buzzed, and he let himself in, took the elevator to her floor.

She met him at the door. It was wide open, no chain on. She was almost so dumb it wasn't any fun. He was a little disappointed. She didn't look as good as her photo. She was small and frail-looking enough for him to break in half, her skin pale, breasts pushing against the loose fabric of the long, blue, sleeveless knit dress she was wearing, like a slip or a nightgown. No underwear, he could have sworn. But her arms had scratches on them, there was a big bandage on one shoulder, and her eyes had dark circles under them. Her hair looked like she'd just run a brush through it and it stood up in places. As for sexy shoes, she wasn't wearing any at all. She was barefoot. What was it with women these days? Here he'd been careful to dress nice, shower, shave, the whole thing, and she looked like she'd just been slopping around the house all day and wasn't even expecting him.

Her face registered the disapproval in his at the same time she realized she had never seen him before in her life. She started to close the door, but he pushed past her.

"Guess you'll have to get ready," he said, with just an edge of command.

"Oh," she said, looking down at herself as if puzzled to see what she was wearing, like she didn't remember. A chick who spent that much on clothes, shoes, and jewelry ought to be aware of that kind of thing, especially when she had a man coming over. Or didn't she think he was important enough? He'd fix that. She'd remember him for a good long time. Oh, yeah.

Then she looked up at him and her eyes were glittery, but not with tears. "But you said on the phone you thought maybe I needed to talk and you'd come over and listen, Joe. Then you mentioned dinner downstairs. I don't want to talk about all this in public, over dinner. Surely you understand?" For the first time, her voice was even, calm, and she sounded halfway bright. It threw him.

"Uh—yeah, yeah sure," he said, taken aback and also

thinking maybe he needed to take it a little slower than he'd figured. "Only—I was just wondering from how you were dressed if you were expecting me after all. . . ."

Now her voice was low again, soft, "Because of this old thing?" she asked, picking up the fabric of the sack dress between her right thumb and forefinger. "I don't like to get my nice clothes all torn up."

That got his blood racing again. She looked up at him from under her lashes, a sly look, calculating, and he was about to ask if she didn't mind if he tore the one she was wearing off—since she seemed to be leading up to that—when she turned, ducked into her kitchen alcove, picked up a couple of pot holders and headed for a door he thought led to a bedroom. He almost followed, but that would have maybe been what she wanted. Put her in the driver's seat. That was not what he wanted. He was driving. He was calling the shots. She was not in charge. Of anything.

She called out, "So why don't you call out for delivery if you're hungry? There's a number for a pizza place taped to the phone. They have a good three-meat, extra cheese, no garlic one."

He gave a little snort. Not real likely. He didn't want to be interrupted.

There was a sound of tinkling, scraping, as of metal on metal, and clanging coming from the other room— sounded like a car wreck in there. He looked around the front room. The most obvious assets were the Navajo rugs on sofa and spread over the carpet on the floor—big ones, expensive ones, seven of them altogether—the collection of pottery and baskets in the antique Mission style sideboard and hutch—a few paintings on the walls, an R. C. Gorman, original, he could tell. That'd fetch a pretty penny, too.

An expensive big-screen TV, VCR, stereo, a couple of new exercise machines. He hadn't noticed those on her charges, but they could still be sold to pay off her debt. There were a lot of nice kitchen appliances, too—coffee machine, bread machine, pasta maker, fancy crystal on the shelves. He opened the freezer. One thing for sure, this girl was no vegetarian and had nothing against beef. After her credit was cut off, she must have paid cash for more of those gourmet steaks she'd ordered on her card. The freezer was full of them.

He decided to check out the bathroom. He didn't ask first. Most likely she had a drug habit—cocaine or something. That'd fit in with *all* his plans real well. He fully expected to see the little mirror, the little spoon, maybe even some powder she figured people would take for the kind she put on her nose instead of up it. But there was none of that. Just the bathroom mirror. He opened the medicine cabinet and boxes of Nair and plastic sacks of disposable razors fell out. Huh. She had a little linen closet and he opened it, to see that the towels and washcloths, her cosmetics, perfume and so forth, had all been crammed onto a top shelf while the rest of the closet was stuffed with more COSTCO-sized boxes of toiletry items like the Nair and the razors, two cartons of toothpaste, plus another carton full of those heads you buy for electric toothbrushes.

Her purse was lying on the white leather upholstered sofa. He sat down, reached over, unzipped the purse and took out her wallet. He just had time to see that it was stuffed with bills before he heard a clanking behind him and dropped it back into the purse.

She walked around the sofa, and dumped a box on the coffee table in front of him. He gaped. The box was filled with jewelry. Silver jewelry. Big silver jewelry—a lot of it Indian jewelry—big cuff bracelets, brooches the size of dessert plates, at least three of those whaddaya callem—squash blossom necklaces—earrings that looked long and heavy enough to break her slender little neck.

"Here," she said.

"What's all this?" he asked, backpedaling. He wasn't ready to let her off—let her go—this easy. He wasn't finished yet. Hadn't even got started.

"What you came for. You're the bill collector Countrybank sicced on me, right? This stuff is worth more than enough to pay my bills. Go ahead. Take it. The Ray Tracey butterfly set my ex gave me is worth six thousand dollars alone. Most of the rest is dead pawn and that's worth a small fortune. I've had the older pieces appraised. It's worth more than enough to cover my bills."

"Yeah, but, wait a minute here. If it's worth more, you should sell it and give us the money."

She shook her head and hung back. "I don't want to touch it. I won't ever wear it again. Just take it. That's what you're here for. I didn't send your money, so you came to take it." She sounded teary and upset again, not mad so much as lonesome, sad.

He softened his approach again, accordingly. "Now, that's not strictly the truth. Do you see me huffing and puffing and trying to blow you away? Normally, I don't make house calls," he lied. If they didn't pay up, eventually he always made house calls. But he wasn't going to tell her that. "You sounded real upset on the phone, said you'd been in the hospital, been attacked. I didn't want to come down hard on you when you'd had all that trouble. Hell, I'm a human being like everybody else, and you sounded like you needed somebody to talk to. Why don't you sit down here and tell me what's the matter?"

He patted the sofa beside him. She sat, near his arm, near enough so he could feel the heat from her body, though her skin was goose-pimply from the cold air coming from the air conditioner. He could smell her, the same smell as in the bathroom.

"Thanks," she said. "That's why I let you come in, even though I knew what you were. You sounded human—nice, I mean. You didn't yell at me."

"Well," he said, starting in on one of his favorite themes. He did like to talk and mostly his conversations were over the phone, with people he couldn't say much to. "A lot of doing any job well is knowing human nature. I used to be a cop, you know, before I wised up and started working in the private sector, so to speak. You've got to know people, read their voices, watch their faces, pay attention. You have to have a little sixth sense about people. And you have to know what people want. Most people I meet in my line of work think they need money more than anything. But if you talk to them right, you find out that's not the case. There's usually something more important to them, whether it's family, friends, a pet, their job, their health. I came up with this death-and-dismemberment-policy idea for my clients. The debtor gets a free $1000 policy that will pay off that much of his bill to my client in the event he should die or suffer dismemberment. So my client gets paid even if that happens, especially if that happens, and the debtor pretty soon begins to realize that." Her eyes were wide now, the pupils dilated in the increasingly dim light of the room. She gave a little whimper, and he figured it was time to pull back a little. She apparently got it that his insurance idea made certain that when he was on the case his clients always got their cash. Actually, now that he remembered it, she hadn't signed the policy. He gave her what he hoped was a disarmingly concerned look and said, "So anyway, I know about people and I could tell how upset you were. You gonna tell me about it?"

She relaxed a little, took a deep breath, let it out in a sigh, then glanced at the window. You could see the sky from the seventh floor of this building—see clear out over the Gulf. Really, with a water view like that, they could be getting more for these units than they were. Maybe he'd have to talk to a real estate magnate he knew and see if they couldn't work out a deal. Condemn the building for some kind of public project, buy out the owners at a fraction of what the place was worth and put up a classier establishment where you could charge what the view was worth. The sun was just turning the waters of the Gulf pink now, and in a few minutes, it would be gone and the moon would be up. Real romantic.

"Funny that you mentioned death and dismemberment," she said. "I haven't been the same since the attack. I was hurt really bad. I spent two weeks in the hospital. In spite of how bad the wounds were, I healed really fast, but I never have felt the same since and they couldn't find out what was wrong. I'm hungry all the time. Don't sleep well. I have horrible dreams. And—other symptoms."

"Is that what the bandage is from?" he asked.

"Oh, that," she said, shrugging it off.

Maybe, he thought. The sight of that bandage aroused him even more than he was already. He knew he was on the right track here, in spite of the couple of little surprises he'd had from her. She would have been with other guys like him. This kind of woman always drew his own kind. "I thought maybe that was one of the wounds he gave you, during the attack," he said, leading her a little.

She shook her head impatiently. Her hair was very thick and dark. The little blonde streaks didn't show much now. The backs of her arms and what he could see of her calves had little dark hairs on them. No wonder she needed the razors and the Nair. The bones of her face were really prominent—high cheekbones. Like Cher's. "I bumped into something in the dark and got cut," she said. "The attack was three months ago. All the wounds were healed inside a week. Good thing, too. The hospital bills make what I owe Countrybank look like peanuts, and I haven't got insurance." She gave a nervous little giggle. "Guess I should have taken out your policy. I told the doctor I thought I'd gotten an infection from the attack, but he didn't even treat me for that." Her voice rose into whininess again. "Just sent me home. I couldn't pay, but I can't work either. Can't concentrate. Can't do anything much but eat and have bad dreams and—"

"What kind of infection?" he asked, more sharply than he intended. "You get tested for HIV?" He wanted no part of that.

"You don't have to edge away," she said, a little snappish. "They do that test automatically now when you go in. No, nothing like that. But something."

"Sorry," he said. "I thought if you were raped . . ."

"Raped?" she laughed. "Oh, I see, you thought because I said attacked, that's what I meant."

"Yeah," he said, and let his fingers run along her shoulder, up her neck. "I sure did. Pretty little thing like you says she's been attacked, it's what naturally came to mind."

"Maybe some minds," she said. She was watching his face now, and he realized she could see he was close to drooling. She looked sad again, and as if he had slapped her. "I think you'd better take that stuff and get out," she told him.

His hand tightened on her shoulder just at the base of her neck. Her skin was tight, hot, and throbbed under his hand. He squeezed a little tighter and she yelped. "Nah, I don't think so, Sharon. I think you want me to stay. You didn't invite me up here to bend my ear—or to take this stuff, did you? Now, tell me about this attack."

"It was nothing like you think," she said, still as if in a daze. Behind her, in the window, the moon began to rise over the Gulf. "I was up visiting my sister in the Hill Country and while I was out for a walk on the ranch, I got attacked by a wild dog. A couple of campers heard me scream and ran it off but not before I got torn up pretty baa—'scuse me." And she bent forward, retching convulsively. He pulled his creased blue jeans legs back abruptly. She jerked away from him with more strength than he would have thought she had and ran into the bathroom, slamming the door. He could hear her puking. Or maybe not. Maybe this was a tactic to get rid of him. They told women to do this to turn men off.

He went to the bathroom door. Locked. "I'm not going anywhere, Sharon. I want a better story than that, with details. Now open the door and let me in."

"You'd betterr g–go," her voice said, very rough now with what the puking had done to her throat.

"Have it your way. I'll be waiting," he said. "Brush your damn teeth before you come out."

He walked away from it, away from the noises she was making. He couldn't help it. They had cooled him off considerably, but she wasn't getting off that easy. He walked over to the bedroom and opened the door. Maybe seeing some of the sexy underwear she'd bought, spike-heeled shoes with little straps to wrap around her ankles, maybe. That would get him going again.

The bedroom was a bit of a mess. Steak bones, well-gnawed ones, littered the floor. The bed looked as if it had been stirred instead of slept in.

He opened her dresser drawers, but there was nothing in there. The wastebasket beside the bed, however, was overflowing with ripped lace. He opened her closet door. She had been telling the literal truth. A lot of her clothes were ripped or had holes in them, and the shoes . . .

The shoes lay in a pile on the floor, shredded, chewed. Some were the high heels he imagined, but some were running shoes, moccasins, a lot of house slippers, tooth marks all over them. *Big* tooth marks.

He heard the bathroom door open through the door behind him and turned, ready to nail her if he heard the locks of the front door clicking. But they didn't click. Footsteps padded toward the bedroom door and then she was there, outlined against the door by the light of the moon that was just rising. At first he thought she'd put on a fur coat, using it for a bathrobe to keep him from looking at her. And then he realized that he didn't want to look at her, didn't want to see any more of her, ever. Wanted nothing more than to get away from her and from this room with its gnawed bones and chewed-up shoes.

She cocked her head, her hair on one side lifting like the ear on the RCA dog. "You still herre? I told you to go." Her voice was so husky he could barely make it out.

"Yeah," he said, and his excitement came back—a different kind, the kind that made all the hairs on his body stand at attention. "You're not ready for company, are you? This place is a real pigsty. You're sloppy, too, with your hair all messed up." He was feeling powerful now, okay. Putting her in her place. "You dress like a pig, too, with that shapeless sack you're wearing. Makes you look fat. You need someone to shape you up, you sloppy little sow. Well, here I am. Big, bad Joe Wolferman here to make you pay. You need guys like me and you know it. You *want* me. You *like* it rough."

She closed the door behind her and locked it, and the room was completely dark. But he could feel her smiling. "You'rre rright," she said, her voice roughening even more around the r's and he could hear her slink toward him, smell her. "I do." She was panting now.

She dug her nails into his chest, and he fell back across the bed. Her tongue, smelling like Listerine, was long and wet as it swiped his face. The light from the luminous dial of the clock radio reflected off her large, sharp white teeth.

He tried to shove her away but she was very strong, and very heavy. "Get off me, you pig!" he yelled.

She didn't budge, except to give him another playful lick, "I'm the pig, and you'rre the big bad wolf, huh, Joe?" She snapped her teeth near his nose and he let out a yelp. "But don't you rrrrememberrr, Joe? The happy ending? The wolf doesn't eat the little pigs. The pigs cooked the wolf. Only," she licked him again, "I'm not rreally a pig. I'm a werewolf in piggy clothing. And I like mine rrraw."

# THE CASTLE AND JACK
## by Tim Waggoner

Tim Waggoner wrote his first story at the age of five when he drew a version of King Kong vs. Godzilla on a stenographer's pad. Since then he's published over forty stories of fantasy and horror. His most recent work appears in the anthologies *Prom Night*, *Alien Pets*, *A Dangerous Magic*, and *The Darkness and the Fire*. He lives in Columbus, Ohio, where he teaches college writing classes.

The Castle blamed itself for its master's death. If only it wasn't so old, if only it hadn't been sleeping when the grotesquely huge beanstalk had violated the delicate cloud upon which it rested. If only it had been awake when the tiny thief who climbed up the stalk had broken in and prowled the Castle's corridors in search of booty. If only it had prevented the thief from taking the master's harp and magic goose. If only.

But it hadn't. It had been asleep, wakened only by its master's cry of rage and loss when he realized what had happened. And then it was too late; the thief had escaped and was shinnying down the stalk as fast as he could—although precisely how he could shinny at all while carrying both a harp and a goose was beyond the Castle's powers of comprehension.

The master had given pursuit, and the Castle, while ashamed at its dereliction of duty, nonetheless tried to console itself. Its master was the most powerful of giants. Hadn't he created the Castle and the cloud which bore it aloft through the heavens? Surely he would be able to catch one little thief.

This wasn't the first time the Castle had made a mistake. Just last year it had been daydreaming about a cute little villa they had recently passed over, and didn't notice when they drifted out to sea, directly into the path of a hurricane. The master had been so angry that he painted the Great Hall a hideous chartreuse—the Castle positively loathed chartreuse.

The Castle was afraid of what its giant master would do to it for this latest failure, but the Castle really didn't feel it was to blame this time. After all, what were the odds they would be burgled? They lived on a cloud!

The Castle waited for its master's return, so worried about what its eventual punishment would be that it was barely able to sleep at all. But it was old, and sleep it did. And when it awoke, it noticed that the beanstalk was gone, and that the cloud was drifting again. Assuming that its master had returned successful and was already mixing a color of paint even more hideous than chartreuse, perhaps even—shudder—*puce,* the Castle searched, its awareness moving throughout its rooms, halls, and corridors, attempting to locate its master. But the master was not inside.

The Castle then checked its outer structures. Its towers,

turrets, and spires, its parapets, walls, and courtyard. But still no master. Concerned, it searched the surrounding cloudland, but found nothing. It then stretched its senses to the limit, and probed the ground below. But it had drifted too far. It was no longer above the place where the beanstalk grew. At best, the master had been separated from the Castle by the removal of the beanstalk and the cloud's drifting. At worst . . . The Castle didn't want to think about "At worst."

Alone, truly alone, for the first time since its creation, the Castle drifted with the wind and thought about what to do next. Castles are not fast thinkers, and after several weeks it finally came to the conclusion that there wasn't anything it could do. While it did have some mystical abilities at its command, they were limited.

Without its master's assistance, it couldn't direct its course and was at the mercy of the wind. And it had no way to communicate with its master. So it had no choice but to float about and wait for its master to find some way to return. But this time the Castle would not sleep. It would remain alert and vigilant, guarding its master's possessions until the day he came home.

So the Castle drifted and drifted and drifted, and without the giant to take care of it, the Castle fell into a state of terrible disrepair. Without its master around to sop up the excess moisture—one of the hazards of living on a cloud—the Castle grew moldy. And without the master's presence to frighten them off, all manner of filthy birds took to roosting on the Castle, befouling its stone in the process.

But the Castle didn't care. It just kept drifting, and watching, and waiting.

And finally, after four years of floating about across

the face of the world—and not sleeping once in all that time—the Castle came to realize an unpleasant truth: its master was never going to return, for its master was surely dead.

How the Castle mourned! Its stone wept and cries of sorrow shook its timbers. Its master, he who had raised the Castle, made it the magnificent edifice it was today and set it soaring amongst the clouds, was no more.

And it was all the Castle's fault!

No, not the Castle's fault. The thief's. Somehow that little man had done his master harm. The Castle was sure of it, as sure as it was of its own foundation. Someday, the wind would carry it once again over the area where the beanstalk had grown. And then, somehow, the Castle would make the nasty little thief pay.

Decades passed.

Jack, old, fat, and quite content, strolled across his manor grounds, two of his many grandchildren—two of the legitimate ones, at any rate—tagging along beside him.

"Tell us about how you killed the giant again, Grandpa!" said the boy.

"Yes, please do!" echoed the girl.

Jack stopped and removed a silver snuffbox from the pocket of his gold brocade coat and took out a pinch of snuff that was so expensive it would have taken the peasant he had once been a lifetime of work just to afford to smell it. He inhaled, and waited for the sneeze, embroidered silk handkerchief in hand.

"ACHOO!" The sneeze was a loud, healthy one that echoed through the hills. Jack blew his nose, folded his handkerchief like a proper gentleman, and replaced it within his sleeve.

"Did you really find a goose that lays golden eggs, Grandpa?" asked the girl.

"I did." Although the goose had long since passed on. Jack had the bird stuffed and mounted, and he kept the last golden egg in a glass display case next to his bed.

"And was there really a magic harp?" asked the boy.

"There was." Jack had never been able to get the damn thing to play for him, though, so he'd melted the stubborn instrument down and sold it for scrap.

They headed back in the direction of the sprawling mansion where Jack and his family—and the chambermaids who served as his mistresses—had lived for so many years.

"Grandpa?" the girl asked after a bit.

"Hmmmm?"

"What happened to the beanstalk? After you cut it down, I mean."

"Oh, well, back in those days, this was an extremely poor region, and the folk who lived here were very hungry. The beanstalk fed them for quite some time. I was glad to have the opportunity to help them." *For a nominal charge, of course,* he added mentally.

"And the giant," the boy said, "what happened to the giant after you killed him?"

"Ah, well, he was, er, removed." As Jack had said, this had been a poor region, and the people were hungry. And as hard as vegetables had been to come by, table meat had been even harder.

"Come now, children. You should go inside. It's getting dark."

"But, Grandpa, it's still afternoon!" the girl protested.

"It is?" Jack frowned and checked his diamond-encrusted pocket watch. By George, the girl was right! He looked up into the sky and saw the cause of the darkness. A cloud, a particularly black and angry one, was drifting overhead.

Jack got the children inside before it began to storm, but he couldn't escape the feeling that there was something strangely familiar about that cloud. So after he had the younglings settled, he came outside for another look. He walked far out into the garden where he had a clear view of the cloud and stared into the sky.

The Castle almost didn't believe it at first when its senses revealed that the thief—far older and rounder but unmistakably him—stood directly beneath its cloud.

Finally, after all this time . . . The Castle concentrated and the cloud upon which it sat began to grow thin, changing from dark cotton to wispy fog before finally dissipating altogether.

And as the Castle began to plummet toward the ground, it had a last, satisfying thought.

What goes up . . .

# BARON BOSCOV'S BASTARD
## by Jacey Bedford

Jacey Bedford is a new writer who lives in England. Other fiction by her appears in *Warrior Princesses*.

Ella felt the early morning cold strike up from the stone floor through the thin soles of her shoes into the bones of her feet. It was still dark outside, and she negotiated her way around the cavernous kitchen by the light of one stubby candle, stuck by its own melted wax to a cracked china saucer.

It was her job to get up first and light the fires, so they'd be ready when the household began to stir. She always started with the bedroom ones because Miss Celine hated getting up in the cold.

The bedroom ones were easy, but the enormous black-lead kitchen fireplace was a monster to clean out. The fire, the heartbeat of below stairs, slumbered at night, damped down and dull. Coaxing it into flame was almost an art form. In the early morning the ironwork grills were still hot. Every curlicue of metal held a blistering trap for tired and shaking fingers.

Ella knelt in front of the fireplace, reaching below the firebox to scoop up yesterday's ashes into a bucket. The handle of her shovel was too short, and she flinched as the heat gnawed into her workworn knuckles. She opened the damper a little to let air blow through the gray-black cinders. They began to glow red at the edges.

The coal scuttle was empty. Wearily she got to her feet and picked it up. The coal cellar was next to the kitchen, but it was dirty and cold and full of frightening shadows. She took her stubby candle, wishing she had a safe light that could be taken into a cellar full of coal dust, and put the cracked china saucer down on the floor in the corridor. She propped open the rough oak door with a large wooden wedge. Then one, two, three, four, down the steps into the dark she went.

Something scurried away from her feet into the shadows. She hoped it was only a mouse.

"Away with you," she said, and her voice sounded loud in the echoing stone vault.

"Away way way," the gloom replied.

There was a faint otherworldly sound. The cellar was haunted; she knew it even though the Baron wouldn't tolerate such talk. He was a modern man and cared little for the old magic of the common folk. But she *knew,* as did all the servants.

"Sun and cheer, my way be clear," she chanted, thinking happy thoughts to ward off the lingering wraith.

Despite her best efforts, she shivered. Sometimes she pretended she was living in a fairy tale. But if this was one, fairy tales weren't all they were reputed to be. She'd like something nice to happen now, please, like her mom had promised. A genie with a lamp or a fairy with three wishes or something.

"Hello." A disembodied voice came from the kitchen. She jumped so hard she nearly dropped her shovel.

"Hello, Ella."

She breathed out steadily. It was all right. It was just Jimmy Buttons, the stable lad.

"Jimmy! In here, fetching the coal."

Jimmy picked up the saucer to shine the candlelight into the far reaches of the cellar. There was a flicker of the candle-powered shadows as he came up behind her. "Here, you know I said I'd carry that for you."

Gratefully, Ella let him heft the weight of the coal scuttle and took the candle stub from him.

When she held the candle low, Jimmy's shadow was seven feet tall, but in reality he was little more than her own height. He was strong, though. He carried the scuttle through and put it next to the fireplace.

"I'll do this. You go wash your face," he said.

"It doesn't need washing."

"It does now." Jimmy reached out and smudged coal dust on her nose.

"Oh, Jimmy you . . . you . . ."

She pretended to get angry, and he dropped to his knees.

"Don't beat me, Miss. I promise to be a good boy from now on. I'll lick the floors clean and polish the meat pies and iron the doors. Please, Miss, don't beat me."

Ella relented and laughed. He could always make her laugh. She dropped a kiss on top of his fair hair.

"Arise, Sir Buttons," she said, "and become Lord of all you survey."

"Aww, Ella, that's mean," he said, getting to his feet, "when all I survey is this damned kitchen and you."

"The kitchen's all yours," she said and smiled.

He made a kind of disappointed sound. "I thought that was what you probably meant."

His face was close to hers, and she got the strangest feeling that he was about to get closer still. He made her feel warm and wanted, but . . .

"Ella! Ella! Where are you, girl?"

Ella and Jimmy jumped away from each other guiltily.

"Oh, Lord, it's your ugly sister Celine."

"Shh, don't say that. It's not funny. She's gorgeous."

"Maybe on the outside. It's the inside that counts."

"Ella!"

"In the kitchen, Miss Celine," Ella replied.

"Why isn't my bathwater hot?" They could hear her shrill voice getting closer. Celine was deigning to descend below stairs. She only did that when she was in a foul temper and wanted to vent it on someone. Ella was usually that someone. "And there's no orange juice by my bedside, and the towels are not aired and . . . Buttons." The tone of her voice changed from indignant to frosty as Celine reached the door and realized that Buttons was in the kitchen.

"Good morning, Miss Celine, you're up early."

She ignored him completely, but her anger was concealed now. She never let anyone see her shrewishness, even the other servants. Celine, the kind and beautiful, was worshiped by all. Her voice dropped almost an octave and became velvet soft.

"Ella, this is too bad. I've got such a busy day ahead. This morning I ride with Miss Foxworth, then lunch with

Doctor Porter and his dear wife Amelia-Anne. This afternoon I take tea with Miss Jones and her mother, and this evening Daddy and I go to the Major's for cards, and if I don't have my bath now, this instant, I shall be jolly late for all my appointments, and Daddy will be frightfully cross with you."

She wiped across the mantle shelf with a finger and checked it for dust. There was none. "Daddy's been so kind to you, as he was to your poor dead mother. He keeps you here out of a sense of obligation to her, so come on now, hurry up, don't disappoint him."

She swept out, leaving a lingering scent of lily of the valley. It reminded Ella of funerals.

Jimmy waited until Celine was out of earshot, stuck his nose in the air, and mimicked her cruelly: "You know he only keeps you here out of a sense of obligation to your poor dead mother."

"Hmph! So she keeps telling me. He didn't have any sense of obligation to my mother when he got her pregnant, did he?"

"He doesn't need one, he's a baron. He's *somebody,* and you're . . ." Jimmy's voice trailed off.

"A bastard, Jimmy. You can say it. I don't even think it hurts anymore. It's what all the servants used to call me."

She could never bring herself to refer to the Baron as "my father." It was dangerous to rely on anything like a blood tie between them. It took more than begetting to make a father.

"Now I hear the townsfolk whisper it when they think I can't hear. Baron Boscov's bastard they call me. My mom used to say I was as pretty as a fairy tale. She said if I waited long enough, I'd get my happy ending. But I've waited and waited. When do I get the big break? When do I get my Prince Charming? It's not fair."

Tears began to trickle down her cheeks. She wiped them away quickly, ashamed that they'd caught her out.

"You know, Ella, life's not like that. Your mom, she . . . well she *romanced* a bit. Instead of waiting for your Prince Charming, you should do something positive to get yourself out of here."

"But everything I've ever known is here. I couldn't go. I couldn't leave y—" She stopped with the word unsaid.

"Me? You couldn't leave me? Why, if I thought I meant anything to you, I'd leave with you tomorrow."

"I didn't mean it that way. It's just that we've been friends all our lives."

"Friends. Yes." Buttons turned away. "Remember what I said. Don't wait for someone else to make your fairy tale come true."

Cook arrived as Jimmy went back to the stables to begin the morning round of mucking out and grooming. Ella was pleased to see her. She ruled the kitchen like a tyrant, but she was fair, and she was the only one who ever gave Ella the kind of mumsy advice that all growing girls need.

Cook banged the breakfast pots on to the stove top mercilessly and gave Ella the awful job of scouring out the porridge pans, but while they worked, she chatted.

"Lord, what a scandal, young Ella," she said as they worked. "The whole town's abuzz with it."

"Abuzz with what?" Ella asked.

"Why the Prince. Haven't you heard?"

"Heard what?"

"The King has changed the rule of suc . . . of suc . . . of

suc-something. You know, to do with who's the king after him."

"Succession."

"Yes, that's it. Suction. He says if the Prince doesn't
stop all this wild partying with his drinking friends and
settle down and produce heirs, he's going to name his
cousin, John, as the next king."

"Settle down. That'll be a sad day for trade. It's Charming's drinking habits that prevent half the wineries in this
province going bankrupt."

"Yes, well, the King says it's got to stop. He's giving a
big party, a masked ball, and inviting all the nobles' un-
wed daughters. Miss Celine will be going, I'm sure."

Ella felt her eyes hot with tears. Celine would be going, but what about Baron Boscov's bastard? Jimmy was
right. Fairy tales were for kids and there was no such
thing as magic. What was the point of being as pretty as a
fairy tale if no one ever saw you except the cook and the
stable boy? She bit her tongue. It hurt enough to take her
mind off the tears and they stayed behind her eyelids
without betraying her emotions.

The masked ball was the whole topic of conversation
both above and below stairs for the next two weeks.
Dressmakers came and went, jewelry was delivered on
approval, rejected, and taken back again. Celine's personal maid, Rosie, was worn to a frazzle by her mistress'
high excitement and nervous anticipation. She often visited the kitchen when Celine took her little beauty sleep
at five, and now Ella had to listen to all the details of the
arrangements for the party, how much Celine's gorgeous
silk taffeta gown had cost, and what piece of jewelry she
had finally chosen to enhance it.

"She's got a plan," Rosie confided. "If she gets the Prince's attention and looks as though she's in with a chance, she's going to play hard to get. Everyone will be falling over themselves, but she's going to make him come after her. He's rumored to like the thrill of the chase."

At last it was party night. Jimmy Buttons spent all day polishing the trim on the Baron's best coach and making sure the matched bay horses shone like mahogany.

Rosie was in a flap. When she finally came down to the kitchen at five, her normally neat hair was flying out of its pins in long strands and she had her cap on skew-whiff.

"Oh, my. I bet I look a sight." She borrowed Ella's cracked mirror. "Oh, my goodness. I'll have to fix that before her ladyship wakes." She pulled off the crooked lace cap and brushed her long straight hair until it crackled.

"You've got beautiful hair," Ella said, "What a pity you have to keep it tucked away all day under that cap. You spend all day making Celine look lovely, and then you have to hide your own looks away."

"Oh, I never think about the way I look, as long as I'm clean and tidy. A pretty face is a disadvantage in my line of work. You mustn't compete, you see. Your lady is all you have to think about. Will she be the most beautiful, the best turned out, the most desirable? And tonight it's especially important. There's a crown at stake. A crown. And I want *my* lady to win it."

"A crown." Ella repeated the words out loud when the front door slammed somewhere up above and sixteen hooves and four carriage wheels scrunched over the pebbles of the driveway. Celine was going to the ball to win the Prince.

"Oh, Momma, where are you? It's time for my fairy-tale ending. I'm the Baron's daughter. I should be going to the ball tonight." She began to cry, huge convulsive sobs.

"Ella. Ella." A voice broke through her misery. Jimmy was behind her. He tapped her on the shoulder and she turned into his arms. They were strong and comforting. "Come on, gal," he said. "Quit that. You'll make my shirt shrink."

She sniffed. "It needs a wash," she said at length. "It smells of horses and old leather."

"Good honest perfume," he laughed. "Better than lily of the valley."

She smiled.

"Good girl. Remember what I said about taking charge of your own future. Well, this is where it starts. Make up your own mind about what you want to do. There's no use waiting for a Good Fairy to come along."

"I suppose you're right, but Mom was so convinced."

"Well, try it if you don't believe me. Shout for one now."

"What?"

"Shout now. Shout Good Fairy. As loud as you can."

"But . . ."

"But nothing. Have you waited all these years for your Good Fairy to come along and rescue you, without even trying to contact her?"

Ella felt stupid. Buttons had her backed into a metaphorical corner. He was right, she'd never called for a Good Fairy, even though her mom had told her one would come.

"Good Fairy," she called.

"Pathetic," Jimmy said.

"Good Fairy," she yelled louder.

He shook his head. She tried again at the top of her lungs.

"Good Faiiireeee!"

"All right, all right. No need to shout. I'm not deaf!"

Ella's eyes opened wide, and all the color drained out of her face. Jimmy Buttons whipped his head around. There, in the warm corner of the kitchen, near the fireplace, stood the oddest human being either of them had ever seen. Ella looked again. Maybe human being was debatable terminology.

She looked something like a cross between a market researcher and a washer woman, but she had an eerie incandescent sort of glow to her. She wore an old felt hat jammed down tight over coarse gray curls. Her spectacles, taped together clumsily at the bridge, had dropped halfway down her beaky nose. She wore a bag lady raincoat and carried a document case and a clipboard with a messy, almost organic, sheaf of papers sprouting from it.

"Who are you?" Ella asked.

Jimmy doubled up. At first Ella thought he was in pain or having some kind of attack but then she heard his stifled laughter.

"She's your Good Fairy," he finally managed.

"There's no need to be like that, young man," The Good Fairy said. "I may not be one of the flashy, spangles and magic dust kind, but I am qualified. The department's a bit short-staffed at the moment and I'm filling in for Esmerelda. We can't afford a regular substitute. Downsizing you know. There's just not enough in the annual budget to keep a department like ours running smoothly."

"What do you mean?"

"Look, it says here. Ella has to have a magic spell to send her to the ball when left behind by her ugly sister."

"It says what . . . ? Here let me look." Jimmy went and peered over the Fairy's shoulder at the clipboard.

"Ella, she's right, it does say so." He read, "Ella goes to the ball, and the Prince, stunned by her beauty, dances with her all night. On the stroke of midnight, knowing the magic spell must end, Ella runs from the palace, leaving behind only a shoe. The Prince searches for Ella in vain and eventually decrees that whoever the shoe fits will be his bride. Ella's ugly sister keeps her below stairs when the Prince comes to call, but the Prince's faithful manservant finds her and takes her to the Prince. The shoe fits, and Ella becomes the Prince's new bride."

"Given the game away, now, young man." The Good Fairy snatched the clipboard back from him, only half angry.

"But my sister's not ugly," Ella said.

"That's just her outside," the Fairy replied. "It's what's inside that counts."

"That's what Jimmy said."

"Did he, indeed? Then this young man has a sensible head on his shoulders." She raised her spectacles and looked under them at Jimmy Buttons, staring down into the depths of his eyes until Jimmy blinked and turned away.

"Hrrmph," she said, sounding like one of Jimmy's horses. "You'll do." The last bit was muttered under her breath, but Ella caught it and wondered what she meant. This was all so confusing.

"So am I going to the ball?" she asked.

"Well, now. That's not really my shot to call," the Good Fairy replied. "I don't even *know* the pumpkins-to-coaches spell, let alone the mice-into-footmen one, so there's not much I can do about that. I told you, I only answered because Esmerelda was away. You're not one of my regular clients.

"I've got so much of my own work to do today, you wouldn't believe it. My caseload is shocking. I've been up since before cockcrow. I was four hours sorting out that mess down at Beauty's castle. It took two goes of the spell and a lullaby to finally get her off to sleep even after she pricked her finger on the spindle. And I'm not sure, now, that the spell will last for a hundred years. All I can say is that her prince had better not be late.

"Look at this work sheet." She rattled the papers in her clipboard. "I've still got to go and order breakfast for three bears, clean out the Billy Goats Gruff, collect eggs for Mother Goose, and then take the night shift on the Hansel and Gretel stakeout. It's too much to ask of anyone, you know, but they keep loading more and more on to us."

She looked at Ella's face. "Awww, I'll see what I can do, dear. It's not your fault we're short-staffed." The Good Fairy pushed her broken glasses back up her nose with one jab of her bony finger. She opened her document case and rifled through it.

"Ah, there it is." She took out a long slender stick that looked remarkably like an orchestral baton. She unscrewed the bulb-shaped grip and peered inside it. "I haven't even got a full magazine of spells in my wand. It should take eight, rapid fire, but—well, I'm giving no secrets away if I say they only give us one day's supply of spells at a time. If I haven't got a suitable one, there's not much I can do."

Ella's eyes began to well up with tears. What was wrong with her? She didn't usually cry, and here she was again. Eyes like fountains.

"It'll be all right, Ella." Buttons put his arm round her shoulder to comfort her. "Don't get all upset again."

The Good Fairy stared at both of them with her head on one side. She had a funny kind of look on her face.

Jimmy Buttons might not have believed in fairies, but now that one was under his nose he wasn't going to let her get away so easily. It might be Ella's only chance to make good.

"Please," Buttons said, "haven't you got some kind of spell that will help?"

The Good Fairy's expression softened. "Maybe, though it might have lost some of its vigor. I've used it once today already on Beauty."

She waved her wand three times round and muttered under her breath:

> *"By Candle dim and flickering fire,*
> *This spell shall get your heart's desire.*
> *The Prince must to this Castle keep*
> *To end the spell of lingering sleep."*

On the word "sleep" she made a sign in the air which sparkled like a firework and then vanished. Ella's eyes glazed over and rolled back in her head as her eyelids came down like drawbridges. Jimmy caught her as her knees buckled. He scooped her up into his arms.

"What have you done?"

"I told you it wasn't her spell. It was the one I used for

Beauty this morning. It's a heart's desire spell, she'll sleep for a hundred years or until her Prince comes calling."

"Sleep? Wait a minute. No! Come back. Where are you?"

But the Good Fairy had gone and Jimmy Buttons was left standing in the middle of the gloomy kitchen with Ella, the only person he cared about in the whole wide world, unconscious in his arms. Now what?

"So that's what happened, only I can't really tell anyone, can I? The Baron doesn't believe in ghosts or magic. What can we say? She's asleep and won't or can't wake up. He'll want to dismiss her, but how can you fire someone who's too far gone to hear you?" Jimmy Buttons sat by Ella's little box bed in the back room off the kitchen and looked up at Rosie and Cook. All the time he was talking he was holding Ella's hand, rubbing it gently as though he might coax her back into her own body by contact and willpower alone.

"We can hide her for a day or two," Rosie said. "I'll do her bedroom fires. Miss Celine will never notice, she's in such raptures since the night of the ball. She says she's got the Prince dangling on a thread, and she's expecting him to send for her any time now."

"Dozy woman," Cook said "Doesn't she know the Prince's reputation better than that? Well, if it keeps her above stairs it's all right by me. You're right, Rosie, we can keep this to ourselves for a bit longer till we understand it better. Aye. And I'll come in early to light the kitchen range. And if anyone asks, we'll tell them Ella's got the flu."

"What then? What happens after a few days if the spell doesn't wear off?" Jimmy asked.

"I don't know, lad. Perhaps a doctor could help if we could afford one."

"What about the Baron?" Rosie said, "She is his daughter, after all."

"He'll not want reminding of that, especially by us," Cook said. "Ella's always been an embarrassment to him, only . . ." She wiped a tear from the corner of her eye with her grease-stained apron. "I reckon he really did have a soft spot for her mother. Maria was her name. She came here about six months after the Baroness, Celine's mother, died and . . . well . . . the Baron took a fancy to her, and I think she took a fancy to him. It wasn't just that she wanted to keep her job. It was one of those things that happens a lot and never gets spoken about, 'cept below stairs and behind closed doors.

When little Ella was born, the Baron never wanted to set eyes on her, but after Maria died, when Ella was about eight, he gave orders that she was to be taken into service and paid an annual wage, just like any other servant. I reckon it was as close as he wanted to get to doing right by the child. Poor little mite. Since then she's been treated no better than any other scullery maid, worse, in fact, because she's got enough brains to be more than she is, but she'll never get promoted to Upstairs."

"So do we just keep quiet?" Jimmy asked. "I was hoping you could do something to help."

"We could send for Old Mother Anya. She might know what to do."


"This is Maria's girl?" The old woman bent over Ella. "The Baron's bastard?"

"Aye," Cook said.

"Pretty little thing, isn't she? I brought her into this world, you know." She put her fingers under Ella's chin to feel for a pulse, then put her ear down to her face to hear her breathe. "And I laid out her mother. How long ago? It must be ten years or more."

"All of that."

Jimmy stood in a corner listening to them, his eyes on Ella. Old Mother Anya was thorough. She lifted the girl's eyelids and stared into her pupils, then let them close again.

"Witchwove," she said. "Spellbound."

"Does that mean you can't do anything?" Jimmy came forward into the candlelight.

"Nothing at all, Jimmy Buttons. Nothing at all. And neither can you. It's like she's frozen in time, she'll need neither feeding nor washing, nor anything else. She's asleep, locked at one point in a dream. Now think very carefully. What did this Fairy say?"

"She said it was a spell that would bring her heart's desire, and that she'd sleep for a hundred years or until her Prince came to call."

"Then you must hope that Miss Celine's plan works and the Prince does come calling, or you'll have to find some other way to bring him here."

"She's to marry the Prince. That's what the Fairy said. It's her destiny. But how that's going to come about when she didn't even get to go to the bride-ball, I just don't know."

"That's a problem that's in the future. Just look after her well for now. Dust her off if the cobwebs settle, and see she's not disturbed."

\* \* \*

For two weeks Jimmy, Rosie, and Cook took it in turns to cover for Ella. By now the whole of the downstairs staff knew what had happened, and they all helped where they could. Ella was well liked for her sweet nature.

"Have you heard?" Cook bustled in one morning as Jimmy, bleary-eyed, came out of Ella's little room. He was beginning to think of it as her mausoleum, but he insisted on staying with her each night in case something happened and she needed him. Cook said it wasn't proper, but since the circumstances weren't exactly normal, she ignored the improprieties.

"Have I heard what?" Jimmy staggered over to the fire and began to coax some warmth out of it.

"The King has decreed that the Prince has to be wed before the month is out, so the waster is out of the alehouses and on the hunt for a bride. They do say he's looking for the girl from the ball now."

"That's Miss Celine." Jimmy woke up fast. "All she has to do is send a note to the Palace, and he'll come here and then . . ." His face split into a big grin. "The spell will be broken. A Prince will have come. Where's Rosie? Let's find out what's happening."

"Whoa." Cook only just stopped him in time from dashing up the steps to the main body of the hall. "You can't go up there, above stairs. Rosie will be down here presently."

It seemed like forever before Rosie managed to get away from Celine, who was being more demanding than ever today.

"Oh, my aching back. You don't know what she's been like since the ball. She came back so full of herself. Then when the Prince didn't follow the clue she left, she sank into a real black temper."

"She should be happy again after today's announcement. She just needs to send a note to the palace."

"Ha! She's tried that. Her note arrived with forty-six others. Each one claimed to be the masked beauty."

"But she left something behind to lead the Prince here, didn't she?"

"Her shoe. She's got such dainty feet, no one else could fit into it. It was handmade for her by Leonardo Alvolio, right here in the city. He's the most famous shoemaker in the country. All the Prince has to do is call and ask. Alvolio will recognize it as Celine's immediately." She sighed. "But it seems as though the Prince is not such a good detective."

"Either that or he doesn't want to be such a good detective," Cook said. "I hear he'd rather carouse with his men friends and wants to put off the day of his wedding just as long as he can."

"He's announced that he plans to visit each of the forty-seven claimants and see who the shoe fits. He's declared he'll marry the first one who can get her foot into it."

"There's nothing like doing it the hard way," Cook said.

Buttons slammed his fist into the wall. Damn. If he found someone with a small foot, the Prince might never come here at all.

It took three more days and thirty-two ladies well-endowed in the foot department before the Prince finally came to the open gates of the Castle Boscov.

From the gatehouse Jimmy Buttons watched the royal cortege riding up the hill. Besides the Prince, decked out in the finest royal purple, there were footmen, menservants, and some of his drinking companions, not terribly sober by their manner. In front of them all marched a young page with the shoe on a white velvet cushion.

Jimmy rushed back to the kitchen. "They're nearly here," he yelled at Cook as he ran into Ella's room. "Where's Rosie?"

"Up with Miss Celine, of course. Where else would she be? That little madam has changed her gown eighteen times today."

Jimmy knelt by Ella's bed.

"Come on, Ella, wake up, love. Wake up. The Prince is here. The Prince has come to the castle. Wake up!"

He took her hand and chafed it. "Oh, please."

There was a disturbance in the air and the Good Fairy was standing at the head of the bed.

"You." Jimmy stared at her belligerently. "What do you want? Haven't you done enough damage?"

"Tut tut. Jimmy Buttons. You can speak ill of me when you know more. Do you want to break this spell or not?"

"Of course I do."

"Then it's simple. Just kiss her."

"What?"

"Kiss her. On the lips."

"But . . ."

"You mean you never wanted to kiss her?"

"Of course I did, but . . ."

"You were always too shy."

"I always thought she'd want someone better, being a Baron's daughter."

"Well, now's your chance to kiss her without fear of rejection."

Jimmy gave the strange old bag lady a funny look. He bent down low over Ella and kissed her full on the mouth.

He was quite surprised to find that suddenly she was kissing him back, hard.

"Ooh, Jimmy Buttons, why didn't you ever do that before?" Ella said.

Jimmy rocked back on his heels. His heart was pounding.

"You're awake!"

"I hope so. It would be a shame to have dreamed that."

"No, I mean, the spell's broken."

"What spell?"

"The spe— Oh, never mind, I'll tell you later. Come on. We've got to be quick, otherwise it will be too late." He grabbed Ella's hand and pulled her upright. "We've got to get upstairs before the Prince gives the shoe to Celine. There's still a chance."

"A chance to do what?"

"To marry the Prince like the Good Fairy's instructions said. Your mum was right about fairy tales. Hurry!"

Jimmy took the stairs two at a time and nearly tripped over the staid old butler as he burst out of the door into the main hallway, dragging Ella with him. All the servants were gathered to get a glimpse of the Prince. Celine was descending the staircase on her father's arm. The page, with the shoe on the cushion, knelt between the Prince and Celine. There was a hushed expectation in the room. They all knew the shoe would fit. Celine had the daintiest feet in the land, smaller than anyone's—except perhaps her half sister, Ella.

"Stop." Buttons' voice cut through the low murmurs. "Let Ella try the shoe. She's the Baron's daughter, too, even though he's tried to forget it." He came to a sliding stop in front of the Prince.

Ella looked up, and there was Charming, the heir to the throne, possessor of a large personal fortune, and the most eligible bachelor in Christendom. She looked at his long, pale face, his narrow, haughty nose, and his sticky-out ears, barely masked by wispy, fair hair that was already beginning to thin. She shuddered. If this was a Prince, she wanted none of him.

The Prince looked at the ragged servant girl and his nose began, if a nose can, to curl. He looked at the fair-haired, fresh-faced, healthy stable lad and his pupils widened slightly and his pulse began to race.

"That's enough!" The scene froze. Even the breeze from the open door was stilled in its steady roll around the high-ceilinged hallway. The Good Fairy stalked through the human statues, her coat flapping around her ankles. Celine defied gravity, poised halfway between the bottom step and the floor. The Baron was three quarters of the way toward summoning his men, who had anticipated him and already had their hands on the hilts of their ceremonial swords. Rosie's hands were up to her face, and her mouth was frozen in the word, "No."

"Jimmy Buttons, you don't know when you're well off." The Good Fairy scolded him. He could hear her, but he couldn't move or speak. "No one can hear this except you. I told you that the spell I cast on Ella was a heart's desire spell. Let her make her own mind up about what she really wants. You keep telling her she ought to do that anyway. Don't get trapped into this happy-ever-after lark.

"Take a good look at Charming, there, and at Celine. Now there's a marriage made in hell if ever I've seen one. Is that what you want for Ella? Of course it's not." She answered her own question. "Now I'm going to do you a big favor, and it's more than you deserve. I'm going to keep this lot frozen for one full hour, while you and Ella get a head start. With any luck they won't remember your intrusion, since you'll be nowhere to be found. There's a horse out in the yard that you won't recognize. He was mine, now he's yours. Call him a wedding present. Now, I can't rewind time for them," she nodded at the Prince, the Baron, Celine, and their respective retinues, "but I can for Ella. You can explain everything to her later. I just hope she believes you."

There was a sort of swoosh that felt like falling down a hole without quite landing at the bottom, and Jimmy found himself in Ella's arms back in her little room. She was kissing him hard. The Good Fairy was gone.

Ella remembered the Good Fairy, what a funny old bird she'd been. Then she remembered that time seemed a bit out of phase. The next thing she knew, she was being soundly kissed by Jimmy Buttons, who was kneeling by the side of her bed. She realized that it wasn't just a one-way kiss, put her arms round his neck, and settled back to enjoy it.

"Ooh, Jimmy Buttons, why didn't you ever do that before?"

"I always wanted to, but I thought you might not like it."

"Hmmm. Playing hard to get is obviously a tactic I shouldn't use with you."

"Listen, Ella," Jimmy dragged her to her feet. "I think your dad might not be best pleased with me. I'm going to have to go away."

"Away?"

"It's a long story, but will you come with me? I promise I'll tell you everything."

Ella was beginning to suspect that there was quite a lot she might need to hear.

She looked around the kitchen. It had been her home for nineteen years. She'd seen nothing of the world, but now that big scary place, Outside, didn't seem quite so scary if she could explore it with Jimmy.

"Here, you two." Cook came in from the yard. "There's a going-away present in your saddlebag. Some food. It should last you until you reach the border. That Good Fairy of yours said you can keep whatever you find in the saddlebag with her blessing. I don't know what's in there. It seems pretty small on the outside but much bigger on the inside. It wouldn't surprise me if there wasn't something a bit fey about it. And that horse seems to know more than he's telling."

"Thanks." Jimmy gave her a peck on the cheek and Cook blushed. Ella threw herself into her arms, feeling hot and snivelly in the back of her nose. "I'll miss you."

"Me, too." Cook wiped her eyes with her apron.

"Tell Rosie good-bye."

"I will."

"And if the Good Fairy ever comes back, tell her I still believe what my mom said."

"Then you two had better live happily ever after."

"If we don't, it won't be for lack of effort."

Ella heard hooves clatter in the yard. Outside the kitchen door Jimmy was already mounted on a big, bold gray horse with intelligent eyes. With the sunlight glinting gold off his fair hair, Jimmy looked like a Prince.

She ran out, gave him her hand, put her tiny foot into the stirrup he'd vacated for her and swung up behind him. She'd never learned to ride, but Jimmy was an expert, and she trusted him. She trusted him in all things. But this Fairy story of his—it had better be a damned good one!

# THE EMPEROR'S NEW (AND IMPROVED) CLOTHES
## by Leslie What

Leslie What is the mother of two high school students. She is a writer whose poetry, prose, and essays have appeared in several publications, including the anthologies *Prom Night* and *The Fortune Teller*. See *http://www.sff.net/people/leslie.what* for more details.

Stop me if you've heard this.

Once upon a time—in a central European palace as crumbly as blue cheese—there lived a rich and greedy Emperor.

Meanwhile, across pine-covered hills and turnip-infested dales, there lived two hooligan brothers (or *schmaltzovniks,* as they were called in their native land), current owners of the proverbial magical cloak. Times were hard, and these two schmaltzovniks were in a deep funk. Their country had suffered greatly during the postwar years; realism had replaced fantasy as the dominant literary form. To top things off, the Commies had seized power.

Jusef, the bully, practically *screamed* fashion statement, dressed, as always in the primary colors red and blue that subtly complemented his fair skin and Stalin-black hair. He was the Leonardo di Caprio of fairy-tale bullies. A) Children cheered him. B) Women loved him. C) Men feared him. D) All the above. He had it all, and don't think his slight but very shrewd younger brother, Shecky, didn't notice.

Shecky sat back in his rocker, cradling a home-study leather-bound legal text in his lap. Whereas Jusef had inherited the brawn, Shecky had been stuck with the brains, which had never done him much good.

Jusef stood in the center of the one-room luxury garden apartment, thinking up new ways to fleece and swindle the masses. He stomped one of his boot heels against the slate floor, then adjusted the massive filigree codpiece adorning his velvet pants.

"Brother," Jusef began in a deep baritone, "I hear of a greedy Emperor who's still got zlotys in his pants. What do you say we pay him a little call?"

Frankly, Shecky was little conflicted. He wanted to get out of the business, but his long and relatively successful career as a fairy-tale swindler had ruined him for other types of work. Funny thing—the boys came from a good family: a virtuous mother, who had died young; a kindly but impotent dad, who had wasted no time before taking up with a lovely but extremely evil wife. Shecky knew that Jusef worried about him. He had always felt uncomfortable being a thug and to this day, he struggled with his inner nice guy.

Yet it was hard to argue with destiny. Here was his brother, suggesting a way out of his funk. So Shecky put aside all misgivings over Jusef's newest devious plan.

"Never say 'no' to adventure," Shecky said.

The late afternoon sun streamed through an open window, lighting the fine hairs of Shecky's beard to a mottled brown the color of potatoes (incidentally the national crop). A niggling suspicion took hold: that his brother was about to get the better of him. He decided to turn things around to his advantage. "Say, Jusef," Shecky said. "What do you suppose ever became of our old invisible cloak?"

Being a jock, Jusef was faster on his feet. He ran for the coat rack before Shecky could react.

"Out of sight, out of mind," Jusef said. He batted his arm through the air until he felt a soft web, transient and cool as drizzle. "Got it," Jusef said, "I think." When Jusef tugged the cloak free from its hook, his hand vanished beneath invisible fabric.

It was a cool effect, but eerie.

Shecky remained nonplussed. "No way, Jose," said Shecky.

"It's my turn to be invisible, remember? You used the cloak last time, in that Grimm's fairy tale about the twelve dancing princesses."

Jusef's face warmed and he grinned broadly. "Yeah," he said, "that was one mighty fine adventure." He smacked his lips together as if still tasting the memory.

They had been away from the life far too long.

Shecky shrugged. "I want the cloak! It's my turn for a little fun. Gimme the garment!"

Jusef thought about being nice, but saw no reason to go against type. He pointed to Shecky's legal text and stuck out his tongue. "You're the one who's always saying 'possession is ninety percent of the law.' Tough luck, bro, 'cause I'm bagging the cloak. Ciao," he said, disappearing beneath the fabric.

The front door opened and Jusef's footsteps could be heard pattering across the cobblestones. He made his way through a quaint courtyard leading to stables that were converted into one-car garages back in the thirties. There was only one car in all the land, a station wagon that coincidentally belonged to the brothers.

Shecky shut his book and slid it into his valise. He closed the small-paned window and locked the front door, headed toward the station wagon, which waited ever prepacked in the event adventure called.

"Wait for me," Shecky screamed.

Jusef, who figured he could use some brains for this caper, did just that.

"You drive," Jusef said.

Shecky started up the engine. "Say, Jusef," he said. "Take a good look in the back seat and see if we still have that mysterious trunk." An experienced swindler went in prepared. One never knew just what might come in handy.


Okay, now let's talk Emperor.

This particular Emperor, Konstantin the Thirteenth, had stolen all the gold and fine jewels he could from his subjects, and now schemed to turn the scenic landscape into a coal-and-uranium-mine wasteland. He spent his waking hours kissing the Kremlin's *kanakas* to maintain his position of authority. These were the futile acts of a desperate man. Konstantin was about to be overthrown and replaced by a despot half his age, but he didn't know that.

Konstantin was richer than triple-cream Camembert, yet he remained unhappy and dissatisfied. See, he was the kind of character who always wanted more than what he had—really all it takes to be a villain, in case anyone was wondering.

Now, no villainous Emperor gets to be in a fairy tale without the requisite dead wife, bless her innocent soul, who forgot to bear him sons, and this guy, Konstantin, was no exception.

The poor dead Empress had been a beautiful though delicate woman, always in frail health. She had managed to produce the one daughter, Wilma, a few moments before the deadline (in the empress' case this was death by childbirth).

Modern readers familiar with fairy-tale literature can surmise that Wilma was a lovely and honest princess, clever as she was kind. The only flaw even worth mentioning, and I wouldn't bother mentioning this if it didn't figure prominently into the plot, was Wilma's annoying tendency to faint unexpectedly.

As the schmaltzovniks schemed about extracting riches from the Emperor, Konstantin schemed of destructive methods to extract uranium from turnips.

Wilma, who had dated a guy from the Green Party until her father got wind of it, wanted to be both a loyal daughter *and* an environmentalist—an impossible situation for anyone. Emotionally, she was a wreck.

Too bad for the schmaltzovniks, their station wagon broke down in the *burbs* near Warsaw. The engine became a worthless paperweight the moment a fan belt popped; there wasn't a spare part to be had east of the Berlin Wall. The brothers would have been stranded still if not for Shecky's bright idea to trade a pack of Camels for a mule.

Jusef, the magic cloak now snugly hidden in his magnificent codpiece, insisted he be allowed to steer the rig, which left Shecky to clean up after the mule.

Shecky was not pleased.

They drove across the land and finally arrived in the appropriately idyllic village.

Jusef pulled in the reins to park. He whipped out the magic cloak and disappeared beneath it. "Back in a flash," said he.

Shecky growled. Once again he had been left to manage the scutwork while his lazy brother gallivanted about. But being a practical man, Shecky immediately got down to business. In a matter of minutes, he talked a reticent yokel into leasing out an empty storefront apartment facing the town square.

Shecky carted in the brothers' luggage, folding chairs, mysterious trunk, sewing machines, garment racks, a small round table, and his valise. He switched on an overhead lamp and found his place in his law book, then read the entire chapter on family law before starting the one on tort reform.

The hypocrisy of the moment bore heavily upon him.

As if sensing the grunt work was finished, Jusef reappeared. He crumpled up the magic cloak to hide where Shecky would never dare look for it, beneath his codpiece, and set to work hanging a sign outside the door that said "The Schmaltz Brothers' Emporium. Purveyors of Sartorial Expertise."

When Jusef had finished, Shecky asked, "How you want to do it this time?"

"Extortion?" suggested Jusef.

Shecky scratched his head. "I was thinking more like fraud, but we're arguing nits? I assume your Emperor is a rich-and-greedy type?"

"It goes without saying," said Jusef. "What I want to know is this: does he have a beautiful daughter?" He squatted close to the floor and began practicing his isometrics.

"Now, hold on a second," Shecky said. "I agreed to let you wear the cloak, but it's my turn to get the girl."

"I suppose that's only fair," said Jusef, "but then what's in it for me?"

Shecky snapped shut his book. "Trust me," he said.

"Like I would my own stepmother."

Both brothers laughed.

"All kidding aside, what is your plan?" Jusef asked.

"Take a letter," answered Shecky, nonplussed. "Inform said Emperor that if he's truly worthy, for a limited time only, we'll custom-fit his cummerbunds for free."

The next morning, the letter had arrived at the castle.

Konstantin and his lovely, honest, clever, and kind daughter, Wilma, grew excited upon hearing that not only had new purveyors of sartorial expertise come to town, but they were discounting cummerbunds.

The two immediately rushed right down to the square to take advantage of this limited-time offer. Konstantin and Wilma waltzed into the store and found both schmaltzovniks hard at work.

Shecky peeked out from behind a sewing machine and waved them away, thereby creating dramatic tension until the final inevitable moment. "Take a number," he said. He smoothed an invisible wrinkle from the invisible fabric, and marveled at its fine texture.

"Now, brother, settle down. How may we help you?" asked Jusef, who sat at the table, squinting at something unseen. He held a needle as if threading it with air. High-lights shimmered about his fingers like the glint of fire reflected through crystal.

"Perhaps we can interest you in some garments light as cobwebs?" Jusef said.

Try as he might, Konstantin could not fathom what it was the brothers were doing. He looked to Wilma for ad-vice, but she seemed mesmerized by Jusef. Honestly, he thought, at times, bringing a princess along to shop was useless.

Jusef took advantage of Wilma's fixation. He stood and approached, reaching out to take her hand.

You should already know, from your careful reading of Andersen's seminal work, what happened next.

Just in case you missed it, here's a recap: The virginal Wilma fainted from the shock of seeing Jusef's bulging codpiece, which led Jusef to assume that, for sure, he had won the girl.

Meanwhile, the greedy Emperor was wooed and wowed by the younger brother, who easily convinced him to or-der some dry goods from the rack.

But what that other competing fairy tale never explained was the science of how their scheme worked.

See, these schmaltzovniks ran their con by making full use of their advanced knowledge of color theory. They knew which colors made one beautiful; they knew which colors went with green eyes or splotchy skin.

In olden times, Shecky had studied with enchanted cave bats who had taught him how to make magic suits from infrared thread. This thread was invisible unless viewed through a special type of goggles.

The next thing you know, the schmaltzovniks had

carted out their mysterious trunk and demanded that the Emperor and his now revived daughter each wear a set of goggles before being permitted to view the Brothers' fabulous designer line.

See, here's the gimmick: the real money wasn't in the clothes, it was in the goggles!

And Shecky and Jusef had managed to corner the goggles market worldwide. The invisible clothes were what was called, in retail, a loss leader. In fact, the suit the Emperor picked was on sale, sixty percent off!

Now we come to the parade part, always a favorite.

Picture the virginal Wilma, eyes averted so as not to see her father in the buff. At her side walked Shecky, who waved to the crowds.

Jusef trailed behind, pushing a wheelbarrow filled with infrared goggles.

Segue to that critical moment in the story when that obnoxious little boy jumped out from the bleachers to yell, "Look, Ma. The Emperor has no clothes!"

The crowds were scornful. The Emperor was humiliated.

Wilma fainted, but recovered with the help of some of Shecky's smelling salts, at which point she pleaded with her eyes.

"Help my evil father repent his ways, stop this senseless destruction of the environment, and in the process, cover up his keister, and you shall have my heart," was what Shecky took her pleading eyes to mean.

If you really must know, she was simply doing her princess best to keep from slobbering over Jusef's codpiece.

But love is blind, so Shecky believed his feelings for

Wilma were reciprocated. "Of course I'll help," Shecky said. He pulled a set of goggles from his pocket and tossed them to that obnoxious little boy, who, thank God, got eaten by a hideous troll in the fairy tail coming up next.

"Wear these goggles," Shecky shouted to the boy, "and tell us what you see."

The spoiled brat did as he was commanded. A miraculous thing occurred! He gasped to see the Emperor. "Excellent! Magnificent!" he said. "And *so* thin! All hail!" The kid fell to his knees in supplication.

You'd have thought this would be enough, but the throngs continued to scoff, unable to confirm what the child had seen. This was one tough audience.

The Emperor shouted to his guards, "Grab those goggles at once and disperse them to the throngs!"

But before the guards could obey, Jusef pulled out the magic cloak from his magnificent codpiece, covered himself and the wheelbarrow, and utterly disappeared.

Pandemonium ensued.

The Emperor had never felt so exposed.

Wilma probably fainted maybe three or four times before finally getting it out of her system.

At which point, Shecky winked at her and rubbed his hands together, anticipating the reward that would soon be his.

"I bet you'd like an estimate on outfitting the masses," Jusef said to the Emperor.

The shamed Konstantin had no choice but to negotiate on the spot.

Shecky had the contract ready. "My brother can have the money, but I, as the older brother, am thereby entitled by law to marry first. The castle, I might point out, comes with the girl," Shecky said, thankful he had taken the time to study law.

The deal was struck. The goggles were passed out and the Emperor's keister covered.

The final finagling and tallying was left to the accountants and later, a widowed wedding consultant who took the train all the way down from Minsk.

For the most part, everybody lived happily ever after, but it being a fairy tale, there were some consequences.

The land was temporarily spared from environmental destruction, but when that got old, they held a nuclear meltdown in Chernobyl.

Konstantin and the marriage consultant fled to the east to elope. Konstantin got on as a doorman at KGB headquarters and eventually worked his way up to comptroller.

Shecky and Wilma married without haste and were soon blessed with twin sons, only a couple of months premature. One of the boys bore a strong resemblance to Jusef, causing quite a stir before all the newspapers were again taken over by the state.

Sadly, both little tykes suffered from astigmatism, flat feet, and dental caries—afflictions which, while not life-threatening, were severe enough to keep them out of the literature of the fantastic. When last anyone heard, the twins had been put in charge of janitorial at EuroDisney.

With the boys finally out of the house, Wilma discovered the works of Betty Friedan. She returned to school to study biology and destiny, and was awarded the Nobel Prize for her discovery of the princess gene. By the turn of the century, fainting became a relic of the past.

Alas, poor Jusef was left angry at being stuck with

only a magic cloak, a magnificent codpiece, and an empty mysterious trunk to call his own. He now lives bitter and alone in a decrepit warehouse north of Newark, where he endlessly plots his revenge.

# ONE FAIRY TALE, HARD-BOILED
## by P. Andrew Miller

P. Andrew Miller has been publishing fiction for close to a decade now. His stories have appeared in *Dragon, Sword & Sorceress XIII*, the British magazines *Valkyrie* and *Odyssey*, and many other publications. He hopes to soon add a novel or two to that. A former library clerk, mall survey taker, and talking reindeer, he is currently a lecturer in creative writing at Northern Kentucky University. He lives in Cincinnati, Ohio with his two cats, Circe and Medea.

### Monday

I knew she was trouble as soon as I saw her. I had seen the type before. The poor-girl-made-it-good-and-married-the-king type. And they were always trouble.

You had to know what to look for. At first glance, she appeared just like she should have, gold hair done up in fancy curls, a necklace of gold and rubies. (Which meant the shadows behind her were bodyguards 'cause in this neighborhood, if she had been alone, she would never had made it in here with her head still attached.) Her dress was silk and satin.

But I could tell she was new royalty. She walked too stiff, like she was trying to imitate noble walk. She had on some classy bracelets and a wedding ring with a rock the size of my kneecap. But she hadn't managed to get rid of the calluses at the base of her fingers. This dame had done hard labor for a long time. Probably a wood-cutter's or miller's daughter. That was the usual case. Somehow or another she got lucky and married the king or prince or duke. And now she was wondering if Mr. Pointy Crown was still being faithful to her. And I hated those cases. Kings and company tended to get nasty when you peeked in on their royal "activities."

"Mister Thorn?" she asked.

A good guess, seeing as how I had scratched out my ex-partner's name from the window. Poor bastard. I told Ashe not to pursue any missing virgin cases without tak-ing the dragon gun. Anyway, I nodded at her, but I didn't get up or offer her a seat. She paused for a moment, like she was used to getting her own way. I expected her to pull a "high and mighty" on me, but she didn't. Instead, she came up to the desk and sat at the one empty chair. I took my feet off the pile of paperwork and lowered them to the floor so I could look her in the face.

She met my gaze. Behind that put-on haughtiness, I caught a glimpse of something deep in her eyes. Some-thing I knew well enough from the mirror. Fear. This dame was scared.

"Mister Thorn, I need your help," she said.

"Why else would you be here?" I said.

She ignored me. "I need you to find someone for me."

Uh-oh. A missing person case. Probably an old lover

blackmailing her about their past lives. Seen that one before as well.

I didn't let on that I knew what was coming. I am, after all, a professional.

"If you can't help me, I . . . I just don't know what I'll do. I just can't give up my baby!" she cried.

Whoa! Baby? That was a new one. She had my attention now.

"Look, lady . . ." I started, but she just blurted out, "Please, you have to help me!" and then the faucet came on. The tears just poured from those blue-painted peepers. And me, I'm just a sucker for the damsel in distress, you know what I mean? I knew it was going to get me killed some day, but it didn't stop me from trying to comfort her and promising to take the case.

As soon as I said that, the tears shut off. My instincts kicked me like a flea-bitten unicorn. I was being played like a magic harp, but there was no turning back. I had given her my word, and I never go back on my word no matter what that cheap little tramp with the red cloak says.

"So tell me the story," I said as I poured myself a drink. My memory works better with lubrication.

She launched into a sorry tale about how her father told the king a whopper about her spinning talents, and she thought she was a goner until this little guy shows up to help her. I stopped her there.

"What kind of little person?" I asked. "Elf? Leprechaun? Dwarf?"

She gave me this look like I just crawled out of her cereal. "How should I know?" she said. Then she started spouting off more details, including a description of the suspect. Definitely a dwarf. He showed up three nights in a row and on the last night, she promised him her first-born child. The next day the king married her, and she forgot all about the little guy. Figures, doesn't it? A few weeks ago, she gave birth to the little bratling. And who pops up but the little guy. But the guy must have had a heart. He made another deal with her. She only had to find his name. I had a feeling this is where I came in.

"So I want you to find out the name of this," she paused, trying to decide what to call him before she decided on "person."

Bingo.

I leaned back in the chair. "Well, that shouldn't be too hard," I said. "I can ask around, check out some of my sources in the otherworld. I should have a name in a week."

"You have three days," she said.

Damn the little folk and their obsession with numerology. I hated deadlines.

"Piece of cake," I answered, and drained the rest of the bottle.

I decided to start where I start every case: Grimms' Place. It's a seedy little dive on the edge of the Enchanted Forest, but it was run by a honey of a bartender named Rose. It was early in the day, just past noon, when I walked in the swinging saloon-style doors. I had to blink a few times to adjust to the light. Rose liked to keep the place dark.

When the lumps in the gloom finally started to look like people, I saw Rose sitting at the table in the corner playing cards with a tough looking bunch. A woodsman with a big ax and a wolfskin coat. An elf with a cigar hanging out of the corner of his mouth. And some dame with a thumb the size of a banana. I walked over so Rose could see me, but not too close. I didn't want them to think I was looking at their cards.

The elf glared at me, and his cigar bobbed up and down as he chewed on it. The woodsman and the dame ignored me.

"Your turn, Hans," Rose said.

The woodsman looked at the elf. "Got any threes?"

The elf smirked. "Go fish," he said.

The woodsman pulled a card out of the mess in the center. "Picked up a three!" he crowed. The elf bit his cigar in half.

The game lasted another fifteen minutes with Rose winning. I had yet to see her lose a game in her own joint. The woodsman and the big-thumbed dame were good-natured. The elf grumbled and glared. He turned his back on Rose and started mumbling and twisting his fingers. I walked up behind him and grabbed his shoulder. He jumped.

"Now, you wouldn't be trying to put a curse of the Little People on Rose here, would you?" I asked.

"Bite me," he answered.

I leaned close and flashed my teeth. "Don't tempt me. I could use an appetizer."

He looked startled for a minute, and then I heard Rose behind me. "Trouble, Thorn?" she asked.

"I don't think so," I replied. "Trouble?" I asked the elf. Still glaring, he shook his head.

"By the way, you don't know any dwarfs that can spin straw into gold, do you?"

He wrenched free of my grip, made a rude gesture, and vanished.

I sat down at the table, and Rose put a tall one in front of me.

"New case?" she asked.

I nodded as I took a sip. "Need to find a dwarf," I said. "Fast."

She grimaced. "You know how I feel about dwarfs. Won't let them in the place."

"Like princes?" I could have kicked myself as soon as I said it. Rose didn't like to be reminded of her ex.

"Sorry, Rose. But, please, what have you heard?" I asked.

She softened. "I've heard there're dwarfs about three miles into the forest."

I finished off the prune juice in one long swig. "Thanks, Rose. You've got the best ears a detective could ask for."

She batted her eyelashes. They were like two cater-pillars getting electroshock. "The rest of me ain't bad either."

I winked at her. "I'll check out that lead when this case is over."

It wasn't much to go on, but then I was used to not hav-ing much to go on. I circled behind Grimms' and found the footpath into the forest.

Me and Nature, we don't get along so well. I'm a town-boy. But too many cases have taken me into the woods, so I've learned to adapt. Of course, three miles was a long way to go, and though I can find my way through city al-leys on moonless nights blacker than a witch's oven, I get turned around in the woods. So I filled my pockets with pebbles before I hit the trail.

The path twisted and turned as I kept dropping the pebbles, but it seemed like it took forever before I heard something. It sounded like sobbing. I'm never one to ig-nore a possible lead, so I left the path and followed the sounds of weeping. But I sure as hell made sure I dropped some more pebbles.

After about ten minutes of getting my face slapped by tree branches, I broke into a clearing. There were dwarfs all right. Seven of the little suckers, all standing around what looked like a coffin on a pedestal. They stood, weepy-eyed and sobbing, wringing their hats and their beards. It made me uneasy. I knew I could handle one or two dwarfs in a fair fight, but seven? I decided I better try subtlety.

I sauntered up to the coffin, walking quietly with my head down, as if I were paying my last respects. I made it to within three feet of the group when they got quiet. I lifted my eyes. Seven faces glared at me.

"Um, sorry fellows. Bad time?" I said.

They didn't answer. A few looked mean. A couple looked thoughtful. I wasn't sure which was worse.

"Um, maybe I could come back later?"

Three of them circled around to block me in. Somewhere, they had gotten pick axes. I put my hand in my pocket to feel the bit of insurance I always carried while on a case. Its cold steel made me feel slightly better. Those pick axes were sharp.

"Do you think he's the one?"

"Doesn't look like a prince to me."

"And how many princes have you seen?"

"Achhoo."

"Gesundheit."

I decided I needed to play it cool and took my hand out of my pocket.

"Gentleman," I said. "I'm sorry. I was looking for a dwarf, but I think I got a bad tip. The one I'm looking for works alone. Unless one of you spins straw into gold?"

The meanest looking one spit onto the ground. "We're miners. We work for a living," he growled.

"I'm sure you do. I'll be leaving now."

The dwarfs behind me didn't move.

"Uh, guys?" I said.

A dwarf wearing glasses and a mean expression moved closer to me.

"Are you a prince?" he asked.

Now, I wasn't sure if they wanted a yes or no to that. I knew enough that princes couldn't always be trusted. Just ask Rose. It could be that a prince had done them wrong and they wanted to go prospecting for my liver. Then again, they might actually want a prince.

"Why do you ask?"

He glared some more, then pointed over his shoulder to the glass casket. I took my first good look at who was in it.

I gasped. It was some broad, but a damned good looking one. She had hair the color of obsidian, skin as white as a daisy's petals, and lips as red as, as, as something really red. Seeing her lying there almost brought a tear to my hardened eye.

The one in glasses continued. "She's our roommate. We need a prince to kiss her and wake her up."

I looked down at him. I looked at the other six. "Your . . . roommate?"

He nodded. My mind skidded into several different mental images all at once. Then I shook my head. No point going there. I looked back at the dame. And I have to admit I was tempted to give her a peck on the lips. But then my mind went off down another corridor. I saw years go by and watched her hair turn gray, her skin yellow, and that healthy figure plump out. Not to mention having seven little people sharing the house. It wasn't worth it.

"Sorry, I'm not a prince."

They didn't look happy. And they edged closer. I looked around and only saw one way out. I ran forward, put both hands on top of the coffin, and vaulted over it. When my feet hit the ground, I was running. I'm good at that, and I figured with their short legs, they wouldn't be able to catch up.

The trouble was, I ran away from the path that I had marked with the pebbles. At the time, though, I just wanted to get away from the dwarfs. But by the time I stopped running, I was really lost. And I had about as much wood smarts as a leprechaun has height.

The trees all looked the same to me, and I didn't see any path at all. I had to decide what to do. Did I wander around the woods, looking for a way out or did I wander around the woods looking for the gold-spinning dwarf and hope I found a way out as well?

I remembered my client's tearful expression and decided I could at least look for the suspect while I found my way out. I still had some pebbles left, so I wouldn't be walking around in circles.

## Tuesday

I woke that next morning stiff and still tired. I had slept with my back against a tree. I felt a little safer that way. I had a hard time standing up. My legs were cramped, my back ached, and I had tree bark in my hair. People who think spending the night sleeping under the stars or under trees is romantic should be shot, that's my opinion.

I starting walking again since there wasn't much else I could do. The sun wasn't visible, but a brighter direction on one side of the forest let me know that was East, so I had a partial guide.

Hunger pains rumbled through my stomach. I tried to ignore them but it was hard. I kept thinking of Rose and a tall, cool glass of prune juice. Forget it, I told myself.

I must have stumbled around in the trees for another hour before I saw the clearing up ahead. I knew it wasn't Rose's, but I could see some sort of house in it. I got my hopes up, and I walked faster.

I popped out of the trees and stopped. I had never seen anything like it. It looked like your average forest cottage with eaves, chimney, small front porch, even gutters. But I had never seen a cottage made out of candy before.

The roof shingles looked like marzipan. The shutters were gingerbread. The front porch consisted of candy canes. And the gutters and drain pipe were chocolate. The whole thing started my stomach rumbling.

I took a few steps closer to the house when I noticed something else. Someone or something had been chewing on the architecture. One shutter was half consumed. Part of the gutter was missing. Two rungs from the porch railing were missing. A couple of shingles had been pried loose.

So I wasn't alone. I slowed down. My brain told me "walk away," but my stomach shouted "GO FOR IT." Guess which one won?

I changed my direction so I wasn't in a direct line of sight from the cookie-dough door or the spun-sugar windows. I saddled up against the wall. The cottage had peanut brittle siding. I snapped off a small piece and put it in my mouth. It was delicious.

Creeping along the wall, I reached the window. I peeked in, but spun sugar isn't actually transparent. I ducked, though, as I crept past it. I broke off some more siding and nibbled on it. I was just reaching for a piece of the porch when I heard something.

"Who's that nibbling on our house?" a voice said.

My hand went for the gun. I knew I had been caught red-handed, but there was something about that voice that gave me the creeps. It was the type of voice that made the hairs stand up on the back of your neck and made dogs put their paws over their ears. It was the type of voice that belonged to a witch.

So imagine my surprise when two chubby kids waddled out on the porch.

"You own this house?" I asked.

"Yeah, what's it to you?" the boy said.

"You just seem a little young to be property owners," I replied.

"We sort of inherited it," the girl said. She absent-mindedly reached out, broke the knob off a porch railing, and started sucking on it.

"So, your parents . . ." I started to say, but I wasn't sure how to finish. I didn't have to.

"Our parents could care less what happens to us," the boy said. The girl nodded her agreement, but while the boy looked belligerent, she looked sad. "They left us out in the woods to die," Chubby continued.

I didn't know what to say to that. I mean, I knew such things happened, it's just that I never had to deal with them before. If I had been back in town, I would have called Social Services. Out here? I had no idea what to do. I could offer to take them with me, but since I had no idea if I was going to make it out of the woods alive, I didn't think that would be fair either. I hated having moral dilemmas pop up in the middle of a case.

"Look, kids, what're your names?"

The girl spoke up around the know. "I'm Grethel, and this is Hansel."

Hansel glared at her. "Don't tell him that," he said.

She glared back. "I already did."

"Hansel, Grethel, are you sure you're okay out here? Isn't there someone else you could stay with?"

Hansel turned his beady little eyes on me. They looked like two shriveled raisins on top of a hot cross bun. "Look, Mister. We're fine. We can take care of ourselves. Now get lost and leave our house alone," he growled. Then he grabbed Grethel's arm and pulled her inside after him. But before she disappeared, she looked at me once more. I think she looked sad.

But I still had a trail to find, two of them, in fact. The one of the spinning dwarf and the one home. Two brats in a candy house couldn't worry me. I yanked off a hunk of drainpipe and went on my way. The chocolate was good, but I still had a bad taste in my mouth.

## Wednesday

When I woke the next morning, it was with the sincerest prayer that I wouldn't have to spend another night in the forest. My back just wouldn't take it. And my knees creaked like old floorboards as I stood up.

I could do without the dreams as well. Fat little kids kept popping through my head all night long. I knew I shouldn't have eaten that whole drainpipe. I also shouldn't have left those kids behind. I kept kicking myself about it

all afternoon and well into last night. I knew it made
sense to leave them since at least they had food there. But
I also knew I'd have to go back for them when I finally
found my way out of this forest. *If* I made my way out and
*if* I could find their house again. At the moment, those
were two pretty big ifs.

I stretched and reached into my pockets. My gun was
still there, but my supply of pebbles was low. I rolled six
of the white stones around in my fingers. The rest were
scattered all through the woods. Considering how far I
had walked in the last two days, I thought I should have
found my way out by now, but with a place called the Enchanted Forest, who knew if standard directions made
sense.

But I knew I wasn't going to get out just standing there,
so I started walking again. My stomach grumbled, and I
wished I had broken off more of that house to eat. Then I
started thinking about those two kids again, and I got even
more depressed.

I'm not sure how long I wandered around in that funk
or how long it was before I heard the voice. I stopped and
listened. It was someone singing. I put my hand in my
pocket and crept forward. Two days in the forest taught
me extra caution.

I edged up on a clearing and peeked around a tree. The
heat and light of the fire smacked me in the face. A dwarf
danced around it singing.

> *"Today I brew, tomorrow I bake,*
> *Then tonight, the queen's child I'm going to take.*
> *How glad am I she hasn't got a clue*
> *That Rumplestiltskin is my name."*

What an awful song. Didn't have good rhyme or meter. But I had the information the queen wanted. I mean, there couldn't be two dwarfs singing such songs. Now I just had to make my way back to the queen before Shorty did.

I was just starting to back away when I heard something else. I looked back. Another little person came up to the fire. Bearded and ugly like Rumpelstiltskin, this one wore a dress. I had never seen a she-dwarf before, but I think I just had.

"Dear?" she said.

Rumpelstiltskin stopped then went to her.

"Yes, precious?"

"It's tonight, isn't it? We'll have another baby tonight?"

"Yes, snookums," he said.

The she-dwarf put her head on his shoulder. She was sobbing. He looked across the fire to the edge of the clearing. I looking in the same direction.

A little bulge of mounded earth stuck up through the grass. A small stone tablet and a lily adorned the bulge. I felt a tear come to my eye. Must have been a bit of ash from the fire. But I looked back at the couple. Another damn moral dilemma. I looked back at the mound. And I made my decision. I walked out of the woods.

"Rumpelstiltskin," I said.

The dwarf spun around, snarling.

"We have to talk," I said.

I finally found my way out of the forest and back to town, with about an hour to spare. I didn't even have time to stop to change clothes before I headed for the palace. The guards must have been looking for me because I hadn't even said "Hi" before they surrounded me and steered me though some back corridors and into a room.

Her Royal Haughtiness was waiting for me, pacing around the room that held only an old spinning wheel.

"It's about time. He'll be here any second. Did you find out his name? You better have if you want to live, I mean work, in this town again."

She said it all in one breath and the effort left her face red and puffy like a tomato starting to turn bad.

"I have a question for you, Your Highness. Do you love your child?"

She looked shocked. The redness left her face. But I was looking at her eyes. I knew I could see the truth there.

"Of course, I do," she said.

"And what would you do if you lost your child?"

"Lost?" she echoed, but now all color left her face. The fear I first noticed in her eyes burst forth and nearly consumed her. "You mean, you didn't find out . . ."

She loved the kid. I knew that for sure now. I just wanted to make sure.

"The dwarf's name is Rumpelstiltskin."

"You found him? Why didn't you tell me?" She nearly floated off the floor she was so happy.

"Your Highness," came a gruff voice behind us. We both spun around, surprised. I jabbed my hand in my pocket.

Rumpelstiltskin stood there. He bowed to the queen and glared at me.

"Who's he?" he growled.

The queen glanced at me and motioned me away. I walked to a corner.

"He's just some hired help," she said.

Rumpelstiltskin shrugged. "The last night, milady. If you don't guess my name, your child is mine."

The queen wrung her hands. "Oh, dear. Is your name Conrad?"

"No."

"How about Henry?"

"No."

The queen clapped her hands together. "I know. Your name must be Rumpelstiltskin!"

The dwarf just stared. Then he shook. Then his face turned scarlet. He reminded me of a teakettle about to blow.

"Rotten stinking fairies! They told you! Didn't they? Damn fairies, can't trust any of them. Why, I'm so mad, I could split myself in two!"

And as we watched, he stamped his right foot onto the floor. It sunk right through the stones. Then he reached over, grabbed his left foot, and ripped himself in half. We stared at the two parts for a few seconds before they vanished in a puff of smoke.

"I think I'm going to be sick," the queen said.

I knew how she felt. Yuck.

Then she composed herself and turned around to face me.

"Thank you, Mister Thorn." She slid a gold-and-emerald bracelet off her wrist. "Will this cover the job?" she said as she tossed it to me.

"Yeah, that'll do it."

"Good night, then," she said and left.

A guard came in and escorted me out. Once outside the gates I fingered the bracelet and stared up at the moon. Then I headed off to Grimms'.

## Friday

The next morning, I felt like I had a lumberjack chopping down a tree in my head. Not the type of morning to be wandering around the forest again. But I had promised, and like I already mentioned, I keep my word.

It only took me two hours to find the candy house. Of course, following the sickly sweet scent made it easier. The kids sure weren't doing well on the upkeep.

I stepped into the clearing and realized how bad matters were. Most of the porch had been eaten. All the lower pieces of siding had been stripped off. The shutters and window panes were gone. How had those kids eaten all that in two days?

"Is this the place?"

I nearly jumped out of my shorts. I spun around to stare at the dwarf.

"Don't do that!" I yelled.

"Sorry," Rumplestiltskin said.

"And not so loud," I added, trying to ignore my headache. "But, yeah, this is the place."

"Doesn't look like much. Where are the kids?"

"I assume inside. I just got here. By the way, that was a . . . an interesting trick you pulled last night, splitting yourself in two."

The dwarf shrugged. "A little something I learned from a traveling magician. No big deal."

I just grunted and turned back to the house. Someone was coming out.

"Who's been nibbling on . . . oh, you're back. What do you want now?"

How nice to know that two more days of eating candy

hadn't sweetened up Hansel's disposition any. It had fattened him up a little more. He looked like he should be lying on a platter with an apple in his mouth.

Before I could answer him, Grethel came out. The girl didn't look good. In fact, she looked green. She reached for a piece of the porch but stopped and shuddered. She turned to face me.

"These are the kids? They don't look like babies. They look like fat brats," Rumpelstiltskin said.

"Who's the short freak?" Hansel returned.

I could the tension getting thicker than Hansel's waist and that wouldn't work.

"Now, listen, you two, I really think this could . . ."

I didn't get a chance to finish.

I heard a pop and suddenly Mrs. Rumpelstiltskin was standing there.

"Where are they? Where are the children?"

The she spotted them. "Oh, aren't they precious?" she said as she clasped her hands around her beard. Then she rushed up to the porch as Hansel and Grethel stared at her.

"Honey bottom! What are you doing here?" Rumpelstiltskin asked, following his wife.

"I heard you two talking, and I wanted to see the poor children for myself," she said. She was already next to Grethel, who stood paralyzed with fascination. The she-dwarf patted the girl's hair, then she hugged her, cooing. Grethel broke down and started sobbing.

"There, there, dear. Don't cry. When we get home, I'll make you some nice stew, and Daddy just baked bread this morning."

"Anything but candy," Grethel wailed.

"Wait a minute," Hansel cried. "What's going on?"

"It's simple, kid," I said. "These two want to adopt you."

"What?" the fat boy asked, glaring around. He tried to look mean, but he looked more scared than belligerent, and just a little hopeful.

"They want to adopt you and give you a good home, isn't that right?" I said, nudging Rumpelstiltskin.

"Yeah, whatever," he said.

"We're doing fine on our own," Hansel said, crossing his arms over his pudgy chest.

Grethel's head came off of Mrs. R's shoulder. "That's not true. I want to go, Hansel. I don't care what you say. I'm tired of living in this stupid house and eating all this," she shuddered, "candy."

"But . . ." Hansel said.

Mrs. R released Grethel from her hug but held onto her hand. The she-dwarf then reached out for Hansel, catching his hand in hers. He jumped and looked at the small wrinkled fingers. He looked up at Mrs. R, and she pulled him into her arms. He went willingly. After a few minutes of hugging him, Mrs. R took them both by the hand and led them off the porch.

"Looks like you got a family now," I said to the dwarf besides me.

"Yeah. Two fat brats, if you ask me."

I looked down at him.

"But I guess they can grow on you," he said.

I nodded and stuck out my hand.

"Good luck," I said.

He shook. "We'll need it." Then he followed his wife. I watched them all disappear into the trees.

That's when I realized I hadn't marked my own path.

"Wait a minute!" I called, but got no answer.

Great. Stuck out here again. I looked at the house and pulled off the least sticky piece of the gutter I could find. I sucked on it as I tried to find my way home.

# FEEDING FRENZY OR THE FURTHER ADVENTURES OF THE FROG PRINCE
## by Josepha Sherman

Josepha Sherman is a fantasy writer and folklorist whose latest novels are *Highlander: The Captive Soul* and *Son of Darkness*. Her most recent folklore volume is *Merlin's Kin: World Tales of the Hero Magicians*. Her short fiction has appeared in numerous anthologies, including *Battle Magic, Black Cats and Broken Mirrors,* and *The Shimmering Door*. She lives in Riverdale, New York.

Now, I'm sure you've heard the story; Princess drops golden ball in stream, weeps and wails till frog rescues it, tells her he's a prince under a spell and she has to let him eat from her plate and sleep in her bed until she, the spoiled brat, gets fed up and slams him against a wall and, ta-da, she gets the prince.

Not exactly. First, my dear Swanilde is neither spoiled nor a brat, and it was my shout from the river—"Hey, get me out of this mess!"—that startled her into dropping that ball.

Second, since there was nothing enchanted about the basic *me* under that froggy shape, we'd gotten to know each other pretty well by the time of the wall-slamming part.

And when Swanilde did throw me against that wall and broke that damned spell, turning me back from a frog into a perfectly human—if stark naked—prince, we both thought that, *hey, wonderful, now we get to enjoy that proverbial happy ending*.

And I don't mean that the way it sounds.

Not exactly, at any rate.

I mean, after the first cries of wild delight and let's draw a veil over the proceedings, we had the Grand Royal Wedding, prince and princess in robes of cloth-of-gold, largesse given to the poor: the works. And isn't it then that we traditionally hear that "happily ever after" bit?

Uh, right.

So, start with a day not long after the wedding was over and done, and my wife and I deciding that all the froggy problems were also over and done.

Foolish us.

Now, one of the obligations of a good ruler—yes, we were declared joint rulers, that much went right—one of our obligations is listening to our people. Predictably enough, our first joint open session after the wedding brought a crowd, most of them just curious to see us and maybe get a royal souvenir (the guards had their hands full making sure bits of royal silver or napkins didn't leave with the curious). Some of the wealthier were carrying those garish Faerie Lights™ that leave a permanent afterimage of the scene on parchment—and a fortunately temporary afterimage of dazzling light on your vision.

We had just about finished the session and were looking forward to retiring together for some . . . conversation (being, as I say, still newly wed) when a small mob of people pushed their urgent way forward. The guards moved to stop them, but hey, these folks were our constituents. Besides, they didn't look dangerous, and everyone had been disarmed at the palace gates, neither Swanilde nor I being quite *that* trusting, so I waved the guards back.

In the lead was a very sincere-looking young woman in a blatantly plain gown as stylish as an unbleached burlap bag. "I represent P.E.T.A.," she began without preamble.

"Uh, what?"

With an impatient sigh, she explained, "People for the Ethical Treatment of Amphibians!"

"I see. Or rather, I don't see—"

"I must protest the cruelty that was displayed to you, Prince Albright," she interrupted earnestly, "when you were a frog—"

"Whoa. First, I never was truly a frog, only a transformed human forced to wear a frog form."

"But you cannot deny that cruelty was involved!"

"On the part of the witch who transformed me, yes. So why don't you go look her up, and—"

"Princess Swanilde," the Amphibian Woman challenged, "can you deny that you hurled the frog, thinking that he was, indeed, a true frog, can you deny that you hurled him against a wall?"

"Of course I knew he wasn't a true frog," Swanilde snapped. "True frogs don't go around saying, 'Kiss me, I'm a prince!' "

"But you don't deny that you threw him against a wall with the intention of wantonly inflicting damage!"

"Now just a minute! Yes, I threw him against that wall—but somehow everyone forgets a crucial section of the story. No, I did not like having a stranger share my food, or my pillow, particularly one who was stuck in that ugly shape, but he didn't stay a stranger for very long. And I did *not* enjoy having to throw him against that wall—even though he, himself, told me I *had* to do that in order to break the spell!"

"Ugly shape!" an indignant voice proclaimed. A grim-faced man of uncertain years and scholarly robes pushed his way forward to join the Amphibian Woman. "I represent the Union of Concerned Amphibiologists, and I must say that I protest this cavalier treatment of so important a natural subject as the life cycle of *rana pipiens* and its fellow frogs!"

I held up a hand. "No one's denying the importance of any amphibian! But—"

"Your pardon, Prince Albright, but you have to admit that no Environmental Impact study was done, either prior or anterior to the transformation incident, regarding your impact upon the natural frog ecocycle."

"What impact? I ate a few flies, yes, but that's all! I didn't have anything to do with the, uh, lady frogs, if that's what you mean."

"Yes, but—"

"About that cruelty issue," a new voice piped up. A scrawny young man who looked as though he hadn't eaten in weeks wormed his way forward. "Princess Swanilde, I represent M.A.D.L."

She gave me a helpless glance. "M.A.D.L.?"

I shrugged just as helplessly.

The young man glared at us both. "That's the Male Anti-Defamation League! Princess Swanilde, you state that you knew this was a man, not a frog, yet you still threw him with all your female strength against a wall."

"I had to break that cursed spell!"

"But can you deny that you *enjoyed* throwing a man against a wall?"

"Of course I deny it! I don't like hurting anyone!"

"That's what they all claim, but—"

"Prince Albright!" A stocky little man in worn home-spun shoved his way through, pushing the man from M.A.D.L. brusquely out of the way. "Prince Albright, I represent the *Weekly Magic News*. What's this about a witch anti-defamation suit?"

"That's the first I've heard of it. And let me set the record straight: Dame Gruesome *is* a witch, or at least calls herself one!"

"Gruesome, eh? Can you deny that bit of name-calling isn't defamation?"

"I certainly can! That's her professional name, Dame Gruesome! She has it printed on all her cards: 'Dame Gruesome, dark spells by appointment.' "

The Faerie Lights™ were flashing like fireflies by now, dazzling me. "Guards!" I shouted. "Enough—"

But before I could get any further, yet another figure, a dignified woman in severely tailored robes forced her way through the mob. "Prince Albright, I represent the S.P.Q.R."

"You're . . . from, uh, Rome . . . ?" I hazarded weakly.

"No, no, from the Society for the Preservation of Quizzical Royalty—transformed royals like yourself or the Beast—as in Beauty and the—we protect your legal rights—"

"They don't need any protecting!" I protested. "I've done nothing wrong, and neither has Princess Swanilde!"

That started up a storm of protests from the frog protectors, the male protectors, the royals protectors. My wife and I exchanged quick, frustrated looks. Then I grabbed her by the hand, and we both raced off before anyone could stop us.

Now, one little fact I've kept from the public is that, as a former, if involuntary, shapeshifter, I still retain a now-voluntary ability to shift. And I can shapeshift anyone with me. Swanilde and I tore off our clothes and dove into the river, changing as we went, and swam to the bottom as two large frogs. Together, we paddled off underwater till the furor behind us was out of earshot, then surfaced.

"That was insane," Swanilde began, since of course, as magical frogs, we'd kept our human voices. "You'd think *we* were the criminals instead of Dame Gruesome."

Dame Gruesome, who was still living in her castle downriver, going totally unpunished because my guards couldn't find one scrap of evidence linking her to my transformation. "Never mind that," I said from between what would have been clenched teeth if I'd been in human form. "Let's just relax for a while."

It's kind of fun being a frog—when you know that you don't have to *stay* a frog. We swam peacefully down the river, happy to be in each other's company, and out of reach of everyone.

"They're going to be waiting for us, you know," I said. "We haven't settled anything."

Swanilde sighed. "I know. But at least—"

"There you are!" someone shouted.

We both jumped. A large frog and a duck were blocking our way, glaring at us, and I asked warily, "You . . . spoke?"

"Damned right we did!" the frog said.

"Don't like doing it either," the duck added.

"Uh . . . you're transformed humans, too?"

"Hell, no!" the frog snapped. "Born a tadpole, nice and normal, thank you very much."

"Me, I hatched from the egg, nice normal duckling," the duck continued.

"But—you—how can you—"

"Dame Gruesome," Swanilde breathed.

"Naw," the frog cut in. "She never laid a finger on either of us. All we did was, you know, swim, down by her castle, and *poof,* there we were, talking. Other stuff going on down there, too, weird stuff: Water snake grew wings and got stuck in a tree, some other frog grew horns and drowned—you're the human, you're the prince, you do something about it, okay?"

"Of . . . course."

Warily, Swanilde and I swam on downstream, ready to beat a hasty backward retreat if the witch sensed us. There was Dame Gruesome's castle on its rocky outcropping over the river, a ramshackle building ugly as proverbial sin, and badly in need of repair. From down here in the river, I could see that sections of wall had already slid halfway down the slope to the river. Even as we watched, a chunk of stone broke off and fell all the way down, hitting the water with a great splash that sent a cloud of magic shimmering over the surface. The water boiled up, swirling with oily iridescence. Magical residue, I thought; the area must be full of it.

"That's it!" I whispered to Swanilde. "That's how we

get her once and for all—and get those damned reporters and cause-ists off our necks, too!"

Well, now, if you follow the media, either the papers or the mindspeakers, at all, you've surely heard about the case that followed. Dame Gruesome was charged with five counts of illegal transformation, cruelty to animals, and magical pollution of water and air—as well as an additional charge of resisting arrest.

Resisting arrest isn't the half of it! She put up quite a fight. Several guards wound up croaking, literally, before she was taken, and two bushes, a woodshed, and a tree sprouted wings and haven't been seen since. But Swanilde and I have placed some good, strong wizards on the judicial circuit, and Judge Rikard, utterly honest and unimpressed by magical tantrums, is one of them. Dame Gruesome finally realized that she was only hurting her case, and grudgingly settled down.

As much as she was going to settle, anyhow. Predictably, Dame Gruesome (whose real name, it turned out during the trial, was Rosemary Higginbottom) denied everything. She tried her best to enchant the jury—but with a wizard judge, she didn't get very far.

Besides, the evidence was far too damning, in the testimony of a very angry frog and duck, as well as in the samples of water analyzed by the E.P.A., the Enchantment Protection Agency, the report of which was read by their agent, a rabbity little man with the intense stare of a ferret.

"We have a thirty-five point three transformation level," he read, his voice fairly quivering with indignation. "That's well above the safety limit. We also registered shapeshifting residues in air and water of well over *fifty-four point eight!*"

"And that means . . . ?" Judge Rikard prodded.

"That means, Your Highnesses," to Swanilde and me, "Your Honor," to Judge Rikard, "that what we had was bigger than a few random transformations—"

"Random!" the duck quacked, but hushed at the judge's glare.

"What we had," the little agent continued, "was nothing less than an environmental disaster just waiting to happen!"

Well, let's gloss over Dame Gruesome's reaction, since those words aren't suitable or safe for print, and ended with Judge Rikard gagging her before more of the jury turned into newts. Dame Gruesome was, naturally, found guilty on all five counts, with an additional charge of tampering with a jury, and ruled an irresponsible wielder of magic, and a danger to society. Her sentence was the standard one in such cases: Banishment to a Realm of Science.

Hey, now, don't waste any sympathy on her: You know why Dame Gruesome enchanted me in the first place? It's not usually part of the official story, but she'd attempted to, well, forcibly get to know me, and wouldn't understand that "no" meant "no!"

Back in the palace after the trial, Swanilde and I let out mutual sighs of relief. Nothing to do for these precious few moments, no one to speak with or be ogled by. We waved away the attendants and walked together in the palace gardens like the newlyweds we were, hand in hand, enjoying the splashing fountains and pretty flowers, alone at last.

Oh, right. That damned reporter from the *Weekly Magic News* popped out of the bushes where he'd been hiding, flashing one of those thrice-cursed Faerie Lights™ at us and insisting as we blinked, "Now that the trial's over, how do you feel?"

Swanilde and I exchanged quick, if dazzled, glances. *Go for it,* hers said. "How do you think I feel?" I asked.

"Come closer. I've got a real exclusive for you." He came closer, practically panting with eagerness. I caught him by the scruff of the neck, dove with him into the deepest of the fountains, shifted both of us—and left him there.

"What—wait—you can't leave me like this!"

"Why not?" I asked, climbing out of the fountain, dripping wet but back in human form.

Which was more than he could say. "I'm a—a *frog!*"

"See? You've got an exclusive right there. Don't worry. I'll turn you back. Eventually."

I winked at my grinning wife. Ignoring the plaintive cries of, "You can't do this!" and "I *hate* frogs!" we strolled off together arm in arm, just two nice, normal utterly human beings.

This time, dammit, we were going to live happily ever after!

# A LEG UP, or THE CONSTANT TIN SOLDIER (GONZO VERSION)
### edited and annotated
### by Gary A. Braunbeck

Gary A. Braunbeck writes poetically dark suspense and horror fiction, rich in detail and scope. Recent stories have appeared in *Robert Bloch's Psychos*, *Once upon a Crime*, and *The Conspiracy Files*. His occasional foray into the mystery genre is no less accomplished, having appeared in anthologies such as *Danger in D.C.* and *Cat Crimes Takes a Vacation*. His recent short story collection, *Things Left Behind*, received excellent critical notice. He lives in Columbus, Ohio.

> "Either those drapes go, or I do."
> —Oscar Wilde's dying words

There once was a little tin soldier who—
   —mistake, forgot something, sorry—
   —there once was a little *constant* tin soldier who fell in love with a ballerina in a castle and proceeded to get himself into all sorts of trouble because of it—which only goes to prove, as you'll soon see, that not everyone who spends their life pining away for a love they'll

never know should be an object of pity. Ridicule, yes; unsavory rumors about what they do in the privacy of their own home, you'd better damned well believe it; but never pity.

Onward.

There were twenty-four other of these tin soldiers, and all were brothers because they had been born from the very same spoon. They were a splendid-looking bunch, what with their red-and-blue uniforms and tall hats and muskets and the way they always stood perfectly straight when arranged in a line by the little boy for whom they had been a birthday gift—in fact, he had cried out, "Tin soldiers!" upon opening the box in which they nested, proving to his parents and older sister that he was indeed a very gifted child, as those had been his very first words. That he had not spoken these words until the age of six was never brought up, what with the mother being an unstable sort and the father's drinking problem and the sister's mysterious "night job" that was also never brought up because it often sent the mother into a nervous fit and the father down into the wine cellar where he'd remain for days on end, but the sister often brought in more money in a week than three households did in a month, so everyone just grinned and bore it and became accustomed to their debt-free lifestyle.

*(It should be noted here that the little boy in question was none other than—no, wait, sorry, don't want to divulge that information just yet. Forget you ever read this part.)*

The gifted little boy arranged his twenty-five tin soldiers upon his table, noting with pride how most of them were exactly alike—except for one, who is of course the hero of our story: What made out hero different from his

brothers was that he was the last soldier cast from the tin
of the spoon, but there had not been enough tin remaining to finish him, so, as a result, he had only one leg, but
this did not stop him from standing just as still and proud
as his brothers.

*(First actual note here: The little boy, whenever his
playmates came over from the neighboring kingdom,
would often invent very elaborate stories concerning the
loss of the tin soldier's leg. Some of these stories were
brief and brutal—"He stepped on a land-mine and was
blown—WHOOSH-THUMP-SPLAT—clear to the other
side of the field"—while others were long and even more
brutal, usually involving slow, sadistic torture at the hands
of the enemy—which the little boy detailed in all its gory
glory—and reduced more than a few of his playmates to
tears. The rest are still in therapy. Oddly enough, his
family never wondered why it was that none of their son's
playmates ever came over more than once, but that is a
matter for the kingdom's counselors to debate and, besides, there are some other things on the table you need
to know about.)*

The table on which the tin soldiers stood was very
large, and there were several other toys upon it, the
largest of which was a magnificent cardboard castle that
had been built by the little boy's sister *(whose own draw-
bridge didn't reach all the way to the moat, if you know
what I mean)*. In front of the castle lay an oval mirror that
served as a lake. Swans of wax drifted upon it and were
mirrored in its surface. Around the lake there were trees
*(leafy branches ripped from trees, truth be told—remem-
ber, this was long before the Environmental Movement or
vandalism fines)* that formed a lovely, deep, dark forest.
*(You didn't really expect there to be a shallow, **bright** for-*

*est, did you? Good God, have you never **read** one of these
things before?)*

Onward.

This was all very pretty, of course, the castle and swans
and forest and the soldiers guarding the entrance, cha-
cha-cha, so on and so forth, but the prettiest thing of all
was the little lady who stood at the door of the castle. She
was also made of paper, and wore a dress made from the
finest gauze. Draped around one shoulder was a bright
gold ribbon, and in the center of the ribbon, hanging just
below her face so as to accent her angelic features, was a
tinsel rose. Now, because she was a ballerina, she stood
on one leg only, with the other pulled so far up behind her
that it could not be seen. The constant tin soldier saw this
and thought that, like himself, she had only one leg.

That would be the wife for me, he thought to himself.

*(What he actually said was, "Whoa—you do Shakes-
peare from her balcony!" because he was, after all, a
member of the Armed Forces and as such wanted to fit in
with his fellow soldiers, all of whom had undergone training at the kingdom's equivalent of the Citadel and none
of whom had ever uttered anything more tender than
"I'd like to pull up your rear!" when referring to the female sex. He was, naturally, ashamed to have said it, but
peer pressure can be an awful thing for a tin soldier—add
to that his being a **handicapped** tin soldier and, well . . .
you can imagine how his nightmare of forced bravado
and machismo caused him to lose so much sleep. Tragic.
We could go on for pages about the deep psychological
scars this left him with but there's no need to depress you
this soon into the story.)*

That would be the wife for me, he thought to himself.

But she is so grand, and I am but a tin soldier with no discernable source of income, living with twenty-four brothers in a box with no indoor plumbing or cable television. It would be no place for her. Still, she is very beautiful, and I must meet her, if only to say that I once stood close to such perfection.

So he looked around and found a hiding place behind a silver snuffbox at the edge of the table, and lay down there so that he could better see the little lady in the castle without her being aware of him.

*(Note: Stalking laws were several hundred years away from being put into the books.)*

He remained there all the day long. The sun set, the rest of the soldiers were put back into their box, and the little boy and his parents went to sleep while the sister went out to her night job that no one ever mentioned.

As soon as they were sure the people in the house were asleep, all of the toys came alive and began to play at "visiting" and at "war" and at "giving balls." *(Not going to touch that one.)* The Pencil drew fantastic pictures on the paper, the Nutcracker threw somersaults, the Jacks made all sorts of racket, and even the Mechanical Canary came awake and began to speak in verse. The tin soldiers wanted to join in the mirth and merriment, but could not lift the lid from their box and so had to settle for rattling around in the dark.

Everything was alive and moving around, except for the Tin Soldier and the Dancing Lady; they remained perfectly still, watching one another. *(Our hero had stood up several minutes before, having become bored with the cramps in his leg and elbow from trying to keep himself hidden behind the snuffbox.)*

The Dancing Lady stood on the toes of one foot, her

arms stretched out toward the Tin Soldier, who was just as enduring on his one leg.

They never looked away from one another.

Until, that is, the clock struck midnight and—*Ta-Da!*—the lid flew off the snuffbox and a Black Goblin emerged.

"Tin Soldier!" he snarled. "Is your name George, and have you some information on the rabbits?"

"Huh?"

"Why are you looking at the Dancing Lady?"

"Because she is so beautiful, and I love her."

The Black Goblin cocked its terrible head to one side. "Love, you say? Ha! Go back to your box and remember your station in life."

"I'll do no such thing."

"You're willing to risk my wrath so that you can stay here and gawk at her all night long?"

"You wrath cannot possibly be any worse than your breath."

The Black Goblin started. "I'll have you know my breath is a serious medical condition, thank you very much, and should not be interpreted as being the result of snorting sulfur or any of that overdone Demon-from-the-pits-of-hell, black-arts crap."

"I apologize if I have offended you."

"Yes, well," said the Black Goblin, "be that as it may . . . do you really think you've got a chance with the Dancing Lady? I hear she's very refined."

"She is perfection."

"You don't get out much, do you? *She's made out of paper!*"

The Tin Soldier would not be swayed. "I have never been against mixed marriages."

"You're very weird," said the Black Goblin.

"I'm truly getting annoyed with you. You're blocking my view."

Fine," said the Black Goblin, retreating back into the snuffbox to nurse his wounded pride. "But if you want the best, I mean *the best of all possible* views, you should haul yourself up to the windowsill."

The Tin Soldier glanced away from the Dancing Lady and saw that the Black Goblin was, surprisingly, telling the truth. "It would seem to offer the best vantage point, that sill." He tipped his hat to the Black Goblin. "I thank you."

"Go away before you hurt my feelings again." And with that, the Black Goblin slammed closed the lid of the snuffbox and began laughing hysterically.

The Tin Soldier, thinking that the insane cackling laughter was just something that Black Goblins did because the union required it to maintain membership in good standing, made his way from the table and onto the sill—which, unbeknownst to him, was exactly what the Black Goblin wanted him to do.

*(There was originally a very long sequence here detailing the Tin Soldier's journey to the windowsill, but it went on for about six pages and the gist of it was this: He stole some string, made a rope, shimmied down it, crossed the floor, engaged in battle with the Garden Gnome—who turned up in the house for God-only-knows-what reason—then used the rope and a pile built from the shattered remains of the Garden Gnome to get himself up onto the windowsill. I can't for the life of me figure out why this had to take six pages, unless the author was originally being paid by the word, but I digress. Here he is, on the windowsill, and morning approacheth.)*

As morning approached and the sister was returning from her night job, she decided to air out the room and opened the window nearest her—which, of course, was the one upon whose sill the Tin Soldier was standing, pining away at the Dancing Lady.

As she opened the window, the sister's arm bumped the Tin Soldier, knocking him out the window and down into the bushes far below.

Oh, shit, he thought.

*(What he actually said cannot be repeated in a PG-rated story such as this; suffice to say it was extremely salty and colorful and involved his suggesting impossible physical acts the sister should perform as soon as possible with handcuffs, two watermelons, a Doberman, and the little one-eyed hunchbacked fellow who was always muttering, "surrender, Dorothy!" as he raked up leaves outside the asylum; very colorful, that: Would've make a truck driver blush. But here's the Tin Soldier, lying there in the bushes, and we must press on.)*

It began to rain, which irritated the Tin Soldier no end, because he had landed upside down on the ground, his leg sticking straight up, his hat and musket tip embedded in the muddy ground. The water splashed against his leg, ran down its length, and began dribbling down into his nose, choking him.

This isn't good, he thought to himself. If I do not do something soon, I stand the chance of drowning in a quarter inch of water, and that would be most embarrassing.

As luck would have it, there was another Garden Gnome nearby who noticed the Tin Soldier's predicament and waddled over to see if he might be of assistance.

"Is your name George?" asked the Gnome.

The Tin Soldier, realizing that he might not get out of

this position if he identified himself as anyone other than this George fellow that everyone seemed so concerned about—and at the same time realizing he'd never been given a proper name—coughed up some rainwater and said, "Yes."

The Garden Gnome pulled him out of the ground and stood him upright. "Will you tell me about the rabbits now?"

"What rabbits?"

"You know."

"I'm afraid I don't."

*(This strained exchange goes on for another page, the author evidently thinking he had to hammer the satire into the ground, and elicits not so much as a chuckle. Trust me on this.)*

The Tin Soldier bid a sad farewell to his friend Chaney the Garden Gnome, and was setting about the task of getting himself back into the house when two little boys came along.

It must be said that you would be hard-pressed to find a little boy anywhere in the kingdoms who had not, at one time or another, been subjected to the horrid tales spun by the little boy who owned the one-legged Tin Soldier. These two were no exception.

"Look," cried out one of them. "Isn't that . . . ?"

"It certainly is," replied the other.

"I wonder how he came to be out here."

"Who cares? Let's do something terrible to him."

"Why?"

"Because we're two little boys with no names in a fairy story and we're always mischievous, if not outright sadistic, and it's not up to us to alter archetypes."

"Archy-whats?" asked his friend.

"Never mind."

They pulled some papers from a nearby trash bin and fashioned a boat out of it. Then they placed the Tin Soldier into the boat and set him asail in the gutter, where the water was rushing in a torrent down the street, toward a large drain.

Oh, dear, thought the Tin Soldier, so frightened by the probability of what was about to occur that he could not even muster forth a decent profanity on this occasion, when it would have been completely understandable.

The boys ran along behind the paper boat, clapping their hands and laughing and having a high old time.

Meanwhile, the Tin Soldier was in the throes of an apoplectic fit.

"Are you crazy?" he screamed at them. "Do I *look* like I can swim, I ask you! It would be deeply appreciated if you would kindly, if it's not too much trouble, please, please get *me out of this boat!*"

But he was very tiny, his voice even more so—even though he was screaming—and the boys heard not a word.

He turned back and saw that the evil-looking drain was only a few feet away, and silently cursed the Black Goblin for having put him in this position—for something like this was undoubtedly what the Black Goblin had in mind.

*(This was before cell phones and personal injury lawyers, or you can bet the farm that he'd have been calling up his attorney who'd be suing the banonga-loo-loos off not only the Black Goblin and the two little boys for what was about to happen to his client, but the publisher of the paper out of which the boat had been made, the manufacturer of the snuffbox where the Black Goblin*

*lived, the factory where the window had been made, and the poor slobs who had installed the thing.)*

The boat fell into the drain, and before he knew what to do, the Tin Soldier found himself engulfed in a darkness even more oppressive than the box in which he lived after the lid had been placed on it by the little boy whose name you still don't need to know just yet.

This displeases me, he thought to himself. I need to take a moment.

He took a moment to rally himself, thinking, If only the Dancing Lady were in this boat with me, it could be thrice as dark for all I'd care! But while he was doing this the boat rounded a corner, and he became aware of all the debris in the water surrounding him, then realized he could see, *then* realized he could see because of the light from a torch held by a rat; it illuminated a small ledge that ran the length of the tunnel he was now floating. Behind the rat the Tin Soldier could see an opening in the wall, and within that opening were rows and rows and rows of bookshelves crammed to bursting with tomes and papers and file-folders.

"Have you a name, good sir?" asked the Tin Soldier.

"You must be George," replied the rat.

"Maybe I am and maybe I'm not," said the Tin Soldier, deciding there on the spot that if he got out of this alive, he would make it his mission in life to hunt down this George fellow and punch his lights out. "Have *you* a name?"

"Maybe."

"I asked first."

"Rumpelstiltskin," replied the rat. "Are you here from Personnel?"

"First of all," said the Tin Soldier, "I have no idea

what you're talking about. Secondly, you are most certainly *not* Rumpelstiltskin. He was—"

"—I am so!" snapped the rat, and his snapping was a most fiercesome sight to behold. "I am, always was, have been, and will be a rodent, but they didn't bother telling you *that* little tidbit in the story, did they? Oh, no—they had to make me into a little misshappen dwarf and give a bad name not only to dwarves but rats, as well! And does anyone ever stop to wonder about all that straw that the King has the miller's daughter spin into gold? Heaven forbid! Do you know how much livestock died of starvation as a result of spinning all that gold? No, of course you don't—they decided to leave that part out because it would make the upper class look even more crass and greedy than they already did, and the dear Brothers were nothing if not upper-class butt-kissers, and who bears the brunt of their little editing frenzy? Me. So here I am, down here in the Footnote Sewer, trying to keep all these little historic facts organized, doing my best to make sure that every version and revision and retelling of all the stories are properly catalogued by year, month, language, and translator, all by myself, and what happens when I ask for an assistant? *Nothing.* Not a bloody thing! So I think, that's okay, they'll send someone down here eventually, and I go on busting my hump while the weeks turn into months and those turn into years and next thing I know, my fur is turning gray and I'm no closer to getting this mess organized that I was when I first got saddled with this gruntwork, so you'd better be from Personnel or I'm going to start mixing up the stories and characters and pages until you won't know Little Red Riding Hood from the Whore of Babylon—and just between you and me, there's a flying squirrel and talking moose who've offered me *mucho wampum* to do just that."

"I don't suppose you could just kill me now and get it over with?"

"Why would I do something like that? *I need some help!*"

"That you do," muttered the Tin Soldier, grabbing up a small outboard motor that was floating in the debris and attaching it to the back of his boat. "I really must dash now, but I'll be sure to pass your comments along to the Personnel Department." And with that he fired up the engine and sped away—

—right into the mouth of a gigantic fish.

"This is just ducky," he mumbled to himself in the slimy darkness of the fish's great mouth.

*(There appears here a long and very graphic description of the fish's innards. The author never bothered to explain how it was that the Tin Soldier was able to see in the darkness, as he did not take the torch from the rat earlier on, but that is secondary to the fact that for the next **fifteen pages** we are treated to an urp-inducing description of fish guts that rivals the whale-production section in* Moby-Dick, *only without the snappy wit and whimsical irony, and so I have chosen to cut this section, loss of satire notwithstanding. My apologies to any scholars of fish innards who were anticipating this section.)*

Eventually, he sat there in the fish's great belly trying not to think about the possible Biblical implications of his predicament, the Tin Soldier became aware of someone else in the belly with him, and for a moment—he was quite stressed by this time and not thinking clearly—he thought—nay, was *certain*—that the Black Goblin had somehow tricked the Dancing Lady into following him and here they were, alone at last in the dark, and he would profess his love for her and they would be as one, forever after, so happy and snuggly-snug you'd just want to bring up your dinner.

"Hello?" said a distinctly male voice.

The Tin Soldier's heart sank as he realized that this was not, in fact, the Dancing Lady. Unless of course she suffered from some hideous hormonal problem of which he was not aware.

"If you ask me if I'm George," began the Tin Soldier.

"Oh, no. I wouldn't do that," said the voice.

*(See what I mean? For fifteen pages we can see every disgusting organ and slimy secretions within the fish, but here's our hero talking to someone not an inch away from him and can't see who it is. Belive it or not, folks, this is why editors and proofreaders are needed, despite what many writers will tell you. But I'm getting off the point here, and there's a scene to finish.)*

"So who are you?" asked the Tin Soldier.

"I'm the punchline to an extremely dirty joke," replied the faceless voice.

"Oh. And your name would be . . . ?"

"Help Me Find My Car Keys And We'll Drive Out Of Here."

"That's quite a name."

"It's a classic joke."

*(An aside: I am ashamed to admit that I have heard this joke, and it is indeed extremely filthy and was often cited in the Freedom of Speech controversies during the 1950s and 1960s; I believe R. Crumb even did a cartoon*

*based upon it, which ought to give you some idea of its content.)*

"I don't get it," said the Tin Soldier.

"No one ever does, when I appear out of context like this," replied his faceless companion, who then set off to find his car keys.

Very soon the Tin Soldier saw the fish once again open its great mouth, and into it came a very large and very sharp hook which very nearly latched onto the Tin Soldier's boat.

Everything became very confusing after that, for the fish was lifted up out of the water and the Tin Soldier fell out of his boat and he could hear voices outside the fish talking about supper—

—but then the fish was flopped down onto a counter and cut open and a hand came in and pulled out a bunch of fish-guts, then the paper boat and a set of car keys and, finally, the Tin Soldier himself, who shook off some of the slimy secretions he'd fallen into, cleared his eyes, looked around—

—and found himself in the very room in which he had been before!

He was back home!

It must be Destiny!

*(Strictly editorial note here: I have chosen the word "Destiny" in place of original word, which I assumed was "fate." I say "assumed" because the translator was either nearsighted or dyslexic—possibly both—because in every instance where it appeared in the manuscript the word "fate" read as "fart." Somehow I don't think this was the author's intention: "It was fart undid the Tin Soldier." "They were farted to be together." "The garden*

*smelled just lovely until someone let fly with a whopper of a fate." Things like that. I'm done.)*

He saw the same play table. And there were the same toys in the same place, and the same children, and the cardboard castle was still standing—and there, oh, *there* was the most glorious sight of all: The Dancing Lady still stood at the castle door, her arms extended, balancing herself on the toes of one foot. She was faithful, too. This moved the Tin Soldier so very deeply he was close to tears, but knowing that a good soldier never cries, he remained strong, smiling toward his True Love and saying not a word.

Then the little boy, Hansel, took the Tin Soldier and flung him into the stove. He gave no good reason for doing this. Then his sister, Grethel, having had a bad night, flung the Dancing Lady into the stove, as well.

*(Yes, you read right: Hansel and Grethel, the notorious Cannibal Twins of Fairyland, who some time later were responsible for the disappearance, fattening up, cooking, and eating of some seventy-two minor characters from the storybooks—including the witch who was purported to have tried to do them in. Now, even though this was long before the esteemed psychoanalyst Dr. Heinrich Von Earshplitenloudenboomer wrote the definitive book on recognizing sociopsychopathic behavior in children,* You Should Have Seen It Coming (So Let the Victims' Deaths Be on Your Heads), *everyone in the house, mother, father, and servants included, suspected that there was something not-quite-right in the way the children behaved. But hindsight is easy, and it really worked out for the best because the parents wrote a best-selling book about their children and became even*

*more rich and very famous and appeared on lots of talk shows.)*

The Tin Soldier felt a great heat, and saw that all his colors were melting away. He looked at the dancing Lady and smiled at her. He would not die with fear on his face. He shouldered his musket and stood firm and in the final moments, before the Dancing Lady was turned to ashes and he to a clump, he managed to say, "I love you," to the Dancing Lady.

"And I you," she replied.

When the servant-maid cleaned out the ashes the next day, she found him in the shape of a little tin heart. But of the dancing Lady there was only a tinsel rose that was black as coal.

*(Okay. The ending's a bummer, I know. But there were some interesting notes accompanying the manuscript— which has an alternate ending that we'll get to in a second. The translator's notes point out that the author was infamous for knocking off his characters, especially the female ones. "They either turn to foam or are thrown dead upon a heap or freeze to death selling matches on the street. He should have dated more."*

*I am in full agreement on this last point. A lot of fairy tales have bummer endings, and yet people still read them to children. Is it any wonder the world's got so many problems, what with little ones going off to Dreamland with images of wicked stepsisters hacking off their toes so their bloody feet would fit in the glass slipper or children being fattened up and shoved in ovens or being abandoned in deep, dark forests or swallowed by wolves? Jeez, the story of Caligula seems tame by comparison!*

*The point is that if you want a happy ending, it de-pends entirely on where you choose to stop the story. Face it, folks, the ending of every character's story is Death, like it or not, and unless you belong to one of those goat-worshiping cults—in which case you wouldn't be caught live reading a story like this in any version—then you want happy endings to your fairy tales and damn any moral. I can get with that. Therefore, not only as a public service to ensure that this story doesn't cause any unsuspecting child to have nightmares, but also in the spirit of fairness, I offer to you the alternate ending which was patched together from notes provided to the translator by none other than the rat Rumpelstiltskin—who has, I've been told, since gone on to have a very lu-crative career in cartoons.*

*Anyway, here's the other ending, the happy one, the one where you can stave off your children having to deal with the reality of Death.)*

He saw the same play table. And there were the same toys in the same place, and the same children, and the cardboard castle was still standing—and there, oh, *there* was the most glorious sight of all: The Dancing Lady still stood at the castle door, her arms extended, balancing herself on the toes of one foot. She was faithful, too. This moved the Tin Soldier so very deeply he was close to tears, but knowing that a good soldier never cries, he re-mained strong, smiling toward his True Love and saying not a word.

A gentle breeze blew in from an open window, and caught the dancing Lady in its arms, lifting her from the castle door and allowing her to fly gracefully across the room to land before the Tin Soldier, who could no longer contain his feelings.

He took her in his arms and kissed her, and a sweeter kiss there has never been.

"Oh, my love," he whispered in her ear. "My fair Dancing Lady."

And she breathlessly replied: "Oh, George."

# MRS. MYRTLE MONTEGRANDE VS. THE VEGETABLE STALKER/SLAYER

## by Elizabeth Ann Scarborough

Elizabeth Ann Scarborough won a Nebula award in 1989 for her novel *The Healer's War,* based on her experiences as an Army nurse in Vietnam. She has collaborated on four books with Anne McCaffrey, three novels and one anthology, *Space Opera*. Her most recent novel is *The Godmother's Web,* which uses Native American folklore as a backdrop. She lives in Washington with four cats, Popsicle, Kittibits, Trixie and Treat.

"**A**nd so we lived happily ever after, at least until certain parties dropped in unexpectedly and began making wild accusations," said the mother of the accused. She was a respectable looking woman, her white hair professionally braided with bright and expensive ribbons into a crown on her sleek head, her chic designer apron and custom matched kerchief making the most of her newly well-padded figure.

The counsel for the defense, a calico cat in high leather boots, a fine feathered hat, and embroidered surcoat and gauntlets, purred sympathetically at her. "So, to sum up then, Mrs. Jackson, you sent your son, the accused, to market with your only cow, which he exchanged for magic beans. These beans he cultivated into a magic vine which provided access to the deceased Mr. Montegrande's kingdom. Your son then climbed said vine, and was then invited by the plaintiff . . ."

There was a rustle of wings. A raven perched on one slope of what appeared to be a mountain of black veiling, and squawked, "Objection, your honor. Counsel is asking the witness to verify events she has only hearsay knowledge of."

"Sustained," said the owl at the bench. "Counsel will confine its remarks and questions to events of which the witness has personal knowledge."

"Then the next thing you knew," the cat said with a courtly bow to the bench before returning to his client's mother, "your son returned from the beanstalk with Exhibit A, the hen that lays the golden eggs. Is that correct?"

She nodded.

"And on two subsequent visits, he returned with a bag of gold and a golden harp?"

"Bang on," Mrs. Jackson said with an approving nod.

"And you lived happily ever after? Improving your home and farmstead and contributing to a number of worthy charities?"

"Very grateful they was, too. Called my Jack a hero, they did."

She nodded to the various groups in the back of the courtroom, bearing signs with legends such as "Widows and Orphans of the Ogre-Eaten" and "Victims of Property Damage Inflicted By Persons in Seven League Boots."

"Thank you, Mrs. Jackson. You've been very helpful." The cat bowed to the raven. "Prosecution's witness."

The raven fluttered forward and perched on the railing of the witness stand. He cocked an eye and regarded Mrs. Jackson quizzically, as if trying to figure out how a nice lady like her could have a son such as the accused. "Mrs. Jackson," the raven said, "when was it you decided to go on a vegan diet?"

"I beg your pardon?" the lady asked, flushing.

"A vegan diet. When did you decide to change?"

"Objection!" the cat said with impatient jerks of his tail. "The prosecution's line of questioning is irrelevant and immaterial."

"Your honor, I beg the court's indulgence. Mrs. Jackson testified that she sent her son to market with their only cow, and that times had been very hard and they had little to eat at home. Therefore, I can only conclude, since she was relinquishing their only remaining source of food and gaining a bean vine in exchange, that the Jacksons must have decided to change their dietary habits and the cow was of less use to them than a bean vine."

"Overruled, but please make your questions more direct in the future, counselor."

"Very well." The raven cocked his head to the other side and squinted at the witness with his other eye.

"Witness is directed to answer the question," the owl said.

"We did no such foolish thing!" Mrs. Jackson said. "I sent the cow with my boy to the market hoping the beast would fetch enough money to buy us a bit more food to last us the winter."

"Aha! So you did not send the accused specifically to purchase bean seeds?"

"Of course not! Why, any fool knows that ordinary beans wouldn't yield anything till early summer at least."

"You were, in fact, most unhappy with your son when he brought home the bean seeds, then?" the raven asked. "Isn't that a fact, Mrs. Jackson?"

The woman stole a look at her son, who shrugged. "I was, a bit, until he told me they were magic bean seeds, and he planted them and they started to grow."

"Which was it, Mrs. Jackson?" the raven asked.

"Which was what?"

"When did you cease being angry with your son? When he told you they were magic bean seeds? Isn't it true that you thought he had been taken for a fool? Isn't it true that you said, as you were overheard to say, that he was a simpleton to fall for an old trick such as that one? Isn't it true you suggested that if you had another cow and sent him to market with her, he would no doubt return with a bridge?"

"Well, yes, but of course, when he planted the seeds and the next morning there was that stalk, well, I . . ."

"Objection!" the cat spat.

"Sustained. Please make your point, counselor."

"Your honor, my point is this: Even though he and his mother were starving, young Jack, showing sociopathic tendencies, sold their only resource, their cow, not for money or food, as his mother told him to do, but for allegedly magic seeds! Is it any wonder that he went on to behave with similar lack of respect for the home and belongings of the plaintiff and her late husband when he would disregard the instructions of his own mother for the chance that potentially worthless seeds were, indeed, magic, and might enable him to embark upon some tawdry little adventure?"

"Objection! Counsel is attempting to lead the jury . . ."

"Sustained."

"Mrs. Jackson," the prosecution continued, spreading his wings slightly. "What did your son tell you about his trips up the beanstalk? How did he explain returning with such treasures? And why, Madam, when you already had a hen that laid golden eggs, did your son feel compelled to return to Mr. Montegrande's home and burgle it a second and third time?"

"Oh, that's easy. The fairy told him about us, you see. Our noble beginnings and that."

"Can you be a little more specific, Madam? What was the name of this fairy who allegedly told your son—"

"Objection. Counsel is asking witness to repeat hearsay."

"Sustained."

"No matter, your honor," the raven said. "The prosecution may wish to recall this witness later. But for now, I will call another witness."

"Mrs. Jackson, you are dismissed for the moment," the owl said, peering down at the mother of the defendant.

She bustled back to her seat and the raven squawked, "The prosecution calls Ms. Mab Golightly."

"Objection, your honor! This is a surprise witness! The prosecution did not give defense adequate time to prepare—"

"Your honor," the raven interjected before the owl could make a ruling. "Ms. Golightly is here for the prosecution as a hostile witness. It was only with the aid of our investigators that we were able to locate her."

The owl fluffed the feathers of his chest and at length said, "Defense will be permitted ample time to cross-examine the witness. Proceed."

A small female with the elongated arms and legs and

thin, high cheekboned face of a fashion model tripped up to the witness stand. She was dressed in a green velvet miniskirt and blazer which had slits from which poked gossamer wings of a peridot hue. Her hair was a peculiar shade of pink. She giggled as she took the oath, putting a spidery long-fingered hand to her generous mouth.

"Now, then, Ms. Golightly, could you tell the court where you currently reside?" the raven asked with another head tilt.

"I flit blithely here and there among the flowerth and birdth through aaaawwwwlll the kingdom," she said.

"Which kingdom would that be, Ms. Golightly?" the raven asked.

"Fairyland! And adjoining principalities."

"And these adjoining principalities would include the kingdom of the late Mr. Montegrande?"

She nodded so vigorously her wings fluttered enough to lift her off the witness chair an inch or two.

"And how long have you resided at your present location, Ms. Golightly?"

"How long?"

"Yes, ma'am."

She chewed her lip and rolled her eyes and counted on her fingers and the toes of her long skinny bare feet. "Forever and ever," she said finally.

"Approximately."

"Thousands of years, give or take a century."

"And by reason of this long occupancy, you consider yourself an authority on the region?" the raven watched her closely.

"As much as anybody," she said.

"Have you ever to your knowledge had a conversation

with a person in this courtroom prior to being subpoenaed as a witness in this case?"

She chewed her thumbnail, looked around the courtroom, looked straight at the boyish face of the young man seated next to the attorney for the defense, and waved and nodded at the same time, "Hi, Jack! Yes, him. That's him. Jack. We had a couple of nice chats."

"Did the defendant, at the time of these chats of yours, show homicidal tendencies toward the deceased Mr. Montegrande?"

"Oh, no. He—Jack—was just playing tourist. He grew this great big beanstalk see, out of these seeds, and he climbed it to see where it went."

"So we've heard. Did you, Ms. Golightly, at any time, attempt to provide the accused with a history of the area?"

"I may have clued him in on one or two little bitty teensy weensy historical footnotes," she admitted.

"Did you, for instance, tell him of your queen's attempts to annex Mr. Montegrande's property into Fairyland in order to expand her borders and tax base and use the castle as a convention center?"

The fairy's face grew very sly. "No, why would I tell him that? He didn't seem very interested in politics."

"What *did* you tell the accused, Ms. Golightly?"

She swung her feet, which did not meet the ground, and chewed on her pinkish curls, and rolled her eyes and said, "I—um—I don't remember. This and that."

"Perhaps you will be able to recall a bit later, Ms. Golightly, after we have heard further testimony. The prosecution is done with this witness for the time being, your honor."

The owl peered down at the cat, "Do you wish to examine the witness now, counselor?"

"The defense wishes to call the witness at a later time, your honor, when we have a chance to consult with our client."

"Very well. Bailiff will please escort Ms. Golightly to the iron-barred cell in which she will be housed until released by both counsels."

The fairy's lower lip trembled and a large diamond tear perched precariously on the edge of the lower lid of one slitted green eye, but she meekly descended and followed the bailiff, a dragon of stern countenance.

"While we prepare our cross-examination of the young creature just led away by the scales of justice, your honor, the defense will pause in making its case."

"Very well. Prosecution?"

"The prosecution calls the plaintiff, Mrs. Myrtle Montegrande, your honor."

The courtroom shimmied as the mountain of mourning rose to its—her, actually—feet, and walked lightly, for a woman her size, to the witness stand.

Before she took her oath, Mrs. Montegrande was asked to raise her veil, and when she did, everyone could see that she had but a single eye, now red and puffy and wet with constant crying. Otherwise, her features were regular and appealing, particularly if one happened to be a giant or an ogre. Delicate ivory tusks punctuated the sad downward curve of her full red lips. She dabbed at her eye and nose daintily with a square that could be recognized by smaller beings as a lace tablecloth.

"Please state your name, address, and occupation," the raven said with a dovelike coo.

"M-Mrs. Myrtle Montegrande, Giant's Castle, Fairyland Borders. I am—was—a homemaker." She stifled a sob as she said the last and dabbed with the tablecloth once more. The raven shifted, careful not to tangle beak or feet in the lace.

"Mrs. Montegrande, would you please tell the court in your own words of the events leading up to and including your husband's death?"

She sniffled, and the defense attorney's plumed hat was almost sucked into her nostril as a result. "We led a quiet life, Monte and me," she said. "Our little place in the country was just right for us and—we had always hoped—maybe a little one someday. Alas, it was not to be, for I was childless. Perhaps that's why, as Monte always warned me, I was so vulnerable to young con artists."

"There were more than one?"

"Oh, yes. Fairy folk were forever plaguing us, blackmailing us to put milk out for them, complaining when Monte accidentally stepped into some of their little rings, that sort of thing. They played tricks on us until Monte bound our castle round with iron, and then they couldn't get in, and that made them even madder."

The judge said, "Whoo is germane to this case, counsel? The fairies or the defendant? Instruct your witness to stick to the present situation."

The widow's eye, which was large and blue and long-lashed, blinked sadly at the judge, and she nodded. "I'm sorry, your honor. All I meant was that I did *like* little folk, and so did Monte, as long as they behaved themselves. And it was lonely around the castle while Monte was off lending his services to various construction projects. And when he came home, so tired from fitting those tedious little blocks into pyramids or building stone rings for wizards, he wasn't very good company until he had his rest, and I had the whole place to look after myself. Well, you can see why I welcomed the boy—the defendant, I mean—when he came to call. He said he was willing to work, and, frankly, I had to think hard to come up with a job that was small enough for such a puny, ill-fed lad to do so that he wouldn't feel it was charity when I fed him. But the tricks those nasty little fairies had played hurt my Monte's feelings something awful and he wasn't very hospitable, at least not until he'd eaten and napped.

"So I hid the little fellow. Had I but known the grief and sorrow he would bring my Monte and me, I would have hidden him in a hot oven instead of a cold one. But one cannot know the future.

"At any rate, my Monte came in, tired and hungry, and he's very sensitive when he's that way—he was rather psychic, you know, my Monte, and a state of deprivation greatly enhanced his powers. He asked if we had a guest, and I pretended ignorance until I could jolly him into a better frame of mind. Then I served him the excellent stew I had prepared for him from a passing herd of caribou. After eating, Monte always needs some little diversion to help him settle down to his nap."

"And on this occasion, Mrs. Montegrande, did your husband require you to fetch for him his hen that laid the golden eggs?" the raven asked, his voice still imitating a dove's instead of his own raucous squawk.

"He did. He was very fond of chickens, and though you may not realize it, those who lay golden eggs are great pets. They love to be spoken to and stroked and it helps increase their egg production. Monte usually fell asleep muttering to Henny, leaving me time to read or catch up on my mending or spinning or play a hand of solitaire.

"I'm sorry to say that about the time I was ready to introduce our guest to Monte, my poor hubby awakened to find Henny gone and I, upon looking in the oven, saw that our guest had disappeared as well." She started to cry again. "I just felt so betrayed. So violated. And I didn't have the heart to tell Monte, of course, that his Henny had been stolen. So I said I put her away myself."

She sniffled and seemed to get a grip on herself, smoothing her veils with a black glove.

"Please continue, Mrs. Montegrande, to the second occasion on which you saw the defendant. Could you please tell the court why you entertained him again, when you realized he had stolen your property and tricked you the first time?"

"Objection!" the cat purred, "Counsel is making damaging assumptions."

"Sustained."

The witness was answering anyway. "He was in disguise, you see. Had colored his hair and put on a mustache. I suppose I should have seen through it, as I did at once when the second incident occurred, but I basically believe in the goodness of people. I thought we'd had our one unfortunate incident and that was no reason to deny some other little chap our hospitality and myself the opportunity to interact with my fellow creatures. He polished the insides of our drinking vessels for us while we chatted, and later on, I hid him in my wardrobe.

"Monte came home and partook of the nice flock of goose soup I had prepared, but the poor baby was so tired all he wanted was to count his money. I brought out the cookie jar in which we kept our life savings, and he amused himself counting the coins. I was going to keep an eye on the new visitor, just in case, but I became so involved in my new book—a family saga romance about a lovely princess with a wicked stepmother and a fairy godmother with that hunky Charming fellow who is on so many of the covers these days—and I completely forgot all about it until I heard the cookie jar smash on the floor and my honey bellow with outrage and loss." She was silent, but her single blue eye was eloquent. "It was horrible. Horrible. All our years of work, of scrimping and saving, gone. Just like that."

"And the third incident, Mrs. Montegrande? Do you need a recess before you tell us about that?"

She dabbed her eye bravely and squared her shoulders, slightly rearranging the back wall of the courtroom as she did so. "No. No, I want to get this over with. To see justice done. You will think me so foolish, I know. But when the boy returned again, I had simply blotted out the other two incidents, they were so traumatic, and I didn't recognize him. I had a terrible feeling in my belly when I asked him in, but good manners are something that my mother bred into me. He helped me polish the silver while we chatted and he told amusing tales of his recent travels, of the fine parties he had given with lovely food— little did I realize this had all been accomplished with *our* money and the proceeds from the sale of Henny's eggs. When Monte returned home, I asked the little fellow to please wait in the cupboard until I felt it was the right time to introduce him to my husband. Monte, who has a better memory than I, was having a flashback, I believe. He said he thought he could actually smell someone who had done us harm in the past, but I discounted it. Monte can be so paranoid sometimes. It's because of this mercenary service in the various wars of men, you know. Everybody targets the big guy, which is very painful to a sensitive soul like my Monte. Anyway, when he had partaken of the crust of bread and bit of stale wine we had been reduced to, what with all of our wealth spirited away, I set out our last remaining treasure, our dear little singing harp, to soothe away his troubles. I didn't leave the room that time, but our harp's music was so calming that we both fell asleep."

At this point, the witness lost control of her emotions and began to sob piteously. The prosecution patted her top veil with a comforting wing and the judge ruffled his feathers uncomfortably while the cat for the defense disdainfully chose that time to wash beneath his tail. Jack, the accused, looked appalled, dismayed, and as if he knew his hen who laid the golden eggs was getting cooked before his eyes.

"And then what happened?" the raven asked when the lady had regained her composure.

"Our—loyal little singing harp—cried out to us. 'Master! Mistress! I'm being abducted! Help!' the poor little thing cried. She was our dearest possession although all she gave to us was the gift of music. We both awakened to see the tail end of the boy fly out the front door. I tripped on my skirt, but my Monte was after the little thief in a flash. If the boy hadn't had such a head start, it would have been the worse for him, but he ran over to this—this—well, I think it was some sort of vegetable stalk, like the ones we used to grow in our garden when I was a little girl. I cried to Monte to let him go, but Monte was down the stalk after the little miscreant before I could reach the first leaf. In horror I watched the thief

disappear through the clouds while the stalk swayed under Monte's great weight, and then—and then—" She bit
her lip, piercing it with one of her tusks, and continued,
in a tightly controlled voice. "Just as Monte was about to
disappear into the clouds between us and the lower world,
the vine toppled. Monte gave one yell, and then all the
world shook as my darling was dashed to his death and
was—no more."

"What did you do then, ma'am?" the prosecution asked.

"I didn't know what to do. That horrible stalk was
gone, taking my beloved with it. How could I reach the
lower regions to confront the criminal with his murder?
And then, a kindly witch happened by. She had a young
ward, she said, who had an unusually strong scalp and a
great length of golden hair—real gold, mind you, and very
sturdy. In exchange for the use of the ruined tower we
have on our property, the witch and the girl agreed to let
down her golden hair so that I could descend the golden
stair to the ground and plead my case. We wound her hair
a couple of times around the tower in question so that she
wouldn't be taking upon her poor scalp all of my weight—
no, no, I know I am not the daintiest of ladies—and I descended, with a curl or two to spare. Her hair let me down
some distance from where the remains of the stalk and
the final resting place of my husband were located, but
after a bit of searching, I found them, and the lavish
home of our persecuter and his mother. He denied any
wrongdoing and even made up some story about our castle belonging to his father, and that is why I sought the
help of this court in avenging the wrongful death of my
husband and reclaiming the items stolen from his estate."

Sniffles and sobs resounded through the courtroom in

response to this heartrending tale, and the raven bowed to the cat. "Your witness."

The cat prowled back and forth in front of the lady while she regained her composure. "Mrs. Montegrande, do you recall your husband's words when he entered your home on the evenings you described?"

"You mean, other than, 'hello, sweetheart, have you had a nice day?' " the lady asked, her blue eye wide with surprise at the question.

"No, I mean, if the court reporter will read back the statement from the accused—?"

The court reporter, a wizened monkey, mimicked back in the precise tones the accused had used during his statement, "Fe Fi Fo Fum, I smell the blood of an Englishman. Be he alive or be he dead, I'll grind his bones to make my bread."

"Do you recall *that,* Mrs. Montegrande?" the cat spat.

"Heavens! That's what comes of cross-cultural miscommunication," she said. "How on earth would Monte have known what nationality the little fellow was, even if the quote was accurate? No, you see, Monte never liked my first name, which is Myrtle. He always called me Fifi, a little pet name he had for me. What he actually said, I believe, though I'd hardly recognize that interpretation is, 'Fifi, wife, I'm home, hon. I smell *like* a bloody Englishman'—because he'd been working for some, you see, constructing a stone circle, and the wizard could never make up his mind where he wanted the stones to go. The last part is also a misquote. What Monte said, to the best of my recollection is, 'Maybe I'm alive, but I feel like I'm dead, that foreman will grind my bones just to make some bread.' I did *say* that I'd hidden the boy, didn't I?"

The cat gave her a narrow-eyed look and said, "Thank you *so* much, Mrs. Montegrande. Uh—one more thing."

"Yes, Kitty?"

"Can you tell the court how you and your husband came to be in possession of the castle, the hen, the gold, and the harp?"

"Why, yes, Kitty, I can. The castle has been in our family for generations, and giants and ogres are quite long-lived people. Once all of the sky kingdom was populated with giants and ogres. The northernmost climes agree with us, you see, as we're a hot-blooded race. But soon more and more fairies moved into the area for summer homes, and soon they began passing laws and crowning kings and queens, while humankind began to develop a very jaundiced view of we large folk, who have always attempted to use our power and strength to benefit others. Finally, all of our nearby kin moved away or passed on, leaving only Monte and me, childless and alone. The fairy government offered to buy us out, but we are, as you may have guessed, somewhat sentimental. Henny and her ancestresses have been in our family for years, and the singing harp is said to have been made from the hair and bone of the famous giantess minstrel, Celitalinda, or Beautiful Heaven, whose Hi-C could shatter the stars in the sky. The harp was made when she committed suicide after being jilted by the handsome giant, Magnifico, also a minstrel, and an ancestor of my Monte's, so that he might have use of her as a harp as he had not otherwise. As for the gold, well, as I told you, we worked for it, Monte and I. Him with his construction business and me by maintaining our home for him."

"Thank you, Mrs. Montegrande," the cat said, switching his tail with dissatisfaction, and giving her a look that said clearly that she was lying. "The defense is now ready to ask the accused to take the stand."

The boy, his fair hair shining in the light from the courtroom windows, was well dressed in new trousers and a vest embroidered with birds and flowers.

"Now, Jack, you've heard the testimony of Mrs. Montegrande," the cat purred. "Have you any reason to think that you may have misunderstood what her late husband said?"

Jack shook his head. "No, sir. Of course, I don't speak giant, sir. But he was trying to kill me, he was."

"Well, then, Jack, if you felt he was trying to kill you the first time you met him, why did you return to the castle?"

"Why, to get what was rightfully mine, sir! Mine and me mum's!"

"And could you tell the court what that was, Jack?"

"Why, the hen and the gold and that little harp and whatever else I could carry. Giant may have stolen our kingdom and castle, but I was out to get back from him what was ours. Once I knew, of course."

"Once you knew what, Jack?"

"Why, that I was prince, see, and me mum was the queen and me dad had been the king before the giant killed him."

"But Mrs. Montegrande has just testified that the property in question has been in her family and her husband's for generations."

"I wouldn't know about that. Maybe she's just mistaken. Maybe her husband told her that and she believed him. But I remember, now, all about it. And I'm a prince and that castle and all that stuff is mine and Mum's by right of birth. See, the real truth is, me dad was a kind and wise king who ruled his land so everybody was happy and fairies and folk all got along good. But then giant came and murdered Dad and would have murdered Mum and me, but she got me away, with the help of the friendly fairies, and took us to live with Mum's old nurse, who used to have our cottage."

"And why was this not commonly known in your local vicinity?"

"Fairy put a forgetfulness spell on us all, to keep us safe like. Only, when she saw me again, she helped me remember—my—my—ironed? reironed? No, pressed! That's it. She helped me remember my pressed memories of when I was a prince and how it was my duty to get our stuff back and all."

"Thank you, Jack." The cat returned to his table and curled up on it.

The prosecution flew in. "Jack, you say you were a baby at the time of your father's death. A babe in arms, in fact. How then, do you have memories of these events that the fairy could recall?"

"She says babies have memories, too. It's a trade secret the fairies have. And, sir? I didn't mean to kill giant. But he were coming after me and I had to do something to keep him from grinding our bones to make his bread. So I chopped down the stalk."

"Hmmm. Yes. Thank you, Jack. Your honor, the prosecution wishes to recall Ms. Mab Golightly."

Once more the fairy tripped up to the witness stand. "Ms. Golightly, you have stated that you are a fairy. Could you please describe the duties and powers invested in you as such?"

"Well, they don't include pushing around big ol' giants

like that lady said!" the witness replied with a fearful look in the direction of the plaintiff.

"No, but is it not true that fairies are able to help mortals see things, remember things, perhaps, that they would not otherwise be aware of?"

"Well, we do have the glamorie, of course, and illusion, and—well, sometimes, we forget that their time and our time is a little different."

"I see. I will take it that that is a 'yes,' then. The accused spoke of a pressed memory you helped him recall—what sort of power do you use in that sort of thing?"

Mab Golightly's tilted green eyes grew shifty, and her thin face acquired the look of a trapped weasel. "I'm sure I don't know. The term may have come up, but I—"

"You have nothing to do with people's memories, eh, Ms. Golightly? Nothing to do with baby's memories, in fact?"

"No."

"The only thing you have to do with babies is changing them for fairy children who don't meet the standards of your peers. Or making foolish people think that dead leaves are fairy gold. Isn't that true?"

"People believe what they want to," Mab Golightly said with a little shrug. "I never said 'is father was king, I just said 'what IF.' "

"Aha. And what IF Mr. Jackson caused the death of the giant, then perhaps the grieving impoverished giantess could be persuaded to move away from her painful memories and her property could be annexed? Even better, if the giant's death was proved to be the result of theft, perhaps his riches would eventually be returned to the kingdom and its new owner—the fairy queen."

"I—er—golly, *any*thing is possible."

"Your honor, perhaps you and the bailiff, bearing the jurors, the defense, and the defendant on his back, could accompany me on a little journey."

"This is highly irregular, counselor."

"Yes, sir, it is. But it will prove, beyond a shadow of a doubt, Mrs. Montegrande's contention that she and her husband were rightful owners of the castle and property contained therein. Because, your honor, I have already flown up there and the castle is huge and everything in it is gigantic. The defendant himself in his statement affirmed Mrs. Montegrande's statement that he was able to fit inside her oven, cupboard and wardrobe with perfect ease. And yet, no normal-sized man such as Mr. Jackson could do so in a normal-sized oven, cupboard or wardrobe. Why would Mr. Jackson's father, whose birth is on record at the local town hall, by the way, have owned a castle of such proportions?"

"Is there no less dramatic fashion in which you can prove this ownership, counsel?"

"Your honor, there is. I call the Singing Harp to the stand."

The bailiff brought forth the harp, whose strings shivered at the dragon's touch.

In a few short notes, the harp confirmed the history given by the giant's wife. The jury was out only a very short time before returning, and the verdict was read.

"Your honor, we of the jury find the boy Jack guilty of one count of giantslaughter. However, we also find extenuating circumstances, in that he was temporarily pixillated at the time by the influence of the witness Mab Golightly. Therefore, it is our verdict that the money and property taken by Jack be returned to the widow Montegrande, that the witness Golightly be remanded into custody for conspiracy to commit murder, and that Jack himself be banished to Fairyland for the remainder of his life."

The defendant's mother screamed and fainted. Mrs. Montegrande smiled and scooped her up on the way back to call her witch friend and the ward with the golden hair. "Come along, my dear," the widow said to the unconscious woman she carried in the crook of her arm. "I have a recipe for bread I'd like to introduce you to."